Elijah Hael

and

The Last Judgement

By Steve Goodwin

All characters and events appearing in this novel are fictitious. Any resemblance to real events, or persons living or dead, is purely coincidental.

ISBN: 978-0-9873784-0-8 (Paperback)
ISBN: 978-0-9873784-1-5 (Online Edition)

www.ElijahHael.com

Author's Foreword

Elijah Hael and the Last Judgement is a novel that introduces the character Elijah Hael.

I decided to start writing novels to bring to life this character Elijah, who I had been thinking about for some time. My original intent was to give life to Elijah through computer games, but after further thought and considering the resources required to write computer games, I felt I could introduce Elijah to a larger audience through books.

Books have a longer lifespan than video games, which are limited to the lifespan of the platform they are designed on. That is not to say, however, that at some point I will not bring Elijah to life through computer games.

My day job, like my character Elijah's, is writing computer software, which requires a lot of dedication and creativity to bring other people's dreams to life or develop an application that can help satisfy a company's business requirements. The scheduling flexibility the job affords has given me the good fortune of spending some time writing each day.

While out riding my bicycle or jogging, I would be working on the next chapter in my head to get a good grasp of the scenes before writing. Something I have learnt from creating large software projects is that, although any large task is daunting at the beginning, if you spend just a bit of time each day chipping away at it you will eventually complete it.

One thing is for sure: If you never give something a go, you will never know if it is something that could have been. I encourage everyone with an inkling of creative intent to just give it a go and see where it takes you. If it does not work out, well, at least you tried.

I hope you enjoy getting to know Elijah Hael in reading *The Last Judgement*.

I credit this book to my wife Trish who throughout the years has been my rock and foundation in life. We have gone through both tough and wonderful times together, and we are looking forward to the rest of our lives together.

Acknowledgements

Firstly, I would like to thank the original team of manuscript readers: Brady MacDonald, Mary Anne D'Costa, Andrew Argent, Val & Bruce Perkins, and my lovely wife Trish Goodwin. Their feedback was invaluable in bringing Elijah Hael to life. Their insights helped to shape the novel and kept me motivated to churn out more chapters. My sincerest thanks to you all!

Secondly I would like to the thank Scott Stewart, the editor, whose diligent editing tightened the language and polished the writing to a high shine while fixing up issues with grammar and syntax usage along the way. The clarity improved in many areas because of his efforts. I look forward to working with Scott again on future novels.

Chapter 1 - Awakening

"What is your name?"

Elijah looked around, puzzled. He wondered who the man who was asking him questions was and how he had gotten here—wherever he was. "My name?"

"Yes, your name," the man said. "What is it?"

Elijah looked at the man seated across the small rather old wooden desk from him and said, "Elijah. Elijah Hael. But, wait, how did I get here?"

"*I* will be asking the questions," the man said in a stern but matter-of-fact tone. "You will be answering them."

Elijah nodded.

"My name is Uriel, and I will be recording a few details about you before we take you to interrogation."

"Interrogation?" Elijah asked, his voice quivering.

"There you go again, asking questions," Uriel said with an unamused smile.

Elijah turned his head side to side and scanned the small, well-lit room. It had a single door, a window and a desk in the middle where Elijah and Uriel sat. Uriel typed Elijah's answers to his questions on a tablet computer that lay on the desk before him.

"What is your date of birth?"

"June 14, 1971."

Elijah heard shouting beyond the door and the stuttering voice of a frightened man shout: "But I'm innocent! I'm a good person! I don't deserve this!"

Another voice, stern, cold, and commanding replied, "Yeah, that's what they all say. Take him away, officers."

The frightened man continued to yell, but his voice faded into the distance. "Wait, I can change. What can I do to make it right? Please, please, give me another chance. Help me."

Elijah looked Uriel square in the eyes. "What was that all about?"

"Oh, that's the typical response when people realise the gravity of the situation they are in. They always want another chance. They plead their innocence or claim they are really 'a good person' and that should compensate for all the bad things they have done."

"What sort of 'situation' are they in?" Elijah asked. "What sort of 'bad things' have they done?"

"Let me say it again," Uriel said with a sneer on his face. "I will ask the questions. Now we are just about done here, Elijah. Just one last question: Do you remember how you got here?"

"No," he said, shaking his head. "No, I don't. In fact, I have no idea."

Uriel stood up and led Elijah through the door into an adjoining hallway with a door at the end and a single door on each side. The door on the right was marked "Interrogation A" and the door on the left, "Interrogation B." An "Exit" sign hung over the door at the end of the hallway.

Uriel knocked on the door marked "Interrogation A." A quick reply came from the same stern voice he had heard speaking to the frightened man a few minutes earlier: "Bring him in."

Uriel opened the door and introduced Elijah to Detective Stolas, who was sitting behind a desk near the back wall of the room, and Detective Lilith, who was sitting next to Stolas. The room reeked of the pungent and overpowering smell of tobacco smoke. The ashtray on the table was full of cigarette butts and cigar stubs. The room had no windows, only a mirror on the far wall and a recording system mounted on the wall within reach of Detective Stolas.

Uriel pulled out the chair opposite Stolas and told Elijah to sit down. Elijah reluctantly lowered himself onto the chair. Without saying a word, Uriel walked out the door and shut it behind him.

On the table in front of Stolas lay a file labelled "Elijah Hael" that was as thick as the final Harry Potter novel.

Stolas flipped the file open and said, "Elijah Hael. People call you Eli, don't they?"

"Yes, my friends do."

"Mind if I call you Eli?"

"No, that's fine."

Elijah scooted his chair forward and sat up so he could face Stolas squarely. "Am I in some kind of trouble? Do I need a lawyer?"

"A lawyer. Why?" Stolas replied sharply. "Are you guilty of something?"

"No, not that I know of," Elijah said. "But all this—"

"Then why would you need a lawyer?"

Elijah contemplated the question but said nothing.

Lilith smiled, apparently finding some humour in the situation.

Elijah could see his reflection in the mirror and wondered if it were two-way glass. He pictured a group of people behind it watching his every move. Elijah's own reflection was cold—a stark reflection of how he currently felt. He was not sure how—or more importantly, why—he had got here to ... wherever he was. He looked worried. His brown hair was frazzled, his face was contorted with concern, and the whites of his blue eyes were a little bloodshot.

Chapter 2 - Interrogation

"Have you ever killed a man, Elijah?" Stolas asked.

"No."

"Okay, then. What about wishing he was dead or that harm may come to him?"

Elijah narrowed his tired eyes. "Why? That is certainly not a crime, is it?"

"Well," Lilith butted in, "that all depends on *whose* laws you're following."

Stolas pinched his chin between his fingers and nodded. "What about Wade? You do remember Wade, don't you Elijah?"

"Wade?" Elijah drew in a deep breath and rubbed his eyes. "Wade from back in school?"

"Yes, *that* Wade. Tell us about him, Elijah."

"OK." Elijah leaned back and clasped his hands at the nape of his neck. "Wade was a kid who went to the same school as I when I was in year seven."

"What else, Elijah?"

"He broke my nose."

"Oh, and how did that happen?"

"I was walking down the corridor with my bag slung over my right shoulder. As I passed by Wade, he struck me in the nose. It all happened so fast that, at first, I was not aware of what had happened.

Before long I realised that blood was streaming down my face, and I was stumbling about to keep my balance. Then I pinched my nostrils shut to stem the flow of blood and cupped my other hand over my nose to hold it in place while some people came to my aid and called for help."

"Why did he hit you, Elijah?"

"I'm not sure," Elijah admitted. "I believe it was part of an initiation test—or 'hazing'—for a gang he was involved in."

"And what happened after that?"

"I was taken to emergency where they x-rayed my nose." Elijah crinkled his nose at the thought of the procedure. "It was broken. So they admitted me to hospital to set my nose straight. They put me under while they manipulated it back into place. When I woke up, it felt as though they had whacked my nose with a sledge hammer."

"Pity," Lilith said. "So what happened to Wade?"

"Nothing."

"Nothing?"

"As far as I know: *nothing*. You mean did he get in trouble for attacking me or prosecuted?"

"No," Stolas said. "She means, did you wish revenge on him?"

"I can't recall." Elijah exhaled a big hot breath through pursed lips. "It was a very long time ago—a lifetime ago. I was bullied a lot at school, so it's possible that I did fantasize about revenge. Who wouldn't?"

"Maybe everyone would *fantasize* about it?" Stolas answered the rhetorical question. He crossed his arms. "But act on it? I don't know. Isn't it true that Wade had a so-called *accident* a few months after you were released from hospital? Tell us about that."

"It didn't have anything to do with me," Elijah said. He squinted and cleared his throat. "I don't like what you are implying. Wade did have an accident. He fell out of a tree and broke his foot, busted up his teeth, broke a rib or two. He walked with a limp after that."

Stolas leaned forward and lowered his voice. "You had a motive, Elijah, and you have admitted that you possibly wished him harm— and implied that everyone in the world would do likewise—yet, you want us to believe that you had nothing to do with his *accident?*"

"Yes," Elijah said, "I do. It just happened."

"Were you happy he had his so-called accident?"

"At the time I guess I felt vindicated somehow and maybe I was somewhat happy that he had suffered in some way."

Lilith looked at Elijah and with a gentle smile and said, "So you find joy in other people's suffering?"

Elijah looked down at the table but did not reply.

Lilith said, "Well, do you?"

Elijah shifted in his seat. "Listen, it was an accident. I remember him telling the class about it. He did say that he felt it was punishment for hitting me. 'Karma,' he called it. In fact, that karma thing seemed to keep catching up with him. A year later, I transferred to another school hundreds of miles away. At the new school I became rather popular and made quite a few good friends. By some strange coincidence, Wade transferred to the same school. When I told my mates that he had broken my nose, they gave him a hard time. I never asked them to do so. They were just taking it up for me. I guess Wade transferred to yet another school because after that I didn't see him around."

"You didn't see him around after that, eh?" Stolas said. "You didn't answer the question: Do you find joy in other people's suffering?" He raised his voice and leaned in still closer to Elijah. "Well do you, Elijah?"

Elijah replied softly, "No, not anymore."

Stolas relaxed then. "Do you mind if I smoke, Elijah?"

"Yes, I do mind."

Stolas proceeded to slip a pack of cigarettes out of his shirt pocket and worked a cigarette out of it. He placed it between his lips, muttered "Tough," and lit it.

"Isn't it against the law to smoke indoors?" Elijah asked.

"We are the only law here, Elijah," he said. "Let's move on. Tell us about how you hurt Tida."

"Tida?" Elijah said. "How on earth would you know about that?"

"People have a nasty tendency to tell other people when they are hurt, Elijah, and then they tell two people who tell two people and .... gossip gets around."

"I did not intentionally hurt her."

"So you are admitting that you did, in fact, hurt her?"

"Yes, I am. I did. But I was young, living in a strange country, just trying to get by, and I was infatuated with another girl at the time. Tida would spend quite a bit of time with me. She was a good friend. She showed me around Thailand and helped me learn their language."

"A sweet story," Stolas said, sarcastically. "The kind I would expect to have a happy ending. So get to it."

Elijah felt weary. "I guess she developed romantic feelings for me, but I had developed romantic feelings for someone else. And one day Tida overheard me telling this other girl that I had feelings for her. I tell you, that was the first moment I realised that Tida felt more for me than just friendship."

"No happy ending for Tida, then?" Stolas said. "Whatever came of her, Elijah?"

"I don't know."

"She just vanished into thin air as soon as she overheard you gushing to this other girl?"

"Yes, in a manner of speaking, that's exactly what happened," Elijah said, nodding. "She ran off and I never saw her again."

"And this other girl," Stolas said, huffing out a smoke ring and watching it rise toward the ceiling, "the one you had feelings for?"

"It turned out that she was in a relationship with someone else. She actually found it funny that I had feelings for her. The whole thing was a complete mess. I'm certainly not happy with the way it ended up and still feel some remorse about it to this day."

"Poor thing," Lilith said, with that gentle smile again. "Do you think you and Tida could have had something together, Elijah?"

Elijah leaned back in his chair and looked down at his upturned palms. "Possibly. I'm not sure. We were great friends, but.... As I told you, I didn't have any feelings for her other than friendship."

"And just what was it about this other girl that aroused such romantic feelings in you, Elijah?"

"I really don't know," he admitted. "Do we get to choose who we fall for?"

"You broke Tida's heart, Elijah," Lilith indicted him. "You do realise that, don't you?" Her tone and demeanour couldn't have been more patronizing.

"Yes," he admitted. "I do."

"What if we told you that poor, broken-hearted Tida went on to commit suicide after that, Elijah? Over you."

"She did?"

"Please listen carefully. I asked a 'what if' question, Elijah, didn't I? It was a hypothetical question. But if she had in fact killed herself over love unrequited, would you feel at all responsible?"

"Yes, in some ways."

"And taking that into account, would you still consider yourself a good person, Elijah?"

"I, I ... well, I don't know," he said, shrugging his shoulders. "I did not intentionally hurt her."

"The road to hell is paved with—"

"Good intentions," Elijah interrupted. "I know the worn out saying. But did she, Tida, kill herself?"

"We'll get to that later," Stolas said, smiling. "To summarise so far: You have wished harm on someone who ended up in a coincidental accident and you have admitted to breaking a girl's heart. So, now we are getting somewhere."

Chapter 3 - Realisation

A loud knock on the door bellowed throughout the room. Stolas jerked his head around and shouted, "What now?"

The door opened and a large man—tall and well-built—stepped into the room.

"Castiel?" Stolas said. "I might have known you would turn up."

Castiel held out a sealed blue envelope, and Stolas snatched it out of his hand and tore it open.

Lilith glared at Castiel. "Aren't you looking cheerful? This must be an important one for you."

Stolas' face darkened as he read the letter. As he turned to face Elijah, he crumpled the letter into a wad and threw it on the floor. "Go on, both of you," he said, "get out of here. Why do you do this to us, Castiel, when you must know beforehand?"

Castiel cocked his head. "Because I love seeing the look on your face each and every time it happens."

Castiel looked at Elijah and motioned with his hands. "Come on, let's go." Then he led Elijah down the hallway to the door marked Exit.

As Elijah passed through the door he squinted against a quick flash of white and then they suddenly appeared at the side of a road at the bottom of a large hill near a tree.

Castiel asked Elijah, "Do you remember this place?"

"Yes, yes," Elijah said, glancing around and letting his eyes adjust to the light. "This is one of the last things I remember. I was riding my bicycle down this road. There was a slight drizzle in the air and the road was a little damp. It was late in the afternoon with thick cloud cover, visibility was limited. A car passed close by, within a meter, and someone yelled at me from the vehicle and that caused me to lose control of my bicycle, which is why I collided with this tree."

Castiel looked at the tree, then back at Elijah.

"I was in a lot of pain, mainly in my arm, my left arm." He looked down at his arm and moved it around. "It doesn't hurt now, though. Some people passing by called an ambulance because I was a little groggy and bleeding. The ambulance came and took me to the hospital. Everything seemed all right.... The paramedics gave me some morphine for the pain, and we chatted a bit on the way to the hospital. They put me in a waiting room until a doctor could take a closer look at my injuries. The last thing I recall is staring at the ceiling panels while occasionally glancing at a television in the room."

Castiel's face showed some concern. He nodded his head very slowly.

Elijah said, "Am I dreaming? Is this all a dream?"

Castiel shook his head. "Tell me, Elijah, what else happened that day—earlier in the day? What else do you remember?"

Chapter 4 - May 24, 2012, The Accident

At 6 a.m. Elijah was up and getting ready for the second to last day of work on his current project. He had spent the previous 12 months developing a laser-based guidance system for helicopters flying at low altitude.

He looked at his face in the mirror and contemplated what the future might hold for him. The project he was completing had paid enough to keep his bills paid for at least 12 more months so he was in no rush to find another project. He finished getting dressed and headed downstairs. On his way to the kitchen he glanced at the clock and noticed it was just a few minutes past 6 a.m.

His wife Juliana was in the kitchen. "Good morning, Elijah. How many eggs would you like?"

"Two will be fine, thank you," he said. "And good morning to you." He slipped into a chair at the table and awaited his breakfast. The children were still asleep and Elijah enjoyed this time he had each morning with his wife.

"So, Elijah," Juliana said, "how does it feel knowing this is the second to the last day?"

"A little perturbing, to be honest, but I'm sure I'll be fine. I'll find a new project to work on. I'm looking forward to a new challenge."

Juliana set a plate on the table in front of Elijah. "Your favourite: eggs and bacon."

"My favourite," he said with a smile. "Thanks."

Elijah ate as Juliana proceeded to clean up after her cooking and made lunch for Reece, their son in kindergarten. He took his empty plate over and placed it in the sink. "I love you, Juliana. See you tonight." He turned and took a few slow steps toward the door. "I might be a little late; I'm going to stay back and work on updating my CV."

"Okay, honey, but aren't you forgetting something?"

Elijah turned back and planted a soft kiss on her lips while gazing into her deep green eyes. "Sorry," he whispered. "How could I forget?"

Juliana whispered back, "Love you, too, and I'll see you tonight."

In the garage, Elijah pulled out his bicycle and gave it a quick check to make sure everything was in good working order. "Looks good," he said. He put on his helmet, mounted the bike, and headed off on the 15-kilometre ride to Aeroworks.

In just under an hour he was in his office where he had spent several hundred days over the course of the last year, seated behind his own computer system developing the software to operate the Laser Guidance system. The day was busy and passed quickly. He had a lot of work to do to sew up the last few threads for the project.

As 5 p.m. approached, he fired up Microsoft Word and loaded his CV from the cloud and started to work on it. It chronicled his 14 years of programming a variety of software systems in many different industries. He updated the CV with the project he was completing and added several solid lines to his work history—not only some new additions to his skill set but another project completed successfully, on-time and some good references. He saved the document and glanced at the time in the bottom right corner of his computer screen: 5:20 p.m.

It was late autumn and he knew it would be dark by 6 p.m. The ride home was quicker than the ride in, but it was getting late and he wanted to beat as much of the darkness as he could. "Nice," he said, when he stepped outside and saw that it was raining. Just a slight drizzle, but the road was wet and visibility was poor due to the dying light as dusk fell quickly.

The first leg of the ride home was the hardest, and given the hour and wet road conditions Elijah decided to push a little harder and kick up his speed where normally he would take it a little more leisurely.

Elijah had loved to cycle ever since he was a boy. He loved to cruise down hills with the cool air in his face feeling free and loose and one with the bike rolling beneath him. He felt like a bird in flight, gliding weightless, and found the feeling of freedom hard to describe. It melted his stress level and brought him an amazing sense of peace.

As he neared the top of a large hill, he checked his brakes were working before allowing his bike to pick up speed on the descent. He was about halfway down the hill, doing about 50 kilometres per hour, when a car passed and someone hanging out the window shouted out some obscenities at the top of his lungs—which was not uncommon. Cyclists somehow inspired a lot of road rage, especially from young adults with their P plates who, for some reason, thought it was great fun to startle defenceless cyclists.

Elijah was in a world all his own when he heard the horrific shout. He jerked the handlebars, causing the front wheel to lose traction. The wheel slammed into the gutter, which held the bike upright, as the bike careened uncontrollably downhill. The left-side pedal was stuck on the gutter's edge, trapping the bicycle as it hurtled down the side of the road. There was nothing Elijah could do but try to brace himself for the impact with the fast approaching tree. Though his speed was diminishing, Elijah still hit the tree at about 35 kilometres per hour. He tried to soften the impact by extending his left arm and trying to fend off the tree. His arm made a snapping sound—more like a branch than a twig—as the sudden impact was too much for the bone to absorb. His chest jammed against the handlebars. With a loud, painful shout Elijah toppled to the ground at the base of the tree at the bottom of the hill.

Elijah was moaning and a little delirious as the adrenalin pumped through his veins. He could see lights through the misty drizzle. Fortunately, the sidewalk was a busy place with a fast food joint and a restaurant just a short distance from where he lay. He could see people scurrying about, grabbing their mobile phones, dialling 000, the emergency number, and reporting the "accident." Within 10 minutes an ambulance arrived with sirens screaming and lights flashing, and then paramedics were at his side.

A paramedic asked Elijah, "Can you hear me? What is your name?"

"Elijah, Elijah Hael," he said. "I think I'm okay, but—ooh—my arm is killing me."

The paramedics loaded him onto a stretcher and slid him into the back of the ambulance They injected a needle into his right arm to administer some morphine for the pain.

The paramedic started a conversation with Elijah that resulted in some pretty general chitchat. Elijah knew that they were more interested in keeping him awake and conscious in case he had suffered a head injury—especially after giving him morphine—than in finding out about his children and their ages and so on. They needn't have worried. Elijah was quite aware. It was obvious that his arm was broken, and they reported that to the medical team that greeted the ambulance at the hospital's emergency entrance.

The medical team assessed his condition and took his vital signs. One of the nurses took his blood pressure twice and asked if his blood pressure always ran low. Elijah shook his head. He didn't know the answer. She told him it was nothing to be concerned about and then wheeled him into a waiting room until a doctor could have a better look at him.

The hospital emergency room was busy and apparently understaffed. Nobody's fault but the government's that controlled the hospital's resources. The staff were excellent at their jobs, but there were simply not enough of them to provide patient care for everyone who needed it. Moreover, even when they did: it wasn't quick.

Elijah lay on a bed and waited for a doctor. He scanned his eyes from the ceiling to the television without paying much attention to either. Feeling a little groggy, he let his eyes close and ... lost consciousness.

Chapter 5 - June 2, 2012, Goodbyes

"Take my hand, Elijah."

Elijah took Castiel's hand, and when he did a dazzling bright light filled his eyes. As his sight began to return, very gradually, he could see they were in a hospital emergency room with several doctors and nurses buzzing about. He stood at the foot of the bed and saw himself lying there with no shirt on. A surgeon was drawing a line down the centre of his chest with a blue marker. Elijah felt weak and his knees buckled, but somehow he was still standing as though he were weightless.

Elijah shook his head and clamped his eyes shut as if to wake himself. *Am I dreaming? Am I having a near-death experience? What is going on?*

He saw himself lying there still with several wires connecting various parts of his body to a bedside heart monitor that each second was emitting a loud chirp. The display showed a blood pressure reading of 90/60.

A nurse with a controlled panic in her voice said, "BP is dropping— and dropping quickly."

The surgeon hurried to finish drawing the line on his chest and then proceeded to trace that line with a scalpel, making a perfect incision.

Elijah looked at the heart monitor. Blood pressure: 70/40 and falling. The interval between the loud chirps was getting longer and longer.

"We're losing him," the surgeon said. He looked exasperated. Just then the heart monitor let out its last chirp and then just continued whining its monotone *meeeeeeeeeeeeeeeeeee.*

"Am I dead?" Elijah questioned.

"Come now," said Castiel, gesturing for Elijah to take his hand again.

And when he did there was another bright white flash. As Elijah's sight returned, he could see they were sitting on a bench seat in the back row of a church. The mood was sombre, and muted sobs echoed in the sanctuary. Elijah looked around and saw that most people were dressed in black and seated towards the front of the church. He could see a casket with a photo frame set on top and his picture inside. He scanned to the right and recognized the familiar sight of his family, seated in the front row.

The church was quite full. Elijah estimated the crowd numbered about 150 people. Besides his own family, many of his work colleagues had turned up along with relatives and close friends.

I am dead. This is my funeral.

Elijah turned to look at Castiel who looked back at him and nodded gently. Then he turned his attention to the pastor conducting the service. No surprise to find Pastor Nathaniel from the church Elijah attended regularly, standing in the pulpit.

"This is going to be difficult," he said. "Elijah was a close friend of mine as well as a beloved member of our church. I would like to personally thank Juliana for giving me this opportunity, for I am truly honoured to be the one to bid Elijah farewell. It is a great privilege.

"It is not difficult to imagine the shock and horror that Juliana faced just one week ago when she was informed of the death of her dearly beloved husband, Elijah Hael. I am certain that Elijah would be quite proud of this service that Juliana has managed to put together for his last farewell.

"It is touching—even heartwarming—to see all the familiar and not-so-familiar friends who have turned up. I know that Elijah would be surprised at how many people made the time to be here to bid him farewell. Thank you all for attending.

"Although we are all feeling the sharp pain of losing our husband, our father, our friend, Elijah, who no one could deny was taken from us way too early, today is not about grieving. It is about celebrating the life that was Elijah Hael.

"Those who knew Elijah know that he was a man of faith, so please join me in taking a moment to recite a short prayer for Elijah. Please join with me."

Elijah watched as, without being asked, the congregants rose to their feet and joined Pastor Nathaniel in reciting the Lord's prayer:

"Our Father in heaven,
may your name be kept holy.
May your Kingdom come soon.
May your will be done on earth,
as it is in heaven.
Give us today the food we need,
and forgive us our sins,
as we have forgiven those who sin against us.
And don't let us yield to temptation,
but rescue us from the evil one. Amen."

When the congregants were again seated, Pastor Nathaniel continued. "Life takes each of us on our own journey. No two lives are ever the same, and no two people ever experience the exact same things in life. In one way or another, every one of us here was touched by Elijah Hael. He shared an experience with you—and with me, and that is what led us all here today. His life touched each of us, in one way or another, and so did his death.

"David Romano wrote this verse for his wife just before he died, and I believe it fitting to share this because I feel that Elijah would have shared a similar sentiment if given the chance before he passed away:"

"If tomorrow starts without me, and I'm not there to see.
If the sun should rise and find your eyes all filled with
tears for me

I wish so much you wouldn't cry the way you did today. While
thinking of the many things we didn't get to say.

I know how much you love me, As much as I love you, and
each time that you think of me, I know you'll miss me too;

But when tomorrow starts without me, Please try to
understand, that an angel came and called my name, And
took me by the hand

And said my place was ready, in heaven far above, And that I'd
have to leave behind all those I dearly love.

But as I turned to walk away, A tear fell from my eye, For all
my life, I'd always thought, I didn't want to die.

I had so much to live for, So much left yet to do, it seemed
almost impossible, that I was leaving you.

I thought of all the yesterdays, the good ones and the bad, I
thought of all that we had shared, and all the fun we had.

If I could relive yesterday, just even for a while, I'd say goodbye and kiss you and maybe see you smile.

But then I fully realized, that this could never be, for emptiness
and memories, would take the place of me.

And when I thought of worldly things, I might miss come tomorrow, I thought of you, and when I did, my heart was filled with sorrow.

But when I walked through heaven's gates, I felt so much at home. When God looked down and smiled at me, From His great golden throne,

He said, "This is eternity, and all I've promised you." Today your life on earth is past, but here life starts anew.

I promise no tomorrow, but today will always last, and since each day is the same way, there's no longing for the past.

You have been so faithful, so trusting and so true. Though there were times you did some things, you knew you shouldn't do.

But you have been forgiven, and now at last you're free. So won't you come and take my hand, and share my life with me

So when tomorrow starts without me, don't think we're far apart, for every time you think of me, I'm right here, in your heart.

"Elijah Hael's was born on June 14, 1971, in Milton Keynes, Buckinghamshire, England, and thus began his extraordinary life. His childhood was an exciting affair. The family moved to New South Wales, Australia and growing up in the Blue Mountains afforded young Elijah a world of wonder to explore in his own backyard. There was always another tree to climb, another cliff to scale, another valley to navigate, another cave to explore. He enjoyed endless adventures.

"Elijah was very bright and quite often rose to the top of his class in mathematics and science. He was known, however, as a talkative lad whose mischievous behaviour led to trouble more than once. Elijah once told me that he simply got bored and hence created various ways to amuse himself, which his classmates typically enjoyed much more than his teachers.

"Bullying was a problem for Elijah during his early years and was something that, over time, he had to learn to deal with and forgive— not just the bullies but also himself for the retaliatory actions he took against those bullies ... which cost him dearly.

"Elijah was fortunate to have the opportunity to travel to different countries and experience different cultures. He learnt great compassion and grace from these experiences that helped him to realise how fortunate he was in life, even though he had his own challenging experiences.

"From early boyhood on, he dreamt of being able to fly planes—a dream inspired by playing flight simulators on his computer. His dream came true when as a young adult he flew a small aircraft coast-to-coast across Australia.

"Although he was not an avid sportsman, Elijah did enjoy his cycling, mountain bike riding, the occasional game of backyard cricket, and a little squash here and there. More recently he even tried his hand at golf.

"Elijah married the love of his life, Juliana, in his early twenties, and several years later they welcomed their first child, a son, and named him Reece. Reece was followed a few years later by a sister they named Kaley. Juliana, Kaley, and Reece were the driving passion of Elijah's life. He loved his family for, to him, family was everything.

"Elijah was a determined man who accomplished his goals even when large obstacles stood in his way. He believed that truth mattered and would seek truth and speak truth without hesitation. He was not one to hold back an opinion or be 'politically correct.'

"And now the flame that burned so brightly is but a flicker in our memories. Those memories will stay lit and burn inside each and every one of us here today."

"Let us now spend a few moments in silence to remember Elijah Hael in our own way.

The funeral service was drawing to a close, and the designated pall bearers stood up and took their places around the casket. In unison, they raised the casket onto their shoulders and slowly carried it down the centre aisle and out of the church, followed closely by Juliana and the two children. Elijah witnessed the events with a mixture of disbelief and deep respect for the people who attended his funeral.

As Juliana passed by, Elijah could see the grief etched on her pretty face. He tried to reach for her, but his arm just passed through the air as if it were not there. He soon realised there was no use in trying. Reece and Kaley were walking on either side of Juliana, each holding a respective hand. They seem neither happy nor sad.

Juliana was followed first by close family, then relatives, and then friends and acquaintances. Before long the church was empty, and Elijah and Castiel followed them outside and watched as the casket was loaded into the back of a shiny black hearse. Many police were about, which prompted Elijah to ask Castiel, "Why are there so many police here?"

"Your sister Claricia, being a sergeant in the police force, has managed to pull strings and organise a police escort for the funeral cortege from here to the cemetery."

Just then two motorcycle policemen fired their engines, turned on their sirens, and led the hearse and other vehicles in the procession out into the traffic toward the cemetery.

Castiel took hold of Elijah's hand and that blinding white flash occurred again. They appeared in a cemetery overlooking a casket suspended by a pulley system over a large, freshly-dug hole in the earth. Elijah's wife, family, and relatives stood closest to the casket, while friends and acquaintances were a little farther back. Not as many people were here as at the church. The interment itself seemed to be much more of a private session.

Pastor Nathaniel, standing at the head of the casket, spoke:

"John 5:28-29: 'Don't be so surprised! Indeed, the time is coming when all the dead in their graves will hear the voice of God's Son, and they will rise again. Those who have done good will rise to experience eternal life, and those who have continued in evil will rise to experience judgment.'

"As we stand beside this open grave amongst the long-departed we commit the body of Elijah Hael to the ground and pray that his spirit is well received by our Lord.

"Mary Frye penned a poem that I would like to share.

"'Do not stand at my grave and weep.
  I am not there, I do not sleep.
I am a thousand winds that blow,
  I am the diamond glints on snow.
I am the sunlight on ripened grain,
  I am the gentle autumn's rain.
When you awaken in the morning's hush,
  I am the swift uplifting rush

of quiet birds in circled flight.

I am the stars that shine at night.

Do not stand at my grave and cry,

I am not there, I did not die....'"

The pastor ended with one last sentence.

"God sheds a tear for those who know him when they die, not because they are dead, but because they are coming home."

The attendants freed the pulleys from their restraints and began lowering the casket into the grave very slowly.

Reece, who was still holding his mother's hand, turned and looked up at her. "But, Mum," he said, "how will Daddy get out of the hole? It looks very deep."

Juliana did not reply, but a tear formed in her eye and streamed gently down her cheek.

Elijah looked at Juliana longingly. And just then she turned and looked over in Elijah's direction, staring into empty space. "Can she see me?" Elijah asked Castiel.

"No, she cannot," he said, "but sometimes they can sense your presence, and their mind will generate illusions."

Elijah knew that his children did not understand what was going on—that Daddy would not be coming home. Ever. Again. They were just too young to understand. Elijah wrestled with this and the thought that his kids would be without him in their lives, for the rest of their lives. Elijah loved his children very much. They truly did mean the world to him.

Shortly after the casket was placed in the grave the service ended. People started making their way back to their vehicles.

Elijah and Castiel stood by and watched the people leaving, each expressing grief in his or her own way. Elijah overheard someone say, "It's not the departed who suffers when someone dies. The ones left behind who have to deal with the death do the suffering."

Elijah looked over at his tombstone.

Elijah Hael

1971-2012

Husband to Juliana

Father to Kaley and Reece

There is no tomorrow, no yesterday, where I have gone.

"Why are you showing me this, Castiel?" Elijah asked.

"Soon I will be offering you a choice," Castiel said, looking him square in the eye, "and these events may help you to make the choice that is right for you."

"What was in that letter you gave to Stolas?"

"That," Castiel said. "I was wondering when you were going to get around to asking me about that letter. It contained information about a decision you made many years ago when you were going through quite a difficult time in your life. Take my hand and I'll show you."

Elijah took Castiel's hand and squinted ... but this time there was no white flash.

Chapter 6 - 1977, Nightmares

Elijah and Castiel appeared in a bedroom of modest size. A single bed was in the middle and a desk was on one side and a window on the other.

Elijah scanned his eyes around the room. "Why was there no flash this time, Castiel?"

It was nighttime. The bedroom was lit by a single night light mounted in a wall socket by the desk. It was obviously a boy's room. There was a model of a muscle car—a blue Pontiac GTO—on the desk and the bedspread bore a picture of VINCENT the robot on it from the movie "The Black Hole."

Castiel answered. "As you become accustomed to time travel the flashing stops. It just takes a bit to get used to it. Soon, you will not even need to hold my hand but will just move in time with me."

A woman's voice cried out from beyond the bedroom door. "Get back to bed! I don't care about your nightmares. Just grow up."

A young boy entered the bedroom and dragged his feet slowly across the floor, his head hung low. He shut the door behind him and sat on the floor at the end of the bed. He laid his head down on his knees and began to cry.

"That's me," Elijah muttered. "I remember this room. It was *my* bedroom. That boy is *me*. I was having horrible nightmares, terrifying beyond anything I'd ever imagined. I would see shadow figures of different colours all around me in the darkness. They would pin me to the bed and I would be unable to move or scream. They would then inflict pain throughout my body as if they were digging into my flesh with sharp objects." He shuddered. "It was horrific."

"Sounds horrific," Castiel said.

"I was so frightened that I couldn't go back to sleep. I actually fought sleep because I feared they would come torment me again."

Castiel cocked his head. "What did you do next?"

"I prayed. I didn't even know God, or much about Him. I just started praying for God to protect me and help me. I asked him to purify my dreams."

Elijah watched himself, the little boy, praying. His tears at last stopped rolling down his cheeks. He got up, switched off the bedroom light, climbed back into bed, and placed his head on the pillow. He lay on his back and pulled the bedspread up to just below his chin. Considering the terror of the nightmare ordeal the boy looked very peaceful. Night had fallen hard now, and the gentle glow of the night light provided just enough light to make out the surrounding objects in the room.

"Why did you pray, Elijah?" Castiel asked.

"I'm not sure. I don't even know where I got the idea God could help. I just did."

At that very moment, glowing shadow figures shaped like men began to appear around the room. Each one cast a strange stylised glow. They started to gather around the bed. Elijah was still fast asleep, unaware of the shadow figures in the room.

"Castiel, what are they?" Elijah asked. "I thought they were just figments of my dreams."

"No, not figments," Castiel told him. "They are very real. People who experience them describe them with such terms as demons, ghosts, and aliens—to name but a few. They want to learn more about you, to experiment on you, and to influence you to do their bidding."

"Why?"

"They are lost souls trying to find their way in a world they once called home—but lost. They just spread mischief and hate and stir up negative emotions. They create fear in people however they can. You see, fear is what they live on. It is what drives them."

Elijah was puzzled. "But I didn't have any more nightmares after I prayed, so why are they here? My nightmares had stopped."

A bright light flashed outside the window and out of it came forth a barefoot woman who dived through the light. As she passed through the closed window the glass just seemed to melt around her and then reform once she had passed through. She ended her dive with a graceful, whirling somersault.

The woman was about six feet tall. Her black hair fell over her shoulders and down to the middle of her back. She wore a long white silky dress and her emerald green eyes were piercing. The dress, semitransparent in areas, revealed the outline of her pristine body. Two swords glowing white were in sheaths crisscrossing her back.

"Wh- who is th- that?" Elijah stuttered in amazement.

"That is Sophia," Castiel said, "who has been assigned to protect you."

As Sophia rose from the somersault, she crossed her arms and in one swift smooth movement drew the swords from their sheaths. She lunged towards the first shadow figure and sliced it in two while coming over the top and thrusting her left arm straight into the shadow figure behind her. She then twisted and spun in the air over the bed, and as she landed, she thrust out both arms and pierced through the shadow figures on each side of her. The shadow figures yelped in pain as they deteriorated into the air, consumed by the light trails the swords left behind.

Sophia put both swords away and walked over to Elijah who was still sleeping. After gently stroking his hair and planting a feather light kiss on his cheek, she vanished.

Castiel said, "God listened. He heard your prayer, Elijah, and sent Sophia to protect you. From the moment you said that prayer Sophia was assigned to watch over you."

"Did she kill those shadow figures?"

"No," Castiel said, shaking his head. "You cannot kill them. They are spiritual beings. They are just sent back into the confinement that they slithered out of."

"I remember Sophia," Elijah said. "I've seen her before. I saw her when I was depressed. She would come and cheer me up. I thought she was a figment of my imagination that I created like an imaginary friend because at the time I was somewhat lonely. She wasn't a dual-sword-wielding ninja, though!"

"Yes, it seems our Sophia broke a few rules to appear to you like that."

"So what is she?"

"She is a Seraphim Angel. It is time to move on Elijah. Are you ready?"

"I guess so."

Elijah took Castiel's hand.

Chapter 7 - 1978, The Fall

When Elijah's vision cleared after the time jump he immediately recognised where he was. He was standing at the base of a three-story cliff surrounded by the Australian bush. As a child he had spent countless hours playing here after the family moved to Australia from England.

Elijah looked up and saw a familiar little boy. It was Elijah himself, scaling the cliff. As the boy neared the top, Elijah realised what was about to happen. He felt himself shudder and winced. With only an arm's length to go, the boy lost his footing and began sliding down the cliff face, which was all hardpan and jutting rock. Gravity was pulling him down faster and faster. His right foot caught on a protruding ledge and caused the boy to flip over, so that he was now hurtling down head first. With a loud thump, the boy came to a sudden halt as his head landed squarely on a large rock at the base of the cliff. Blood began flowing from a large gash on the back of his head, and the boy's eyes closed as he lost consciousness.

"That must have hurt," Castiel commented.

"To be honest, I don't remember much pain from the fall. The next thing I remember was coming to and feeling dampness on the back of my neck. I realised I was bleeding. I knew I had to find some way to get up and climb back up to the top of the cliff to get home for help. So I rolled over and tried to get on my feet, but I was so shaky and weak that I laid down again and fell back asleep."

Just then Sophia appeared to the left of the cliff base. She walked over to where the boy was lying and placed her hands over his body. A white glow appeared from her hands and extended over Elijah's body. The flow of blood from his wound began to slow.

Sophia moved into the bushes.

Elijah's eyes began to open again. He forced himself to stand up on shaky legs and take a step onto a rock. His knees started to buckle, but he straightened up and took another step. Halfway up, he began feeling dizzy and started to fall. In that moment, Sophia flew through the air powered by large outstretched wings that protruded from her back between her shoulder blades. She caught Elijah in mid-fall, carried him to the top of the cliff, and set him down gently onto the ground. The boy steadied himself and, still in a bit of a daze, struggled to his feet and made his way home.

"So that's what happened?" Elijah said, nodding. "I could never quite figure out how I managed to climb that steep cliff in my condition. I had no memory of it."

"Let's follow."

"You mean climb up after him?"

"No, no," Castiel said. "No need for that. We just need to follow. Just think about where you want to go and you'll end up there."

Elijah and Castiel both thought about being at the top of the cliff and, sure enough, as they did they floated upwards until they were standing at the ledge 60 metres up. They continued following the boy Elijah through the bush.

Curious, Elijah asked, "How come we didn't need wings like Sophia's to fly?"

"Ah, good question," Castiel answered. "You see, we are in what you would call the 'Spiritual Realm' from which we can *see* the Human Realm, but cannot interact with it and are not subject to its physical laws. To interact in the Human Realm requires that you move into it.

Since Sophia was in the Human Realm, she had to obey its physical laws, which required her to fly using her wings and keep out of sight. It is also possible for an angel to be injured physically when in the Human Realm."

"Can I cross over into the Human Realm?"

"No, not now," Castiel said. "That requires certain skills and understanding of rules that you have yet to learn."

"Can people inside the Human Realm see things in the Spiritual Realm?"

"Some people can see things for short periods of time or sense a presence in the Spiritual Realm–the way Juliana sensed you earlier. People occasionally experience the Spiritual Realm when their body is dying and their soul is departing. At that point—the point of death—they cross over from the Human Realm into the Spiritual Realm. If they are somehow resuscitated, they are pulled back into the Human Realm and sometimes they have partial knowledge of the experience."

Elijah and Castiel watched Elijah scramble into the house with one hand slapped against the back of his head to help stem the bleeding. A moment later they saw the garage door open and a car back out. The boy Elijah was in the passenger seat and his mother was behind the wheel.

"Quick, Elijah, let's hop into the back of the car."

Castiel took Elijah's hand and they dashed into the back of the car, passing through the doors, and took their places on the back seat.

"That was a little freaky, Castiel," Elijah said. "Whew. It's going to take me a little while longer to get used to this 'think where you want to be and then you'll be there' thing."

"It will not take you long."

"I admit that I do like being able to simply pass through objects."

"A gas, isn't it?"

"Wait a minute," Elijah said, squinting. "If Sophia was in the Human Realm when she dived through my closed bedroom window and had to obey the physical laws of the realm, how did she just pass through it?"

"You're no dimwit, Elijah," Castiel said, smiling. "Sophia is trained in quantum mechanics, which allows her manipulate the physical world around her. Humans could as well if they only had the knowledge."

Elijah's mum parked outside the hospital emergency unit and led her son into the emergency room. Castiel and Elijah followed.

The boy lay on a hospital bed as the doctor stitched up the wound on his head. The doctor said to his mother, "It's a wonder that our boy Elijah here got such a deep gash in his head without cracking his skull. You have one very lucky little boy."

Castiel said, "Luck had nothing to do with it, Elijah. Your skull *was* cracked—quite badly, in fact, but Sophia healed it for you."

Elijah looked at Castiel. "So what you are saying is that I would have died if Sophia had not turned up."

Castiel nodded.

Elijah's mother thanked the doctor and, after completing some paperwork at the hospital administration desk, led her son back to the car.

"Are we going to follow" Elijah asked Castiel.

"No, we have somewhere else to be. Take my hand."

Chapter 8 - 1980, Separation

Castiel and Elijah were standing outside a modest-sized family home as a car pulled into the driveway.

"This is where I lived when I was about nine," Elijah said.

"Your father is arriving home from work a little earlier than usual. What happens next is the catalyst for your parents' divorce, Elijah. You've heard the story, but I think it is important that you see and hear it for yourself so you will know what actually happened."

Elijah's father parked the car and made his way to the front door. He glanced behind him at an unfamiliar vehicle parked on the curb in front of his house. After fumbling with his keys for a moment, he worked the key into the lock, turned the knob, and pushed the door. It was deadlocked. He could hear music playing inside the house and began knocking on the door. No reply. He began knocking louder. Minutes passed before he heard his wife yell out, "Just a minute." A few more minutes passed before she finally opened the door.

Elijah's father walked in to find his wife alone with a young man in his teenage years named Dean. Dean was tall and thin and dressed like a typical delinquent youth. The guilt written on both of their faces was sending a clear message that they had been up to something. Elijah's father had suspected that his wife was having affairs but always dismissed the notion. His wife frequently had young men in their teens over to the family house. She found these young men with a CB Radio (which was an early form of social networking in the days before Internet chat and Facebook). Elijah's father blamed himself in many ways for what was happening because he was the one who introduced the CB Radio to the family.

"Come, Elijah," Castiel said. "We need to go inside to see what happens."

Elijah and Castiel proceeded to enter the house by passing through a sidewall and appeared in the lounge where they could see Elijah's mother, father and Dean. Several Shadow Figures were lurking around in the corners of the room.

"Why are the Shadow Figures here, Castiel?"

"They have come to feed on the anger and the fear."

Elijah's father questioned his wife in a frustrated voice. "Why was the door deadlocked?"

"We were listening to music," Elijah's mother replied.

"Couldn't you hear me knocking?"

"No, not until a few minutes ago," she said and then added: "Maybe you could have knocked a bit louder."

"Why did it take you so long to answer the door?"

"Are you accusing me of something?"

Dean spoke up. "Nothing was going on."

"I want you to leave my house, Dean," Elijah's father said, his voice loud. "Right now."

"No," Dean said. "I think I want to stay."

"Leave."

"No."

"LEAVE!!!"

Elijah's father's frustration was growing. Tension was mounting. The Shadow Figures gathered around and soaked up a red flowing energy coming from Dean and Elijah's father.

"What is that red stuff swirling around?" Elijah asked.

"Emotions become energy, Elijah. Red is a negative energy while white is a positive energy. The Shadow Figures feed off the red energy but the white energy hurts them. This emotional energy is visible only in the Spiritual Realm."

Dean stepped in front of Elijah's father and shoved him. Elijah's father regained his balance and walked into the bedroom, opened his closet, and pulled out a rifle. He loaded it quickly, proceeded back into the lounge and pointed the rifle at Dean's heart and said, "Leave now or I will shoot."

All Dean's bravado was gone now; his face was pale with fear. He glanced at Elijah's mother as he hurried to the front door and left. A moment later they heard his car door slam. The engine roared and the tires screeched as he sped away.

Elijah's mother stared at her husband with rage in her eyes. "How dare you!"

"How dare *I*? This is my house. I come home from work and find the doors deadlocked and I can't get in. How dare I? How dare *you*? Are you sleeping with him?"

Elijah's mother did not answer but ran off into the bedroom. His father made his way into the study. Some of the Shadow Figures followed Elijah's father while others followed his mother feeding off the red trails of energy flowing from them.

Elijah shook his head. "That is pretty much the way my father described the scene to me when I asked him about it. I asked him because my mother told me that my father had threatened Dean with a gun. I figured there must have been more to the story because I knew my father was a rather reserved, cool-headed man. He is not the violent or hot-tempered type. My mother used the incident as an excuse for not seeing a counsellor to help us work out our relationship issues. She said the psychologist she consulted encouraged her to leave my father. Somehow I doubt that my mother told the psychologist what was really going on."

"Do you love your mother, Elijah?"

"I've learnt to love everyone," he said. "Loving her doesn't mean that I find her behaviour acceptable. She did some damaging things and showed no remorse for any of them. She would never take responsibility for anything. Her way was always to blame others for situations that she was at least *partially* responsible for."

"You sound angry, Elijah."

"No, not angry, just disappointed." Elijah let the words linger a while before going on. "Not long after this my parents told me they were separating and started living in separate houses. I would live with my mother during the week and spend weekends with my father. It was not the best of times. My father was despondent and depressed. I feared he might end up committing suicide or worse take me with him in a murder-suicide. He did neither, of course, and even managed to make our weekends quite enjoyable times. Things were not so good at home though."

"Come, Elijah. Let's go see what your father is doing in the study."

Elijah and Castiel made their way into the study where they found Elijah's father seated at his desk studying a photograph–a family portrait taken when Elijah was around six years old and his sister around nine. They all looked happy.

Noticing that something was not quite right, Elijah moved around to the side of the desk. He could see that his father had wedged his rifle between his legs and placed his mouth around the end of the barrel. Tears were rolling down the man's face. He shivered as if he were freezing. He was fumbling around trying to get his finger to the trigger, but he was shaking too badly. Maybe he took that as a sign that his suicide wasn't meant to be because he calmed down a bit and pushed the rifle aside. He just wept, the way a man weeps when he knows that his marriage is over and his family will forever be broken.

Elijah looked on. He never imagined that his father had gone through such an agonizing moment. He realised now that this event had hardened his father's heart and led to his depression.

"I was right," Elijah said. "He *was* suicidal."

"It is time to continue on, Elijah. Are you okay to continue?"

"Yes, I'm okay. I admit that this is all a bit overwhelming. I've just witnessed my own funeral, fallen off a cliff and seen my father with a rifle barrel in his mouth, but for some reason I sense that this is important."

"It is, Elijah," Castiel replied, his voice warmly compassionate. "It truly is."

This time Elijah did not need to take Castiel's hand because he could just feel where to go next.

Chapter 9 - 1982, Dale

It was late afternoon when Elijah and Castiel appeared in a bedroom where a boy was sitting at a desk in the corner operating a System 80 computer.

"That's me writing some program on my computer system," Elijah said. "I must be about eleven."

"You are," Castiel said.

"This was soon after my parents separated, and my mum and I had just moved into this house. We moved more than fifteen times and I went to eight different schools while I was growing up. It was hard to establish any long-term friendships."

"It was remarkable that you became as stable as you did, Elijah. It's one of the things that really stood out in your file."

Elijah's mother entered the room and called to the boy. "Elijah?"

The boy turned around on his chair and looked at her. "Yes, Mum?"

"Dale is going to be sleeping in my room from now on," she announced. "The bed in the guest bedroom is old and the springs are hurting Dale's back."

"Okay," the boy said.

Elijah's mum then turned and walked out of the room without saying another word, and the boy turned back and recommenced working on his computer.

"I remember this, Castiel. It's another one of those moments that stick with you because of how ridiculous my mother's statement was to me—even at that tender age. I wasn't stupid. I knew exactly what it meant. They had begun a sexual relationship."

"You didn't get on well with Dale did you, Elijah?"

"Considering the situation, I think we got on fairly well. Dale who was only a few years older than me was my mother's next teenage boyfriend after Dean. Dale came from a broken home and was pretty messed up. He was quite violent at times, both physically and verbally, and smoked like a chimney. Dale was twenty-three years younger than my mum. I could never see the relationship lasting. But they did go on to be married and even had a child together—only to divorce twenty-five years later."

Castiel nodded. "Dale started seeing a psychiatrist who helped him heal the wounds of his past, which gave him the courage to leave and start his own life. It was not easy for him to do that, Elijah. He stayed around until he felt his son was old enough to make his own choices."

Elijah shrugged. "My sister had a more difficult time adjusting than I did. She was about the same age as Dale and her boyfriend was actually a year or two older than Dale. It was quite messed up. In some ways, Dale became an older brother and we did have some fun times together. He was a bit like a Jekyll and Hyde character though. You could never predict how he was going to be. He was brought into a family to play the part of father figure, but he had neither the age nor the wisdom to pull it off. I have never blamed Dale for the way things turned out. My mother, who was old enough to be Dale's mother, should have been the responsible one. But, again, she never took responsibility for anything. I am not sure what happened to her that led her to be that way. But I sure can't recall ever having a 'normal' mother-son type relationship with her."

"Do you want to know what happened to your mother to make her the way she was?"

"In some ways, yes," Elijah said, looking down at the floor. "I do have an idea, but it bothers me."

"The Shadow Figures, Elijah," Castiel said. "They exercise a lot of control over the way your mother thinks and acts. They ended up controlling much of what she does in life. Shadow Figures like to attract others who are controlled by them. In your mother's case, Dean and Dale. They find it easy to group together. Humans sometimes call this 'demonic influence' or 'demon possession.' The Catholic Church performs exorcisms for it while other Christian churches hold deliverance services. People often think that those who are possessed or influenced have to walk around like zombies or foam at the mouth or have weird physical attributes. This is not true. Such people can look quite normal, but they are very calculating, even cunning, and bring about as much disharmony as possible to generate the red energy they feed on. They do this by arousing thoughts that lead to fear, anxiety, stress, depression, hatred, idolatry, anger, sexual immorality, selfish ambition, drunkenness, and jealousy. I'm just confirming what you already suspected, Elijah."

"So, how did the Shadow Figures get control over my mother?"

"The same way they assume control over any human being. Here's how it works. When a person sins, cracks begin to form in the body's natural protection against such forces. In your mother's case, it wasn't simply one particular sin, but many. The more sins a person commits the more cracks form. When enough cracks form, the Shadow Figures can enter in and take control of the person's body. It's a downward spiral because at first there are just minor cracks, but they allow temptations to enter a person's thoughts. If a person acts on those temptations, he or she commits more sins, which create more cracks. Your mother started with simple lies, dabbling in the occult, a little deception here, a little lust there, then adultery, and on it went."

"Can she be helped?"

"A person must want to be helped before they can be helped. If she wants help then, yes, there are ways."

"If my mother and Dale had those Shadow Figures in them then, why didn't they get to me while I was living at home? Surely I had some cracks."

"Oh, they tried, for instance when you were having those nightmares, but you asked for protection. They knew you were protected. That didn't stop them from trying, though."

Music began playing on the boy's System 80 computer as he started playing a game.

Elijah nodded toward the boy at the computer. "The only thing I ended up trusting and loving when I was young was my computer. I did not find much peace in anything else. I believed my computer was the only thing that would not turn around and hurt me. I spent many an hour in front of it. I taught myself to program it, which led to a successful career as a software developer."

"Our next stop awaits, Elijah."

Elijah nodded. "Okay, then, let's go," he said as he turned and stole one more glance at his younger self and felt a pang of deep sadness.

Chapter 10 - 1983, Claricia

Castiel and Elijah appeared in the hallway of a mid-sized house, outside a bedroom door. Faint moon rays streaming through the bedroom window cast a bluish tint on the dark bedroom. A teenage girl was lying under a quilt on a single bed. The small digital alarm clock on the bedside table glowed with red numbers: 9:46 p.m.

"This is my sister Claricia's bedroom," Elijah said. "Why are we here?"

"For some time, Elijah, you have wondered why your sister ran away from home, leaving you behind without a word."

Elijah shook his head slowly, side to side, not sure he wanted to know even now.

Just then Dale came to the doorway and spoke: "Claricia, do you mind if I sleep with you tonight? I'm scared of what is happening and I don't want to be alone."

Looking up from her bed Claricia replied, "I'm not sure that's a good idea, Dale."

"Why not?"

"It doesn't seem appropriate," she said. "You are in a relationship with my mum."

He lowered his voice. "But she is in hospital having our pregnancy aborted because our child died inside of her. It is really bothering me, Clar', and I just don't want to be alone."

"I'm not sure," Claricia said, in a voice almost pleading. "It just doesn't seem right."

"It will be fine."

"Well, okay, but I'm going to put on some more clothes."

Claricia rolled out of bed and put her nightgown on over her nightdress. Then she slowly climbed back into bed. Dale followed and slipped under the quilt beside her.

"Castiel," Elijah said, "something doesn't seem right here. Why would she agree to that?"

"Because she was scared and confused, Elijah. Claricia was backed into a corner. She was just a child herself, really. Dale, the 'father figure,' was about her age and so she figured she could control the situation if something were to happen. It was very confusing— mentally and emotionally."

Claricia and Dale lay on the bed facing opposite directions.

"Let's move forward in time, Elijah," Castiel said. "Otherwise we will be in for a bit of a wait."

Elijah noticed the time on the alarm clock time was ticking over faster than normal. The minute display started ticking over every second, then ever tenth of a second. Everything was advancing in fast-forward. After lying there restless for some time, Claricia and Dale eventually seemed to drift off to sleep. The alarm clock eventually came to rest at 3:33 a.m.

Dale rolled over in bed as discreetly as he could, so as not to rouse Claricia, and put his arm around her. He slipped his hand down to the bottom of her night gown and began sliding it up the inside of her nightdress, reaching towards her breast. Claricia woke up, startled she pushed his arm away and Dale reluctantly withdrew it. Then he tried again, but again Claricia refused the advance and moved as far as she could to the edge of the bed.

"What is he doing, Castiel?"

"Making a sexual advance towards your sister, but she rejected him."

Time started passing quickly again, and Elijah watched as Claricia lay agitated on her side of the bed until dawn broke and Dale left.

"Ready for a quick time jump, Elijah?"

"Yes," he said. "Please."

They appeared in the kitchen of the house several days later and witnessed a spirited conversation between Claricia and her mother.

"Why?" Claricia said. "Because Dale asked to share my bed with him the night you were in hospital."

"Why would he do that?"

"He said he was scared and lonely, Mum."

"Why would you let him?"

"Because I felt I didn't really have a choice."

"You expect me to believe that? It's more likely that *you* made an advance towards him."

"No, I didn't, Mum!" Claricia's face was red, her voice loud and raspy. "In the middle of the night he put his hand inside my night gown."

"Don't tell me this stupid lie, Claricia. He would never do that. You're obviously making up a story to cause strife between Dale and me. You're just jealous of our relationship. You always have been. Now, go! Leave me alone."

Claricia shook her head in disbelief and started crying as she did as she was told and left.

"Shortly after this, Elijah, your sister ran away," Castiel said. "There was such tension between your mother and her that she simply couldn't bear it."

"Why didn't she talk to me about it?"

"Your mother dismissed it—and her—and Claricia figured you wouldn't believe her either."

"But I would have," he said.

"She just didn't have the heart or strength to take that risk."

"I guess when your own mum casts you off like that, well, it would be hard to trust anyone." Elijah felt a pang of sadness in his heart. He recalled how she had arranged for a police escort for his funeral cortege. "Though we didn't have an especially close relationship, I did look up to her. Her leaving like that left me feeling quite hollow. Things became much worse once she was gone. Mum and Dale became even more oblivious to my presence in the house. Quite often I would hear them having sex. Being abandoned by my only ally left me with emotional scars for some time. I was very much alone and felt very unwelcome in that house. I longed for the weekends I would spend with my father."

Castiel placed a hand on Elijah's back and patted. "That was a rough road to travel, my friend."

"My father would have probably killed Dale if he had found out about what he did to Claricia. My mum tried to hide the fact that she and Dale were 'involved' and even lied to him about the pregnancy. She told him she became pregnant in a one-night stand. Because they weren't divorced, only separated, she needed him to sign the medical insurance claim for the procedure. I'm not even sure whether the child did die inside of her or she was just having an abortion to hide the truth that Dale was underage by avoiding a birth certificate. If the police had found out the truth she would have gone to jail for statutory rape. Dale's mother was just waiting for something to pin on my mother. I'm quite sure she never approved of the situation. Why should she? My mother actually asked my father to give Dale a job where he was working ... and he did. He wouldn't have done that if he had known they were sleeping together. How could he have been so blind to the truth? To be fair, though, my mother was quite controlling and deceitful."

"Why didn't you tell him the truth at the time, Elijah?"

"I'm not sure," he said, shrugging his shoulders. "As I mentioned before, at the time I felt he was suicidal. I figured there were some things he was better off not knowing. Apparently, he didn't want to believe them. It did come out later, however. My mother tried to lay a guilt trip on me about being off with my father having a grand old time at a theme park while she was having the 'procedure.' I didn't even know she was going to have it. It was one of many such things she used as an emotional weapon to make me feel bad. She would even describe the gory details of the procedure to me. It was difficult for a thirteen-year-old to understand."

"It was nothing to do with you, Elijah," Castiel said, with sympathy in his voice, "That's for sure. Your mother should never have tried to make it about you."

"How did my sister go on to join the police force, Castiel? I would have thought this experience would have mixed her up quite a bit."

"You would have been right then, Elijah. It did mess her up. It took some time for her to get over it, and she went through some very abusive relationships as a result. She got it together with a bit of help."

"Who helped her?"

"You did."

"I did?" Elijah squinted and shook his head. "But ... how? I didn't see or hear from her during those times."

"It will all make sense to you soon enough, Elijah. But for now...," he said, taking hold of Elijah's hand....

Chapter 11 - 1986, Choice

Elijah and Castiel appeared at the water's edge at Wisemans Wharf on a bleak morning. A 15-year-old Elijah and his father were out fishing in the rain on the end of a jetty. Not much was biting, but Elijah loved fishing with his father.

Elijah's dad was showing him the right way to tie a hook onto the end of a fishing line. Elijah was soaking up the information like a sponge. The young man was not short on talent and could learn a new skill from a single showing or simply from reading a book. Teachers were often quite amazed at Elijah's superior performance on exams—without studying. He was often the first one in class to finish, way before the rest of the students. When he handed in an exam, teachers would just shake their heads as he turned and left the classroom, not believing it was possible that he had answered all the examination questions so quickly.

His marks were so high they realised he was gifted academically ... but they also knew that he was easily distracted and quite often too talkative and mischievous in class. He had a sharp mind and superior aptitude, but his conduct held him back from excellence. Quite often on his report cards, teachers would comment: "Elijah shows incredible talent but fails to apply it on a day- to-day basis." Little did they know it was due to difficulties at home. Elijah was less concerned with schoolwork than with finding stability—and he was forever searching for it during his school years.

When Elijah's father had finished showing him how to tie on a fish hook, he said, "Elijah, I will be leaving to work in Thailand for an indefinite length of time.... If you wanted to come with me, I could check with your mother to see if it would be okay? It would mean leaving school, your friends and attending an international school in Thailand."

"Yes, I want to," Elijah responded, without a second of hesitation.

Elijah did not need time to think about it. He saw this as an opportunity to find with his father the stability he did not have at home with his mother. Though he was enjoying year 9 at school and had some great friends, what he wanted most of all was to feel loved.

When Elijah got back home on Sunday evening his mum and Dale had a brief talk with him about leaving. In her own way, his mother was checking to see if it was what Elijah really wanted. It was all he wanted! Deep down, he knew that Dale and his mum did not really want him around anyway, the truth of which was confirmed by how easily his mother agreed to let Elijah go. She didn't even put up a weak argument. It was as if she couldn't have cared less. Elijah knew that was the truth, that he was expendable just like a sack of garbage. At that time, his mother was pregnant a second time with Dale's child. This time Dale was of legal age—barely. Elijah knew that he would be trouble after the child was born. Claricia had said the same thing years earlier when their mother was pregnant by Dale the first time.

That very Sunday night, Elijah began counting down the days until he was leaving Australia. He did not have much to pack, just clothes, the Commodore 64 computer his father had recently given him, and some miscellaneous items that all fit in one suitcase. Elijah had only been on an aeroplane once before, when he was a year old at the time his family moved to Australia from England in search of a better life. The unfortunate part for Elijah and Claricia was that all their relatives—grandparents, aunt, uncles, and cousins—were in England.

After their time jump, Elijah and Castiel appeared in the airport terminal just as Elijah and his father were boarding the plane.

"I don't even remember this, Castiel, leaving Australia," Elijah said. "I don't remember any goodbyes with my mother. You would think she would have been here at the airport to see me off."

Castiel shook his head. "You had left home a few days earlier when your father picked you up for the weekend. There were never any goodbyes, and your mother showed no interest in coming to the airport to see you off."

Elijah lowered his head. "What did I do that was so bad that it caused my mother to never truly love me?"

"It wasn't anything you did, Elijah. Those Shadow Figures were constantly in her ear. She was in a scurrilous relationship with Dale. She developed a bitter hatred for your father. Those three things combined to make her wish that you didn't exist. It didn't help matters that you resemble your father, which was difficult for your mother to accept. One other thing: You also had protection from Sophia that irritated the Shadow Figures that constantly surrounded her. The Shadow Figures encouraged her to distance herself from you for *their* own safety."

Castiel and Elijah watched the teenage Elijah board the plane with his father. The expression on his face and the cut of his jib showed pure excitement and glee.

Elijah knew that the young man would not again experience such excitement and glee for many years to come. He would soon face some of the most difficult challenges of his life to that point. What promised to be a dream come true—having an adventure in another country—was about to become his worst nightmare.

Chapter 12 - Malaysia

Elijah and his father's journey to Thailand was not direct. They had to layover in Malaysia for a week on business. Elijah was fascinated with flight and especially enjoyed the take-off and landing.

A business executive who worked for a company Elijah's father was visiting greeted them at the airport. He took Elijah and his father on a tour of Malaysia that went late into the evening. At one point, they stopped in a red-light district and picked up a lady of the night. She got in the back seat with Elijah's father while Elijah sat in the front. She wore very skimpy clothes that left little to the imagination and seemed to be flirting with Elijah's father. Elijah was curious as to who she was. Before long she began saying things to Elijah's father that the boy did not understand. In time, he came to realise she was offering him sexual favours. Elijah's father rejected them with a slight chuckle. Shortly thereafter, the driver pulled over and the business executive passed the woman some money for her trouble and she left. Later that night they returned to the motel. Elijah stayed in the room while his father again left with the business executive.

The motel was quite nice. Elijah had a room of his own right next door to his father's. Elijah did not mind being left alone for a while and quickly began trying to figure out how to use the television.

* * *

Castiel and Elijah appeared from the time jump and quickly got their bearings.

"This was the start of a 'great adventure,' Castiel," Elijah said. "That is what I thought this would be. In many ways it lived up to the hype.

It demanded that I grow up very quickly because I was pretty much all alone in a foreign country and didn't speak the language."

"You were never alone, Elijah," Castiel said. "See." He cocked his head to the right as Sophia appeared in the motel room. This time, though, she was in the Spiritual Realm.

"Can she see us, Castiel?"

"No, we are on a different time line. Although we are both at the same point in time in the Spiritual Realm we are on different timelines. She can only see what was around at that particular time on her timeline. We can see her because we have come in on a later timeline. If she were to come again on a different timeline after us, she would see her former self and us. Time itself is not linear. It just appears that way to humans. Time is actually perpetual, forever repeating."

"Why is she here?"

Elijah played around with the remote, trying to figure out what each of the buttons did. At last he pressed the power button and the television turned on. Soon after he was changing the channels, he stopped on a channel that was playing an English movie. He lay down on the bed and began watching it.

A vast number of Shadow Figures started to appear in the corners of the room. They, too, were in the Spiritual Realm. They quickly noticed Sophia, who moved to the centre of the room between the bed and the television. The Shadow Figures surrounded her. They seemed more organised than usual and were armed with their own weapons. Some had chains, others had what appeared to be Nunchakus, and a few were wielding knives. Their weapons had a faint red glow about them, while Sophia's swords glowed white as she drew them out of the sheaths on her back. Sophia stood and waited, calm and poised, in a defensive position. She surveyed her surroundings to determine where each Shadow Figure was.

Elijah whispered to Castiel, "Wow, I never knew all this action was going on behind the scenes while I was watching that movie."

"No need to whisper," Castiel told him. "They can't hear you."

The Shadow Figures charged Sophia, and when they did time seemed to slow down, but Sophia moved at an incredibly fast speed as she blocked their strikes and sliced through them one at a time. It seemed as though Sophia could slow time around her as she maintained her normal pace. Sophia performed amazing acrobatic moves which caused some of the Shadow Figures to crash into each other and explode before disintegrating. Before long only a few Shadow Figures remained, and Sophia returned to the centre of the room and resumed her defensive stance. The remaining Shadow Figures looked frightened and began to retreat and then vanish.

As she put her swords away, Sophia sat beside Elijah on the bed and said, "You'll get through this, Elijah. You have a destiny to fulfil." Then she vanished.

"What would have happened if Sophia hadn't come to fend off those Shadow Figures, Castiel?"

"All that matters is that she did come," Castiel said. "Time for us to go, Elijah."

* * *

The next morning Elijah's father told him that he had gone to a massage parlour the previous night. The "massage" started with a bath, was followed by a massage, and proceeded to sex. Elijah was not sure what to think and wondered why his father was sharing this experience in detail. He did not know whether to feel proud of or disgusted by his father. His father seemed to be describing the experience as something wonderful, but to Elijah it just felt false.

A few days later, his father was in hospital for a urinary tract infection he picked up at the massage parlour. His father described in detail how they had to push a probe into the end of his penis to get a urine sample and said it was quite painful. He then went on to describe how the nurses had a good chuckle over it all. Elijah figured it was the price you pay for dabbling in things you shouldn't.

The week in Malaysia passed quickly. Elijah had quite an enjoyable time. There was no school and many new things to explore, and every meal was at a restaurant or made to order from room service. Elijah felt special and very welcome. The staff at the motel were very helpful and took a bit of a shine to Elijah. They could see that he was very much alone and thus took time to become friends with him. In their own way, they looked out for him.

Chapter 13 - Thailand

Elijah peered out the window as the plane made its final approach to Thailand. Through a sea of every colour he could see the buildings surrounding the airport as the plane touched down.

As they walked through the airport Elijah took note of the signs: "If you are caught with drugs you will be sentenced to death." Elijah thought about how people are caught with drugs on them and wondered why they would take the risk. He thought to himself: *Desperate people sometimes do desperate things.*

Soon after they claimed their baggage Kazem, a co-owner of the company Elijah's father would be working with in Thailand, greeted them. Kazem was short and looked physically fit. Elijah guessed he was in his late 20s. The man led them out of the airport and into his late-model BMW. It took about 45 minutes to get from the airport to a gated community of townhouses that would be their home in Thailand.

"Welcome to your home, Mr. Hael, Elijah," Kazem said as he opened the front door of the townhouse and gestured for them to enter. "I hope you like your next-door neighbour—me. I live right next door."

Elijah and his father walked into the townhouse and gave it a once-over. It was a luxurious townhouse by Thailand's standards. It had two stories. The main living area, the kitchen, and a bathroom were downstairs. Upstairs was a master bedroom with an en-suite, a second bedroom, and a bathroom. The second bedroom, which Elijah knew was for him, had a queen-size bed, a walk-in wardrobe, and a small, but new, stereo system. Elijah was quite excited. His bedroom was much nicer than any bedroom he had before and it was air-conditioned, a luxury Elijah had experienced only in motel rooms.

A door on the lower level connected Elijah's townhouse with Kazem's townhouse. A maid would use the door to move between the two buildings. The maid, Lily, a pleasant lady in her 50s, did not speak much English. She became good friends with Elijah and in many ways was like the mother he had never had. She showed great interest in his life and would sit with him on occasion to catch up on how things were.

Kazem invited Elijah and his father over for dinner later that evening. On arriving for dinner, Elijah noticed that Lily had prepared many different dishes and placed them in the middle of the table. The way the Thai people ate was quite different from what Elijah was used to, but similar to the way they ate in Malaysia. They would put many dishes in the middle of the table, and you would take bits of each dish and put it on your plate. This enabled each person to choose what he or she wanted.

Lily guided Elijah and his father to their seats and soon afterwards Kazem and his wife entered the living area and sat down at the table. Kazem introduced them to his wife Nim. Nim was beautiful, like a model in a magazine, and had a gorgeous smile that would melt even the hardest heart. Her voice was extremely elegant. Elijah was beginning to understand the way the Thai people spoke English. While Kazem and Nim could speak English, it was what is known as "Pidgin English." They spoke in short, clipped sentences containing but a few words and relying heavily on body language to express what they meant. In between speaking English, Kazem and Nim would speak Thai to each other and to Lily. Elijah watched and listened very carefully and began learning the meaning of the words they spoke by their reactions and body language. With no formal training in Thai, he was already learning the language through observation and participation.

Dinner was over before Elijah knew it, and he and his father returned to their townhouse through the connecting door to retire for the night.

* * *

Not long after they returned, Castiel and Elijah appeared in teenage Elijah's bedroom as the boy was saying a silent prayer.

In a voice tinged with regret, Elijah said, "Thailand. I figured this would be our next stop, Castiel, for many significant things happened in Thailand."

"It presented many situations in which you learnt a lot, Elijah. Difficult situations allow us to grow mentally and spiritually, and you did a lot of growing in Thailand."

"I prayed every night, Castiel. My prayer went something like this: 'Master, please protect me and purify my dreams. I don't want any nightmares. Let me dream of adventures and exciting things— nothing that will scare me. Look after me and thanks for being with me.' I use to pray to 'Master.' Back then, I really didn't know who to pray to so I ended up praying to 'Master.' I am not sure where I got that idea. Sometimes I would also include 'God.'"

"Your prayers were heard, Elijah," Castiel assured him. "Sophia was always close by when you were in Thailand, watching over you. There was a lot of darkness around, and many resources were needed to keep you safe. "

Elijah nodded. "It always felt as though someone was looking out for me."

"We are going to do some time-skipping here, Elijah, to visit some particular moments. Hang in there, my friend, because our flight through Thailand is going to be bumpy."

That said, Elijah and Castiel jumped and then appeared in a large office with several people in it. Elijah was sitting at a desk with his prized Commodore 64 computer before him.

"I spent a lot of time here, Castiel. Most days I would stay in the factory's office. I became good friends with the office staff during those six months. We became a 'band of five' and enjoyed many exciting adventures together. They took me several places—the zoo, movie theatres, the beach. I did a bit for the company each day with the computers. I wrote a few programs for the business and performed other general office duties. I picked up quite a few skills that would help me later when I studied business in college. I felt safe with them."

"They were good people, Elijah," responded Castiel.

"My father worked in a different part of the factory, in product testing. We didn't see each other much during the day."

Elijah then noticed that his teenage self had a faint white glow, like an aura, around him. "Why am I glowing, Castiel?"

"Sophia has put a temporary protection blessing on you."

"Protection from what? I can't see anything."

"Look at the floor."

Elijah looked down and saw thousands of black things, a little smaller than a cockroach, scurrying about. They had no predefined shape and kind of warped into different shapes as they moved, the way the gobs of lava in a lava lamp change shape.

"What are they?"

"Shadow Scavengers," Castiel told him. "They scour surfaces for any red energy they can find. "

Elijah surveyed the room and noticed that they were not just on the floor but were moving up the legs of the people in the room—except for Elijah—rolling under their clothing and back out.

"Can they cause harm?"

"No, they're just scavengers, not predators. Sophia didn't want them going anywhere near you, so she put a temporary blessing on you that creates white energy, which repels the Shadow Scavengers."

"Why are so many of them here?"

"They're scavengers. They go where they can find easy picking and lots of them. You see them in busy places such as shopping malls, offices, and factories. Basically, anywhere with a lot of people who exhibit negative emotions."

"How come they are mainly on the floor?"

"Red energy has a weight subject to the pull of gravity and ends up settling on the ground if it isn't captured at the source. A bit like dust, which settles, but slightly heavier."

The teenage Elijah stood up from the desk and walked to the restroom in the far corner of the office. The Shadow Scavengers scurried quickly away from where Elijah walked, parting almost as if they were making a path for him.

"Our next stop awaits, Elijah."

Chapter 14 - The Pink Panther

The large neon sign above the entrance to a nightclub glowed with big pink letters: *The Pink Panther*. Several scantily clad girls were standing outside. The Pink Panther was one of many nightclubs in Bangkok's infamous red-light district, where Elijah would learn about a different side of life.

Castiel and Elijah appeared from their time jump just opposite teenage Elijah who was sitting against the wall outside the main entrance to the Pink Panther just watching people come and go. Occasionally, he would talk to the girl at the door who was dressed quite modestly compared to some of the others.

Elijah said, "I spent many hours sitting outside this place because I found it easier to sit outside than inside with the loud music and the dancing girls, many of them half naked, and the ones in the upstairs lounge were completely naked."

Elijah noticed Shadow Figures by the thousand swarming around and Shadow Scavengers were everywhere. The Shadow Figures were leeching the red energy off the men having lustful thoughts or doing lustful things to the prostitutes scouring the streets. The red energy just flowed out of them, and the Shadow Figures were just drinking it all in like frenzied gluttons. It made Elijah shudder.

Castiel said, "It can be quite disturbing when you see what really goes on between the Spiritual Realm and the Human Realm, Elijah. "

Elijah's teenage self stood up and proceeded to go inside the Pink Panther, and Castiel and Elijah followed. The club was very noisy between the loud music blaring from large speakers suspended from the ceiling to men cat-calling the women dancing around poles mounted on the elevated stages. Men were sitting on the various lounges throughout the nightclub enjoying private entertainment sessions with the 'dancers.' Elijah headed over to where his dad was sitting and noticed that his father's Australian boss, Lester, was there.

Lester said, "What on earth are you doing here, Elijah? You are a bit too young to understand what is going on here."

Young Elijah just ignored the comment and sat down next to his father.

Elijah looked at Castiel. "I *knew* what was going on there, but I still don't understand it. Lester and his wife were staying in a motel about five minutes away from the Pink Panther, and he would leave his wife in the motel room and come down to the Pink Panther to meet his prostitute girlfriend and take her into the toilets for a 'quickie'."

Elijah noticed several Shadow Figures feeding off Lester like greedy leeches as he took Sunlee into the toilets.

"This place brings back many memories, Castiel. My father would come here every night. He got so drunk I often had to help him into a taxi and return home. In some ways, I blame myself for the way he deteriorated in Thailand. I told him about Mum and Dale because their child was about to be born, and I didn't want him to think I was keeping secrets from him. He was bound to find out sooner or later. Once he realised that they had been sleeping together for quite some time he lost all hope and his life spiralled out of control into the dark underworld of prostitutes, drugs, and alcoholism, and all I could do was sit back and watch it happen. It was not long before he had a prostitute, Nataya, living with us. There was no surprise that Nataya was simply there for the money. Why he ever agreed to let a prostitute move in with us, I have no idea. Deep down maybe he thought she loved him, but it was pretty clear to me that she was just there for the money. She was a real piece of work. Not all the prostitutes were like that. Not at first anyway. For the most part they were victims whose parents had sold them into prostitution to earn money to help support the family. Prostitution was the way they had learnt to survive. Over time, it devoured them until their souls were destroyed. I guess the Shadow Figures got them, Castiel?"

"Well, it's not quite that cut and dry, Elijah," Castiel told him. "But yes, in many cases they are consumed by sin and eventually drown in it."

The place was full of Shadow Figures and the floor was covered in what looked like a plague of Shadow Scavengers. Elijah realised that this was a feeding ground for them.

"I see that Sophia's temporary protection blessing has worn off, so how come the Shadow Figures were not trying to get at me, Castiel?"

"Think of it this way. If you come across a vicious hungry dog and you happen to have a piece of meat with you and throw it, the dog will go after it. So it is that here there is so much free meat around for the Shadow Figures that they have no need to fight for a feed."

Just then a drink spilled into young Elijah's lap, likely from his father's elbow tipping it over. When his father turned and noticed that the crotch of his pants were wet he chuckled and made several vulgar innuendos about how they became wet.

Elijah shook his head. "The thing is, Castiel, these girls didn't excite me sexually, even with all the lap dances going on around me at the time. I was there for my father, trying to look out for him. It hurt when he laughed at me and made those vulgar innuendos. I was just fifteen. His behaviour showed me a side of him that destroyed any sense of decency I thought he had. The man I thought could save me and shown me love turned out to be just as self-absorbed as my mother."

"Yes, he was, Elijah," Castiel confirmed in his gentle, comforting tone of voice. "Time to go." With that, they vanished into another time jump.

Young Elijah, upset with his father's crass joking got up, walked back outside, and waited until his father was ready to leave.

Chapter 15 - Holiday

Thailand seemed like a holiday to Elijah because there was no school and he was in an exotic part of the Orient with many new places to explore. Today, Elijah was going on a real holiday with his father, Nataya, Sunlee, and another young woman they picked up on the way. The young woman they picked up from a home outside of Bangkok was around Elijah's age and seemed to be part of some sort of match-making attempt. Although she was nice, very respectful, and not a prostitute, Elijah had no intention of striking up a relationship with her and she showed no interest in one, either. In fact, it seemed obvious that the girl really wanted to be somewhere else and that this was something her family had forced upon her.

Eventually, after a four-hour drive, they arrived at a motel across from the beach. Elijah's father had booked two rooms—one for himself and Nataya and another for Elijah, Sunlee, and the young woman. Each room had a king size bed, a bathroom, and air-conditioning. Elijah wondered at first where he was going to sleep but soon realised it would be with Sunlee and the young woman. Sunlee, although a prostitute, was a very nice person. She was respectful and Elijah could tell she was into prostitution because it was the only way she could survive. She had come with them on the trip because she was good friends with Nataya whom she worked with at the Pink Panther.

The beach was about 100 metres from the motel and you could see it through the window of the motel room. It was a breathtaking scene and the weather could not have been better.

Elijah spent the rest of the day in the motel room watching television with the young woman whose name he learnt with the help of body language was Tamarine. Tamarine was a beautiful person and seemed very warm and kindhearted. When it was time to sleep, Elijah would lie on the left side of the bed, Tamarine on the right, and Sunlee in the middle. Although he was in a strange environment with strangers, Elijah felt safe, even though he was not sure exactly why. Sunlee gently stroked Elijah's hair as he drifted off to sleep.

Later that night Elijah and Castiel entered the room through the wall on the beach side of the room.

"I'm still not used to passing through walls, Castiel."

"You will get used to it, Elijah. It just takes time. Do you remember being here?"

"Yes, I remember. Sunlee was quite nice to me. Much nicer than my dad's girlfriend was. I think Sunlee saw me as a younger brother. I guess you could say from this scene that I slept with a prostitute."

"Yes, slept," Castiel said, nodding, "and that is *all* you did."

"Looking back on my time in Thailand, I'm really surprised that I didn't get mixed up in sex, drugs, and alcohol. It was readily available and nobody would have stopped me. Something held me back, maybe a deep sense of morals, I'm not really sure."

Castiel patted him on the back and said, "You were able to withstand temptation even though it was right in front of you on several occasions. That sort of commitment gets noticed. It is one of the reasons you were selected, Elijah."

"Selected for what?" Elijah asked.

"You'll see soon enough. For now, come, let's move next door. There is something you need to see."

Elijah and Castiel passed through the wall and arrived in Elijah's father's motel room. Elijah's father and his girlfriend were in the bed. Shadow Scavengers covered the walls and floor while Shadow Figures crowded into the room in such multitudes that there was almost no free space to stand.

"Why are so many Shadow Figures here, Castiel?"

"It is a process they call 'induction.'"

The Shadow Figures arranged themselves on opposite sides of the room, leaving a space in the middle where a large oval-shaped portal appeared. A Shadow Figure came through carrying a snake-like creature that was glowing green like a nightstick. The Shadow Figure carrying the snake approached Elijah's father while several of the other Shadow Figures started clawing at the many cracks that were oozing red energy from Elijah's father's chest. As they clawed, they ripped open larger cracks until they all joined into one large hole that split open, like a gaping wound, and red energy suddenly came spurting out as if from a ruptured main artery. A few seconds later the stream of red energy spurting out began to subside and left a gaping black hole in Elijah's father's chest within which a blue sphere of energy was pulsating.

"What's that, Castiel?"

"Some refer to it as the soul."

The Shadow Figure carrying the snake moved forward and placed it on the end of the bed. The snake-like being slithered up the bed onto Elijah's father and then into the gaping black hole in his chest, where it wrapped itself around the sphere of energy. The hole started to close itself sealing the creature inside.

"That snake-like being...," Elijah said. "That's inside of him now, Castiel?"

"I'm afraid so, Elijah. When enough cracks have formed in a person, the Shadow Figures are able to place their spawn directly inside the person. This allows them to have better control over the host to create the attitudes that they feed on."

"You mean he is possessed?"

"That is one way to look at it."

"That makes sense because after that weekend my father deteriorated even further. His girlfriend was living with us full-time and his insatiable lust was disgusting. He would brag to me about how many times he had sex in a night and talk about the sexual acts his girlfriend performed on him. Not really things I wanted to know about. He also began smoking a lot of marijuana and he was drinking more alcohol than ever. He became paranoid and turned on his boss in Australia and made some pretty damaging allegations about him to the company he was working with in Thailand. He ended up being taken to hospital in an ambulance one night complaining of chest pain and shortness of breath. They suspected he was having a heart attack, but it turned out he was just having a panic attack. They kept him in hospital for a few weeks. Did the snake-like being cause that?"

"Directly or indirectly, yes. They can cause a lot of physical and mental symptoms, some are deliberate and some are simply a side-effect of the process. The human body does not allow parasites to invade it without putting up a fight. "

"During his stay in hospital his boss came over to Thailand, and well things really got ugly."

"That's our next stop, Elijah."

Chapter 16 - Breakdown

Elijah re-read a copy of a letter he had taken earlier in the day sitting on his father's desk. Elijah knew that taking the letter was wrong, but he was desperate. It reminded him of his thought at the airport on arriving in Thailand: *Desperate people do desperate things.* It was almost as if the letter had been left there on purpose for him to stumble across. The letter described how the Australian company Elijah's father was working for was ripping off the Thailand-based company they were working with. Elijah was not sure where the "rip off concept" originated, but he suspected that Kazem was probably behind it as an act of sabotage. Elijah's father had a rather stormy relationship with Kazem but a very good relationship with Kazem's older brother who called the shots because he owned the Thailand-based company he was working with. Kazem was very jealous of his older brother. The Thai people have succession rights in which the oldest son inherits everything when the father passes away. That left Kazem with very little to look forward to. Elijah knew his father had written the letter because he had signed it.

Elijah thought that one-page letter just might help him. He considered giving it to his father's boss, Lester, which would be a direct betrayal of his own father. Elijah's father seemed so distant from him now due to alcoholism, drug abuse, and prostitutes. Elijah had felt very much alone and abandoned for the past six months and got by mainly due to the friendships he formed at his father's work.

The six months were not all bad. Elijah had learned the basics of the Thai language and how to get around in a foreign country. He helped teach English at a school and enjoyed many adventures with his work colleagues. There was that incident with Tida, which Stolas brought up during the interrogation. Elijah was none too proud about that and wished he could undo it. If he had only known that her feelings for him went beyond just friendship, maybe they could have explored that together.

The question facing Elijah now was: *Can I use this letter to help find some stability for myself?* He pondered what giving the letter to Lester would do for him. What would that net him in terms of stability? Elijah's thinking was not rational. There were too many emotions that confused the issue, and he could not make any sense of what to do. His father was still in hospital so Elijah called his mother and discussed the situation with her. She encouraged Elijah to give the letter to Lester and suggested that Lester would look after him if he did. Elijah was not so sure about that—or about anything else. He did not know who, if anyone, to trust anymore.

A few days later Kazem took Elijah to the airport with him to pick up Lester. When Lester began complaining to Kazem about Elijah's father's behaviour, Elijah seized the moment and handed the letter over to Lester. Kazem made comments such as "What is this?" pretending he knew nothing about it, but Elijah could tell Kazem knew. After he finished reading the letter, Lester instructed Kazem to stop at a hardware store. He purchased a bunch of cleaning supplies. He then instructed Kazem to drive to the townhouse. Once there, he ordered Elijah to clean the place from top to bottom, saying that he did not want to see a single speck of dust in it anywhere. It was obvious to Elijah that Lester was directing his anger over the situation at him.

Hours passed as Elijah cleaned the townhouse. He figured that onerous task was his punishment either for what his father had done or for betraying his father by giving Lester the letter. Either way, Elijah felt responsible for the situation and carried on cleaning.

Later that evening Lester returned and inspected Elijah's work. He dragged Elijah around the townhouse saying it was not clean enough. He pointed out every speck of dust and every little mark and ordered Elijah to get back to work until the place was spotless. Then Lester verbally attacked, calling him a loser and a bastard child. His insults continued flowing like bitter venom and aimed now on Elijah's father. He called him all sorts of derogatory names and words that Elijah just did not understand. Lester raged on to Elijah about how he only gave his father a job because his mum had practically begged him to. Elijah had no idea how his mum knew Lester.

Lester then went back on the offensive and attacked Elijah with words that pierced like daggers and cut him deep, right to Elijah's soul. He just kept stabbing and stabbing, until finally Elijah began to cry. At that, Lester didn't stop but only stepped up his abuse. He called Elijah "weak" and "worthless" and said it was too bad he was too cowardly to kill himself and spare the world his miserable presence. Before leaving, Lester looked back at Elijah with a menacing stare. Elijah fell to his knees, unable to hold himself up. The wounds were just too deep and he broke down. In that moment everything just came crashing down upon Elijah—his sister's leaving, his issues with his mother, his issues with his father.

Castiel and Elijah appeared in the room, stood silently in despair, and watched Lester abuse young Elijah. They felt helpless, for there was nothing they could do. Elijah knew what was happening and what would happen because he had been through it. It bought back painful memories that he thought were long gone.

The pain was more than Elijah's younger self could handle—emotional pain that ripped through him and brought great physical pain. Tears streamed down the boy's face like creeks that swelled to rivers after a freak storm. He could hardly breathe and gasped for breath between the deep, heaving sobs. Then his heart broke and his mind did the only thing that could possibly save the boy—put up walls. The pain subsided, the tears dried, and the boy emerged emotionless.

"That's where I shut down, Castiel. I became 'comfortably numb.' I used to listen to that Pink Floyd song over and over because it expressed exactly how I felt: comfortably numb. Numb to all emotion."

Castiel said, "Come, let's go. You have seen enough here to remember what you needed to." That said, they departed into a time-jump.

* * *

The next morning Elijah met his father at the hospital after he was released. As they walked to his father's car, Elijah told him that he had given the letter to Lester. His father responded by slapping him hard across the back of the head–so hard that the impact made his nose bleed. His father did not say a word but just walked off to his car, leaving Elijah to find his own way back to the townhouse.

Elijah made it back to the townhouse. That evening he contemplated suicide, even to the point of tying the rope to the balusters at the top of the stairs and creating a noose using the slipknot his father had taught him to use to tie a hook on his fishing line. He stood up on a chair and put the noose around his neck, but he just could not go the extra step. Something held him back. He thought to himself that maybe Lester was right—maybe he was a coward.

Lester had gotten in touch with Elijah's mother, who in turn had gotten in touch with his father's sister and brother-in-law. They helped Elijah get his own British passport so he could return home to

Australia to live with his mother. Though he was not looking forward to it, he really had no choice.

As the days wound down to his departure, he and his friends said their goodbyes. His father was not speaking to him and did not say goodbye. One of Elijah's friends from the office took him to the airport carrying only his suitcase with a few articles of clothing and his Commodore 64 computer.

Thus, Elijah had to travel back to Australia all alone. It promised to be a very long trip.

Chapter 17 - The Return

Elijah riffled through the ticket folder in search of the departure gate for his flight "home." There were three tickets in the folder. The first ticket was for a flight from Thailand to Malaysia. The second was for the flight from Malaysia to Singapore. The third was for the longer flight from Singapore to Sydney. Nobody had wanted to pay for Elijah's airfare, so at last Lester agreed to pay for it—no doubt just to get rid of him. Lester purchased the cheapest possible airfare from Thailand to Australia. Elijah followed the signs around the airport to the gate area, where he sat and waited patiently for the boarding call.

A few hours later, he made his way onto the plane for the short flight—just over two hours—from Thailand to Malaysia.

During the three-hour layover in Malaysia Elijah decided to head straight for the gate so he knew where he had to be to catch the next flight. Airline travel was still very new to him, and he had to work out how to get around the foreign airports carrying his single suitcase.

Tired but unable to sleep, Elijah sat at the departure gate comfortably numb and watched the planes taking off and landing through the airport windows overlooking the runway.

The flight from Malaysia to Singapore took just over an hour. Nine hours had passed since Elijah left Thailand. His feet were hurting from shoes that were two sizes too small for him, and he did not think to take them off during the flights. His layover in Singapore was eight hours. He found a spot to sit in the departure lounge and made himself as comfortable as possible. He pulled out some paper and a pencil and just started sketching. A few hours passed, and then Elijah put the paper and pencil back into his suitcase and just sat waiting for the boarding call. It was a long wait with nothing much to do but contemplate where his life was.

The flight from Singapore to Sydney was eight hours. Elijah closed his eyes but couldn't sleep because his thoughts were racing. The flight encountered quite a bit of turbulence and Elijah could see that many of the passengers were getting nervous. Not Elijah. He wouldn't have minded one bit if the plane went down. Just weeks before he had contemplated hanging himself.

The plane landed safely and Elijah had to make his way through customs, but nothing went smoothly for him. The customs officers took Elijah aside because they thought it was suspicious that Elijah at just 15 was travelling alone and had been through three Asian countries. This is typical of drug mules smuggling drugs. Elijah was shown into an interview room where the customs officers interrogated him, but he was so tired he struggled to answer their questions. Elijah had been awake now for over 30 hours and was sleep-deprived, listless, and exhausted. He felt sick from exhaustion. The customs officers presumed he was on drugs due to his behaviour and decided to put him through a full strip search. A customs officer led him into another room where a male officer asked him to undress and stand on a line. Following the instructions, Elijah took off all his clothes down to his underwear. The customs officer, in a harsh dominating voice, instructed Elijah to take off his underwear as well. Elijah obeyed. The customs officer looked Elijah up and down then moved around behind him and asked him to bend forward. The customs officer then proceeded to do an internal search, which made Elijah feel very uncomfortable, but with all that he had been through over the preceding six months he simply did not care anymore.

The body search did not turn up anything, and Elijah was eventually sent on to immigration. He was travelling on a British passport, which did not enable him to enter Australia, and it took over three hours for the immigration officers to verify that Elijah was an Australian citizen. He had obtained citizenship with his mother many years earlier at a citizenship induction. In hindsight, it would have been better if Elijah had returned to Australia on an Australian passport, but nobody thought about that when they were helping him obtain his own passport.

Elijah finally made it through immigration and out into the airport where he ran into one of Lester's work colleagues. The first thing he asked was whether Elijah had any spare money, which he didn't. The new issue was how Elijah was going to get from Sydney to Hervey Bay in Queensland where his mother lived. Lester's colleague took Elijah to the bus terminal where he bought two bus tickets—one from Sydney to Brisbane and another from Brisbane to Hervey Bay. It would be a five-hour wait followed by an 18-hour bus trip to Brisbane followed by a six-hour wait and then another four-and-a-half-hour bus trip from Brisbane to Hervey Bay. Before leaving, the work colleague gave Elijah $50 so he could buy some food on the bus trip. It appeared to Elijah as though he gave the money out of his own pocket.

The bus trip from Sydney International Airport to Brisbane Coach Terminal was very long. The first stop along the way was a typical roadhouse where they served some decent food. Elijah was happy to get off the bus after nearly eight hours. He was travel-worn and quite tired from just sitting. Inside, Elijah made his way to the counter and ordered a meal of half a chicken and chips. As he handed the 50-dollar note over to the cashier, he noticed that someone had scribbled a crucifix on the top right hand corner of the backside of the note. It was drawn with a blue biro pen. Elijah was in his own little world, lost in his rambling thoughts, so he did not pay much attention to it and just handed it over. Elijah took his change from the cashier and then went and sat down until a waitress brought his meal to him. It was not easy to eat. He was so tired that the energy needed to consume the food seemed to make him feel weaker. He struggled for a while and ate some of the chips and a few bites of the chicken and then returned to the bus to continue the journey.

On arriving at the Brisbane Coach Terminal, Elijah had another lengthy wait of several hours before his bus was ready to depart for Hervey Bay. Since the Bus Terminal was close to Brisbane he decided to explore Brisbane a little.

* * *

Castiel and Elijah appeared in the middle of the Queen Street Mall and saw young Elijah walking down the street with his suitcase carrying his clothes and Commodore 64.

"To me, Castiel," Elijah said, "that Commodore 64 computer was all I had left in the world. My hands were blistered from carrying that suitcase around and my shoulders ached from the weight. I would not let it out of my sight. I became a typical computer nerd at the age of seven and fell ever deeper into them as I got older. The world around me just proved to be a cruel place. The computer world felt safe, somewhere I could escape. Whether it was programming or playing a game, it felt safe."

Castiel and Elijah followed young Elijah as he walked down the mall.

"I was out of it, Castiel, by this point on the gruelling trip from Thailand. I remember very little of what happened on the trip back to Australia. I was travelling for more than 60 hours, but looking back on it now I cannot see where the time went. It is all rather blank other than a few moments of the trip."

Castiel nodded. "Sophia was with you, Elijah. She was following you every step of the way and sitting beside you on the plane and the bus where possible. She never left your side throughout that long journey and more than once defended you against some Shadow Figures when you were bleeding red energy from your own emotional wounds. She cradled you with protective love like a mother tending to a newborn baby. "

"So, is that why I feel I had some time loss?"

"Partly."

"Where is Sophia now if you say she was with me?"

"Look up," Castiel said, cocking his head and gazing up toward the sky.

Elijah looked up and sure enough about 100 feet in the sky Sophia was gliding gracefully around keeping an eye on Elijah.

"I always felt as though someone was there for me in Thailand. I could never quite put my finger on it, though. It did amaze me that with everything that happened I somehow made it through safe and sound."

"Even though Sophia was there, you still had to endure everything that happened, and given the circumstances, I'd say you endured it quite well. "

The time for Elijah's bus to depart was approaching so he headed back to the bus terminal and Elijah and Castiel left.

* * *

The bus trip from Brisbane Coach Terminal to Hervey Bay would take five and a half hours. Elijah did not care anymore. Time seemed irrelevant. He was so tired and sore from the travelling that his body had gone into a sort of shock a long time ago. His mind was no longer functioning the way it normally would.

When he stepped off the bus at Hervey Bay in the early afternoon he had been travelling for 60 hours. He wondered what would happen next as he met up with his mother and Dale.

Chapter 18 - Back Home

Elijah was not surprised that he felt like unwanted garbage when he returned home. His mother and Dale had acquired a leaky old caravan and parked it out in the backyard for him to live in. The caravan was connected to the house by a single power cord that allowed Elijah to power his computer and run lights at night. Quite often Dale would pull the power cord to punish Elijah for no real reason other than because he could.

The caravan did not have a toilet, which meant Elijah had to make his way up to the house when he needed to go. This presented a problem for Elijah because the baby, Jack, slept nearly all the time, and Elijah would get punished—either verbally or physically or both—whenever Jack woke up and he was around to blame. So out of fear, whenever possible Elijah would use jars as makeshift "chamber pots" and empty them in the backyard.

Elijah did not return to school that year but instead attended Business Studies College the next two years after passing an entrance exam. Elijah excelled academically in college and received honours in most subjects. In his spare time he developed computer programs for various departments of the college and everything—at least academically—came together for him. Elijah made some friends and in general was doing okay. Living in the caravan kept him at a safe distance from his mother and Dale, and in many ways that was for the best.

A few years later the time came for Elijah to move out of his caravan and go and live with John, a friend whom he met at a computer club. John had his own house and offered to rent his spare bedroom to

Elijah. The two had a lot in common and got on well. Elijah was delighted at the prospect of getting away from home.

* * *

Castiel and Elijah came floating over the backyard fence just as young Elijah was packing up his computer. They stood outside the caravan and peered through the window as young Elijah packed his things.

"This was one of those pinnacle moments in my life," Elijah said. "I had longed to move out for a while, but never had the opportunity until John and I became friends. John's offer of a room to rent was a real blessing—especially after years of living in that caravan, Castiel. I would have moved out sooner, but I had no money because my mother would take my study allowance as rent leaving me broke. In exchange, she did provide the basics. I came to understand that my mother saw parenting more as a job, a duty, rather than something she wanted or enjoyed. Even after I left home, she would send me birthday and Christmas cards and sign them "Love, Mum." It always felt empty, though, because she never once picked up the phone to call, never once made an effort to have a real relationship with me. She did the bare minimum that she believed was required for a mother to do, but nothing more."

Castiel nodded. "People become very robotic in their actions when the Shadow Figures get to them, Elijah. Love is something the Shadow Figures do everything they can to prevent because it creates the white energy that hurts them."

"It almost sounds like a cop-out, Castiel, like an excuse for selfish behaviour."

"Well, there is some of that as well. A person can always exercise free will to resist the efforts of the Shadow Figures. You see, if the person were not so selfish he or she would break away from the Shadow Figures. On the other hand, if they become self-absorbed they will generally isolate themselves in their own little world with very few 'friends' whom they can control. They typically live alone."

"Where are the Shadow Figures, Castiel? I can't see any around the backyard."

"Sophia takes care of them. The caravan made it easy for her to keep a boundary around where you would sleep. She would simply destroy any Shadow Figures that came into the backyard. The house is a different story. Inside, they are feasting on red energy from your Mother and Dale. That's one of the reasons you felt a lot of fear whenever you went inside. It was not simply fear of physical and verbal abuse. It was from the vast amount of red energy and the multitude of Shadow Figures in there."

"Those three years back at home were pretty bad, Castiel. They were tough despite my being comfortably numb in my own world. It was patently obvious that my mother and Dale did not want me around. In every situation, they made it as difficult as possible. At one point Dale's brother came to live with us, but they kicked him out onto the street soon afterwards. They didn't want any of their family around the baby, Jack. As a result Jack had no contact with his aunties and uncles and very limited contact with me, his half-brother, and Claricia was long gone."

Castiel gestured toward the far end of the caravan. "There is Sophia now Elijah, carrying out her regular routine."

Elijah turned quickly and saw Sophia walking around the perimeter of the Caravan. She was etching symbols into the grass with one of her swords.

"What is she doing, Castiel?"

"She is making a perimeter boundary, like a force shield. No Shadow Figures can cross into the circle she is drawing around your caravan."

"What would happen if they tried?"

"They would suffer the same fate as if they had been sliced by one of her swords."

"How does she know how to do this?"

"She was trained by one of the best, Elijah."

Elijah noticed that several Shadow Figures had gathered on the back fence and were just sitting there watching Sophia work. Just then Sophia noticed them. She yanked on the gold chain of her necklace and pulled out a thick crucifix. She flipped it open and inside were many thin crucifixes. She shook them out in her hand and threw them towards the Shadow Figures sitting on the fence. The crucifixes lit up in a brilliant white light and cut through the air like throwing stars as they split off like guided missiles, each one aimed at its own Shadow Figure. They sliced through the Shadow Figures almost simultaneously causing them to scream and then disintegrate into puffs of blackness. Their mission complete, the crucifixes did not stop, but, like boomerangs, returned to Sophia's hand. She smiled as she placed them back inside the crucifix suspended from the chain around her neck.

"Wow!" Elijah exclaimed with great enthusiasm.

"She is one of the best, Elijah. But now, I think it's time we took a quick visit back to the future." That said, they vanished.

* * *

Elijah finished packing and waited for John to pick him up. When the time came for him to leave, his mother did not say goodbye, nor did Dale. Elijah was not surprised. The real surprise for Elijah would have been if they had come out to see him off.

Chapter 19 - August, 2012, Juliana

As she unscrewed the childproof lid on the bottle of sleeping pills, Juliana looked at herself in the mirror. She noted the dark rings under her eyes, her pale complexion, and her frazzled hair. Though she had tried to sleep several times a day since they laid her beloved Elijah to rest several weeks earlier, Juliana found the comfort of sleep elusive. In the end, she had resorted to taking sleeping pills. The devastating pain of losing Elijah would just not go away. She felt so empty inside and found it difficult with the children asking questions like "When is Daddy coming home?" Those words ripped through her like a knife and led her to feel nauseated.

She lay back down on her bed and stared at the spinning ceiling fan, knowing it would be about 30 minutes before the sleeping pills started to work. She did not want to think about anything because thinking hurt. She tried hard to keep her mind blank, but eventually gave up and reached for something to distract herself. She rolled over and opened the drawer of the bedside table. She started to pull out the novel she was reading but noticed the Bible in there beside it and decided to pull it out instead.

Juliana's faith has suffered a major blow. She could not understand why God, who supposedly loved her, would allow Elijah to be taken from her. She found it easier to believe there was no God than to try to understand why an all-powerful, all-loving God would allow such a tragedy to occur. The pain overwhelmed her and she was drowning in it.

She held the Bible in her hands and noticed that something was propping it open to a certain page like a bookmark. She opened to that page and found a 50-dollar note with a crucifix drawn in blue biro pen in the top right hand corner. She scanned down the page and saw that a Bible passage was highlighted in yellow marker.

"I am leaving you with a gift—peace of mind and heart. And the peace I give is a gift the world cannot give. So don't be troubled or afraid." – John 14:27

Juliana thought about that as she drifted off to sleep.

* * *

Close to midnight Castiel and Elijah appeared in Juliana's room from their time-jump. Elijah immediately noticed the 50-dollar note lying on the bed next to the open Bible at Juliana's side.

"There is a funny story behind that fifty-dollar note, Castiel. I went to church with John. I was not a religious person and had never been to church before, but John talked me into going on the pretence that it was a good place to pick up girls. I had just moved in with him and thought I might as well go along with him. So there I sat and it was time for the collection. I was not really into giving, but the sermon did move me and I felt a very special kind of peace in that church. I am not sure what it was, maybe just the atmosphere, but I opened my wallet and had only a five-dollar note left. It was the last five dollars I would have until the following week and I did not really want to part with it, but I did. After the service John offered me a lift back to his house but mentioned that he was going to his parents' place for dinner first and invited me along. I didn't feel like going for dinner so I politely refused his invitation and said I would walk home. It was only a fifteen-minute walk. About half way back to John's house, I looked down and saw a fifty-dollar note in the gutter on the side of the road. I snatched it up and spotted that crucifix in the top right hand corner drawn with a blue biro and remembered it. It looked exactly like the one Lester's colleague had given me for food on the bus trip. I figured that was impossible. The odds of that ending up here in the gutter would be astronomical. That would be some coincidence."

Castiel smiled with a knowing expression on his face. "Maybe it wasn't a coincidence after all, Elijah."

"So I stuffed the fifty-dollar note in my wallet and took it home. I could not bring myself to spend it. I stashed it in a drawer for a while and later used it as a bookmark in books I was reading. And now, there it is, all these years later. Tell me, though, Castiel: Is Juliana going to be all right?"

"I don't know, Elijah," he said, squinting. "You see, that part of her life has not yet been written. She will be presented with many choices and her own free will is what will determine the outcome."

"Can't we just zip into the future and have a look?"

"No, we can't, because it doesn't exist yet."

"But we can go into her past?"

"Yes."

"Is there anything I can do to help Juliana now?"

"You already have, Elijah," Castiel assured him. "But that will make more sense later."

"You are very cryptic at times, Castiel."

Elijah stood and watched his wife sleeping, wishing he could do more for her, until Castiel again said, "Time to go...."

* * *

Later that night Juliana had a somewhat surreal dream.... She was swimming under water but could breathe as though she were breathing oxygen. She was weightless, felt fresh, and had no pain. She swam along with dolphins, whales, and many other sea creatures until she came across an underwater city with large pillars and a gigantic door. She stopped swimming and walked up to the door. How odd it was that she could walk under water and breathe. She opened the door and entered a large chamber aglow with light radiating from mounted glowing spheres on the ceiling. The chamber was magnificent. The walls were covered with exquisite artwork you would expect to see in a museum with masterpieces by Leonardo DaVinci and Rembrandt. On one wall was a large portrait two stories high that resembled a picture she had once seen by Hans Memling called "The Last Judgement." On the left hand side of the picture was a place that resembled heaven with naked people entering it with grateful expressions on their faces. On the right hand side, naked people with looks of pain and anguish on their faces were being cast into a fiery place that resembled hell. In the middle was an angel, and above the angel was a figure who resembled Jesus Christ sitting on a sphere that looked like the earth. Around him were the 12 apostles.

Juliana walked through the chamber admiring the artwork on her way to a door in the far right corner. She opened the door and entered a room about the size of a basketball court. The room was completely white with a single wooden chair in the centre of it. She walked around the room a few times before eventually sitting down in the chair, feeling as though something was inviting her to do so. As she sat on the chair, the water that filled the room started rushing out through the door. She held tightly onto the chair against the force of the water trying to pull her off. Once the room was void of water the walls vanished revealing a vast landscape all around her as she sat on the chair in the middle of a field of rich green grass. Some beautiful white birds flew overheard and trees began to appear in the distance sprouting from rainbows. The beauty of the place was beyond telling, and no words could do it justice. The colours in the landscapes around her were more vibrant than any she had seen before. The grass field started sprouting beautiful flowers in scores of breathtaking hues. Everything around her was alive in a way she had never seen before.

The chair vanished and Juliana fell to the ground, landing softly amongst the flowers. She rolled in the flowers and looked up at the radiant sun without hurting her eyes. She could feel the sun's warmth on her skin. She was wearing the nightgown she had worn to bed, but it was more vibrant than usual and the polyester cotton blend felt like fresh silk. She felt it rub against her bare-naked skin underneath as she continued rolling in the flowers of the field. It felt wonderful.

"Hello." The voice startled her. She sprang to her feet and spun around to see who said it. A barefooted woman with vibrant green eyes wearing a long white semitransparent dress smiled at her.

"Hi," Juliana said.

"I am Sophia."

When she said that Juliana thought about the time Elijah told her about his imaginary friend named Sophia. This green-eyed woman matched his description perfectly.

"I'm Juliana. Where are we?"

"We are nowhere. This place does not have a name. It's been described by many different terms throughout history, but it really doesn't have a name."

"Why am I here?"

"I pulled you here," Sophia said, "so you could see the beauty of what awaits."

"What do you mean?"

"Look around you, Juliana. See how beautiful things are. There is no pain, no suffering. Everything is as you want it to be, how you wish it to be."

"Is this where Elijah is?"

"That will be up to Elijah."

"I miss him."

"I know, and one day you will meet him again. Just not yet."

"Why?"

"It's not your time, Juliana. You have two beautiful children to raise who need their mother now more than ever."

Juliana thought about that before responding. "I know. It's just so difficult."

"Life was never designed to be easy, Juliana. Life is designed to allow humans to grow, to feel, and—most importantly—to learn. To learn, sometimes you have to feel the worst pain imaginable. The deeper the pain the stronger the love you develop in the end."

Juliana started to cry as she said, "But it hurts, Sophia, it hurts so much."

Sophia came and embraced Juliana. "It will be okay. You'll see. Focus on that pain and turn it into grace. The pain will vanish if you become grateful for what you have rather than bitter over what you have lost."

After a while, Juliana's crying subsided and she whispered, "Thank you, Sophia."

Juliana awoke from her dream in the early hours of the morning. She ran to the bathroom and vomited. She remembered that she did not take just two sleeping pills as prescribed but rather 20. She had wanted to end her life, to be with Elijah. Somehow the dream gave her the chance to change things.

She placed the 50-dollar note back in the Bible and put it away. She felt renewed and had a new confidence about her as she walked out of her bedroom with a smile on her face, for the first time in weeks. She went into her children's bedroom and woke them both up, gave them a big hug, and told them that she loved them and that everything was going to be all right. She took them both back to her room where they lay peacefully on her bed and slept soundly until morning.

Chapter 20 - 1995, Elijah and Juliana

Elijah was attending a church service in Sydney where he had recently moved. He did not go to church often but his friend Maryanne had invited to come along. Just as he was going to say "no thanks," he recalled what John told him about church being a good place to pick up girls. Although his mind wanted to keep him away from relationships—to keep those walls he had put up many years earlier strong and solid—his heart felt empty and desired a companion. Church was about the only place Elijah would meet new people other than through work. As a contract programmer he did not meet many people, so the chance of meeting a girlfriend through work was very slim. So, after considering everything in a most logical way, he agreed to attend the church service with Maryanne.

Maryanne was studying law part-time while working for a legal firm, the same legal firm where Maryanne and Elijah had met a few years earlier. Elijah had been doing some programming for them. Elijah was also friends with Maryanne's husband, Michael. The couple had a son on the way and beautiful twin daughters. Elijah often thought of them as little angels because of the way they joyfully danced. It was as if they spread happiness wherever they went.

Maryanne said she could read loneliness in Elijah's eyes and always encouraged him to meet new people. She knew about some of the challenges of his past and always said it was a wonder he had recovered from his deep emotional wounds. Sometimes Elijah wondered if he had recovered from them. Maryanne once told him that it was amazing how he could be so charming on the outside when he must have been hurting so deeply on the inside. "Maybe you should have been a psychologist instead of a lawyer, Maryanne," Elijah had replied with a smile. "Or a match-maker."

The church was quite busy, but Elijah found a nice spot near the back of the sanctuary where he preferred to sit at such events. He sat quietly and observed the last group of people strolling into the church and then the band introduced a guest singer named Juliana and began singing some worship songs.

Juliana sang in such a way that penetrated Elijah's ears and extended deep down into the very depths of his soul. Her voice somehow flowed through the emotional walls he had erected to protect himself, fortress-like, from the pain of his life. In some ways her voice made him feel quite uncomfortable, but in another it hypnotised him. He could not take his eyes off her and the thought went through his mind: *I believe that when I fall in love, it will be with her.*

At one point when Elijah was staring at Juliana for one instant he saw Juliana look right at him and smile. In that moment, his heart skipped a beat, maybe two. The song finally ended and Juliana left the stage. Elijah wondered how he could possibly meet up with her again. *Would it be impossible?*

Maryanne then whispered, "What did you think of Juliana?"

Elijah replied, "She was great."

Maryanne smiled. "How would you like to go to Luna Park tonight with me and Michael and Juliana?"

"You know her—Juliana?"

"Yes, I do," she said. "Juliana is a friend from school and we had planned to go to Luna Park tonight."

"Uh, well," Elijah said, "I'm not sure.... Does she know I would be coming?"

"No, she doesn't know, but I'm sure she'll be okay with it."

Elijah was nervous. He could feel those thick fortress walls wobbling and he did not like it. His heart, however, overtook his mind and responded with some hesitation, "Okay, if you are sure I wouldn't be intruding."

Maryanne just smiled at him. He saw Maryanne nudge her husband Michael and whisper something in his ear. He turned and winked at her.

When the church service was over Maryanne confirmed the time they would meet at the entrance to Luna Park and Elijah went back to his apartment. Elijah was not sure if what he just agreed to was a good idea or not and wondered if he would actually be able to muster the courage to turn up at Luna Park.

Elijah's apartment had a tremendous view overlooking Sydney Harbour. Elijah was not short of money. His income from computer programming contracts and single lifestyle provided him with plenty of money to live carefree. He did not save anything, lived from week to week, and forked out expensive rent to maintain his luxury apartment. Elijah was searching for that something to fill his emptiness—and he tried to buy happiness. He had tried jet skis, fast cars, and motorbikes, all in an effort to fill that emptiness and find some happiness. Elijah kept himself busy, so busy in fact, that he never had to stop and think about his loneliness and the emotional pain he had buried.

The clock in Elijah's apartment read 3:23 p.m. *Could time pass any slower?* Elijah realised he still had nearly two and a half hours to go until he was to meet Maryanne, Michael, and Juliana at Luna Park. He was already dressed and ready to go. He had put on his best pair of jeans and the smartest shirt he could dig out of his closet and hoped that Juliana would like it. He spent some time cleaning some mud off his sneakers to make them look more presentable. And, here he was all ready to go with hours to kill. He wondered what he could do. He sat on the end of his bed and stared out over Sydney Harbour watching the boats go by. He glanced back at the clock: 3:25 p.m. *Two minutes. Is that all?* It was almost as if the clock had stopped. Elijah had not been this nervous and felt so uncomfortable in years. He was not sure if he liked it. He went and drank some water to help calm the butterflies that had taken flight in his stomach. *What had this Juliana done to him?* He did not even know her but felt as if she had some sort of magical power over him.

He lay down on his bed and put a pillow over his face and growled into it in a mad effort to release some nervous tension. It did not work, so he proceeded to head back into the kitchen to get another drink of water. As he drained it he thought: *If I keep drinking water at this rate, I will be running to the toilet all night. What will Juliana think of that?* He then did the maths and worked out that it would be okay to drink until about 4 p.m. and go to the toilet one last time before leaving and he should be fine.

Eventually the time came for Elijah to head out to Luna Park. Feeling somewhat relieved the wait was over he grabbed his leather jacket from the bedside, exited his apartment, locked the door, and made his way over to Luna Park. It was only a 10-minute walk from his apartment followed by a short ferry ride.

Chapter 21 - Luna Park

Elijah arrived about 10 minutes early and stood outside the large clown face that was the entrance to Luna Park. The entrance was actually the clown's mouth with the turnstiles inside it. Elijah had taken the walk through the clown's mouth many times before. He would come here often as it reminded him of the good times he used to have with his father—before Thailand.

Rather than just standing around, Elijah went and purchased tickets for the four of them so they would not have to wait in line once they turned up. Shortly after, Maryanne, Michael, and Juliana turned up. They briefly said hellos as Elijah handed them their tickets. They walked quickly through the turnstiles in the clown's mouth and made their way into the park. Elijah tried to think of words to describe how Juliana looked, but all he could come up with was *simply stunning*.

Elijah was nervous and conversation was difficult. *What if he couldn't think of anything to say? What if he said something Juliana did not like? What if he could not say anything interesting?* So many "What ifs" thoughts were racing through Elijah's mind as he overthought every possible situation.

Maryanne was much more casual and was great at breaking the ice between Juliana and Elijah. Maryanne said, "Michael and I are going to take a ride on the dodgem cars. How about you and Juliana go and explore some of the attractions? You know this place like the back of your hand, Elijah, so show Juliana the good bits."

Elijah felt awkward but eventually said, "Okay, if Juliana wants to."

Juliana replied, "I would love to."

Elijah gestured for Juliana to accompany him over to the clown heads that were eagerly waiting for people to put balls into their mouths in the hope of winning a prize. Maryanne shouted out as they were walking away, "We will catch up with you later, just don't get up to any mischief." Elijah thought *now she is just being cheeky* and continued making their way over towards the clowns.

"Are you any good at these things, Juliana? They used to scare me when I was younger. I find them kind of creepy."

"I've never tried them before."

"Well let's have a go," Elijah replied enthusiastically as he passed some money over to the attendant who reset the clown head he was standing in front of. A bunch of balls fell into the catchment area just beneath where the balls went down. The idea of the game was simple: Drop the ball into the mouth of the clown at just the right time so it will go down its neck and into the corresponding numbered slot. The problem was that the clown's head turns left and right constantly diverting the flow of the ball. When all five balls have been dropped, the numbers in the slots they land in are totalled. If they add up to a certain number, you win a prize.

Elijah pre-calculated that they needed to get a total of 27 to be able to choose a prize from the top shelf, which included some nice teddy bears. Elijah grabbed the first ball and passed it to Juliana.

"What do I do?"

"Just drop the ball into the clown's mouth when you think the timing is right."

"I don't know, Elijah," she said. "I'm not very good at these sorts of things."

"Give it a go and see. We need to get twenty-seven in five balls."

Juliana dropped the first ball into the clown's mouth and it landed in the slot marked 8.

"Great start," Elijah said.

Juliana continued dropping the next three balls into the clown's mouth and the total of all the slots added up with balls in them now equalled twenty.

Elijah passed Juliana the final ball and said, "Okay, with this last ball we need to get a seven."

"You do it, Elijah. You'll have a better chance at it."

"You're doing great," Juliana. "Give it a shot."

"No, I want you to do it."

"I know," Elijah said. "Let's do it together."

Juliana nodded. Elijah gripped half of the ball that Juliana was holding and together they gently moved it over to the clown's mouth. Elijah said, "On three, drop it. One, two, three," and they let it go. It spiralled down into the clown's mouth through its neck and spat into out the tube at the bottom. The ball was headed to the five slot but hit the divider and bounced up and then balanced itself between the three and seven slot before falling into the seven.

"We did it, Juliana. Now you get to pick a prize from the top shelf."

Juliana spent a moment looking them over before choosing a white teddy bear that was big enough to cuddle comfortably. She called it Snuffy. Proud of themselves, they wandered off together and enjoyed some of the other attractions in Luna Park before arriving at the Ferris wheel.

They had been having an enjoyable time getting to know each other. The initial ice between them from nerves had all but melted away. Elijah was smiling more than usual—and not just on the outside but on the inside as well. As they waited their turn to get together into one of the Ferris wheel chairs, they chatted casually about all sorts of things. Nothing was forced.

For the record, Elijah was not fond of Ferris wheels. He had never really liked heights because he always felt that he could just fly whenever he got close to a ledge. That was what made his adventures on the cliffs of the Blue Mountains so daring. Of course, he knew that he would die trying to fly. But, it created an uneasiness in him when it came to heights. So, he thought it best him to avoid them whenever possible. The Ferris wheel was the only ride at Luna Park that Elijah would not go on ... until now. He had ended up queuing to go on it only because Juliana asked and he could not think of a reasonable excuse not to go.

Elijah and Juliana sat down in the Ferris wheel chair and the attendant lowered the safety bar and locked it into place. The wheel then started moving in stages as each Ferris wheel chair was loaded with waiting passengers. Before long it was spinning without stopping. The very top of the Ferris wheel cycle afforded Elijah and Juliana an amazing view right across Sydney. Surprisingly Elijah was quite calm and the height did not bother him nearly as much as he feared it would. He kept himself engaged in conversation with Juliana to distract him from the height. Then came the dreadful moment when the lights flickered and there was a sickly groaning noise. Elijah's stomach flip-flopped. The lights flickered again, but this time did not come back on, and the Ferris wheel ground to a halt just as their chair was at the very pinnacle of the Ferris wheel cycle. Elijah looked around and noticed that it wasn't just a problem with the Ferris wheel but that a blackout had extinguished the lights clear across Sydney. The night was suddenly pitch black and the only lights he could see were the emergency lights around Luna Park and beyond.

In the distance, Elijah heard a man shout: "Don't panic! We will have power restored shortly either by generator or when the power is restored to the city."

In as calm a voice as he could muster Elijah said, "Well, Juliana, at least it is a nice night to get stuck up here."

"It sure is," she replied as she casually looked at the clear night sky that was lit up with thousands of stars and a rising full moon. "It is so beautiful, Elijah." A cold breeze was blowing at this height and Juliana shivered slightly.

Elijah removed his jacket and placed it around Juliana's shoulders to help keep her warm.

Juliana said "thank you" and moved closer until the side of her body was against his. Elijah responded by taking her hand and she clenched it tightly. This gave Elijah's nerves some relief from the height and also provided a strange feeling of comfort inside him that he was not used to feeling.

"Are you scared, Juliana?"

"No," she said. "I find it peaceful and very beautiful."

Several minutes passed as they sat in silence gazing at the beautiful night sky.

"Hey look, Elijah, there is a falling star!"

Elijah turned and looked where she was looking and noticed the falling star. "We should make a wish," he said.

"We should," she replied enthusiastically.

They both made silent wishes.

"What did you wish for, Juliana?"

"I can't tell you that, Elijah, because if I did it might not come true."

"Fair enough," he said. "Then I better not tell you mine, either."

Elijah released Juliana's hand and put his arm around her shoulders, and she responded by nestling in closer to him so he could clasp her tighter to stay warm.

"I wonder how long we will be stuck up here?" he said. "It's been almost fifteen minutes."

"I don't mind, Elijah," she said. "It's rather nice."

"Definitely," he said, "especially being here with you."

Juliana looked deep into Elijah's eyes and he into hers and they moved toward each other very slowly. Just as their lips gently touched there was a shudder and the lights lit up and the Ferris wheel began to move.

"Talk about bad timing," Elijah said.

Juliana just laughed in the most beautiful way Elijah could imagine.

It was not long before they were back on the ground and saw Maryanne and Michael waiting for them.

"How did you guys know where we were, Maryanne?" Elijah said.

"Oh, we had plenty of time to walk around in semi-darkness looking for you before eagle-eye Michael spotted you at the top of the Ferris wheel. We called out to you, but I don't think you heard us."

"No," Elijah said. "We didn't hear you."

"They are closing the park early due to the power interruptions so Michael and I thought we should go for a late dinner over at North Quay."

"Sounds good to me," Elijah said.

"Sounds good to me, too," Juliana agreed.

The enchanted night extended into the early hours of the next morning when Elijah and Juliana parted ways. Juliana went with Maryanne and Michael while Elijah walked back to his apartment, almost floating in fact, for he was the happiest he had been in a very long time.

Chapter 22 - 2001, Michael

"Could we have another five minutes please, Doctor?" Maryanne asked.

"Of course," the doctor said. "I'll come back in a little while."

Maryanne stood bedside and held Michael's hand. Michael was in a coma after suffering a heart attack at work from a rare heart condition. He never saw it coming. One minute he was working away on his computer, the next he was on the floor with the office staff performing CPR on him. That was 10 days ago.

This was the day—Michael's last day—when the life-support machines were to be switched off. Maryanne, Juliana, and Elijah were there to say goodbye to their beloved husband and friend. It was extremely painful, and Elijah was struggling to keep himself together. Over the years, Michael and Elijah had become like brothers. Just a few years earlier, Michael was Elijah's best man at his and Juliana's wedding. It seemed like mere days ago, and now his life was over.

Elijah struggled to come to terms with how could this happen. How could a loving father of beautiful twin daughters, age seven, and a son, age six, suddenly end up like this with no warning? It seemed so cruel and unfair. *Why did this have to happen to Maryanne and Michael?*

Juliana stared at Michael with a look of disbelief on her gentle face. Elijah pulled her close to his side. He knew she felt uncomfortable seeing all those cold machines hooked up to him by various tubes and wires. The large ventilation tube in his mouth was especially disturbing. A valve attached to the end of it caused a small sack to inflate and deflate with a hissing noise every few seconds.

They all knew that keeping him alive like this was something that Michael would not want. The last 10 days had been a struggle. Maryanne has been praying for a miracle but none had come—and none would come. The EEG showed no brain activity whatsoever. Michael's body was dead and beyond resuscitation; the machines were the only thing keeping his heart beating.

* * *

Castiel and Elijah were standing there watching from the back of the room. Elijah felt uncomfortable revisiting the sad scene but trusted that Castiel had a reason for showing him. His trust in Castiel was growing, even though he had only known him for few days.

"Castiel, what is that blue outline that keeps pulsating around Michael's body with a faint glow? It looks as though it is trying to get out but keeps getting dragged back in."

"That is exactly what is happening, Elijah," Castiel said. "The blue glow is Michael's soul trying to leave his dying body, but it can't because the machines keep pumping life back into it, which drags his soul back."

Elijah got the feeling that Castiel was uncomfortable talking about this.

The doctor re-entered the room. "Are you ready, Maryanne?"

"I'm not sure I'll ever be ready," she said, her voice breaking, "but we have to do this. I know Michael would not want to stay like this."

"Did you want to press the switch or would you prefer that I did it?"

"You, please," she said. "I'll just hold his hand."

The doctor stepped over to the head of the bed where the main control box that powered the ventilator was. He flipped the switch and the machine stopped leaving a deafening silence in its wake. It was as if time and all sound ceased in that moment once and for all. Michael did not move at all. He just lay there still and silent, a shadow of his former vibrant self, as the doctor put his stethoscope on his chest and listened for a heartbeat. After a few moments, he looked up at Maryanne and then lowered his eyes: Michael was gone. The tears in their eyes were a mere token of the deep grief they all felt.

Elijah and Castiel saw the blue glow leave Michael's body. It paused for an instant as if looking back and then continued floating upwards where it vanished into the glow of a great white light that appeared before him.

Elijah's voice cracked with emotion when he said, "Castiel, I've seen enough of this. May we move on, please?"

Castiel nodded and then they left.

*   *   *

Juliana stepped over and held Maryanne tight as they both wept. Elijah stood motionless and watched as the doctor began removing the wires and tubes connected to Michael. Elijah had never seen a dead person before and was wishing now that he never had.

The doctor finished by removing the tape keeping Michael's eyes closed and then covering his head with the sheet. He said, "Would you like more time with Michael?"

"No, I think it's time for us to go," Maryanne replied in a quavering voice. "Thank you."

Juliana, Elijah, and Maryanne hurried out—the quicker to distance themselves from the place and go mourn the loss of their loved one privately, each in their own way.

Michael's funeral was held a week later and presented Elijah with challenges he had never faced before. His emotions stirred inside. Those fortress walls he had erected to insulate himself against the threat of being hurt were quaking under the great pressure of his long-buried memories. Looking at Michael's photo or the casket was just too difficult. He tried to direct his mind to something more peaceful. His emotions were buried deep, and Elijah had spent most of his life thinking rather than feeling. If he could make sense of something—a line of code in his computer programs—then he was master of it. Feelings were another matter entirely. He had not really cried since that day many years ago in Thailand when Lester literally brought him to his knees with that blistering verbal assault. He put up walls and buried his emotions deep behind them and tried hard to stay safe. Emotions can be stifled but never killed. They would at times manifest as physical symptoms—headaches, indigestion, nerve issues, muscle pains, and general stress—as they seeped through cracks in the walls. He could hide, yes, but the emotions had a way of letting him know they would eventually find him.

Michael's death raised many questions about life for Elijah. It shook his very mortality and his faith. He wondered why God would allow such a thing to happen to Michael. These questions set Elijah off on a quest to know more about life, to find some meaning, to find out who he was, to find out if life had any purpose at all.

Chapter 23 - Elijah & Castiel

Elijah and Castiel sat on a park bench eating hot chips loosely wrapped in butcher's paper and watched the waves crashing into the rocky beach.

"Nothing better than eating hot chips while watching the ocean, Elijah."

"It brings back many fond memories, Castiel."

"Life is full of difficult times, Elijah. We have to remember to take a break sometimes and enjoy some hot chips and the beauty all around us. It is always there, but we must stop and take the time to notice it."

Elijah looked out at the surf. "Seeing Michael die all over again was a little tough, Castiel. It was bad enough the first time. Seeing it again just dredged up a lot of memories."

Elijah took another chip and casually ate it while gazing at the ocean.

"Michael and I became like brothers, Castiel. We did many things together—mountain biking, cycling, squash, hiking, video games, and fishing, to name just a few. He was my best friend and very much like a brother to me. He helped Juliana and me in the early stages of our relationship in many different ways. Maryanne and Michael would take us to all sorts of romantic places beginning with that magical trip to Luna Park on our first 'date' and going on from there. He was someone I came to trust, which was a difficult thing for me to do."

"Indeed it was," Castiel said.

"Michael went to church every week and was very deeply devoted to God. He brought up his children in the church as well. At the funeral, the pastor said that God had chosen Michael to be by His side. That made me quite angry at the time, Castiel. I wondered why a loving God would do that. Why would God take a father away from his beloved children just so He could have him by His side? Weren't his kids better off with their dad by their side? None of it made any sense and it sent me on one hell of a journey."

"A lot of things make no sense, Elijah, when you see them all as just random bits and pieces. Like a jigsaw puzzle. When you dump the fifteen-hundred pieces out on the table and look at them, it doesn't make sense. It is only when you start to put the pieces together—to work the puzzle—that you see a picture. Remember this: We never see all the pieces, only some."

"The pieces I am concerned about, Castiel, are Juliana, Maryanne, and the children."

"Oh, so am I, Elijah," Castiel said, his tone serious. "That is why these events I am showing you are very important when it comes to your decision."

In a slightly exasperated voice, Elijah replied, "*What* decision, Castiel? You still haven't given me a choice to make a decision?"

"I can't yet, Elijah, but it won't be much longer," Castiel assured him. "There is still a little more for you to see."

Around them, the park was changing constantly. Flowerbeds appeared out of nowhere and sprouted all sorts of colourful blooming flowers. Trees appeared and swayed in the wind only to be replaced a little later by a lake filled with bird life. It was as though they were inside a painting that was forever changing. It provided visual happiness and a sense of peace as everything—the ocean, the wind, the trees, and the wildlife—were working together in harmony.

"Let's go for a walk, Elijah."

Castiel and Elijah got up from the park bench and proceeded to walk down a dirt pathway that had appeared to head off into some trees.

"I always find that walking can help clear the mind."

"Michael used to say that, Castiel, early on in our relationship when he was getting me into physical activities. Being a computer nerd, I was not big on sports. It took some convincing to get me off my bum and into some physical activity. Video games were much easier."

The pathway continued through the trees and into a clearing where a little shack set on the bank of a lake. In front of the shack was a jetty with a little wooden boat with two oars docked at the end of it.

"Feel like a boat ride, Elijah?"

"Sure, why not?"

They sauntered down to the jetty and climbed into the little wooden boat. Castiel sat in the rowing position. He took the oars and started rowing as Elijah released the rope mooring the boat to the jetty. The boat cruised slowly across the smooth lake that reflected a clear blue sky.

"Will Juliana and Maryanne be okay, Castiel?"

"I honestly don't know, Elijah, but I plan to do my best to ensure that they will be."

"How?"

"You have a lot of questions, Elijah, and rightfully so. In time you will be given some more pieces of the puzzle."

"Can't you just tell me, Castiel?"

"No," Castiel said, "I cannot. There are rules and punishments for breaking them. I trust in the greater order of things. I know you are not a fan of order and rules, Elijah, but sometimes it is better to follow them. You remind me a lot of Sophia. She is not fond of rules, either, and is constantly in trouble. She does get results, however, so somehow she always escapes the punishment side of things. In some ways I think they admire her daring to go outside the rules and test the boundaries. In many cases, the rules are there to keep us safe. Sophia does not mind putting herself on the line if she believes that what she is doing is right. She typically ends up caring too much and that leads to her stubbornness, which in turn leads to her bending the rules."

"You're starting to sound very cryptic again, Castiel, with all this talk about rules and the greater order of things. I have no idea what are you talking about."

"Sorry, Elijah. I tend to say too much at times."

"And too little at others," Elijah said, smiling. "Like not telling me about the decision I have to make."

"Touché," Castiel said. He continued rowing the boat while they sat in silence watching the water life around the lake. Birds of various feathers swooped down into the lake to catch fish, and the fish were leaping out of the water to catch bugs. The sound of the oars gliding through the water and the serene noises of the wildlife created a deep sense of serenity.

"I miss my children and my wife, Castiel. They were everything to me. I would do anything for them."

"When it comes to making your decision, Elijah, that is what the powers that be are relying on."

Chapter 24 - Channelling

Several months after Michael's death Elijah went to the Hilton Hotel in the centre of Sydney to see Marsilla, a woman who claimed she could channel a 40,000-year-old male spirit called Rimmon. Elijah spent some time reading about it and found it fascinating. If that is possible, he thought, then he might just be able to communicate with Michael in some way.

Juliana dropped Elijah near the entrance to the hotel for the seminar and then went into the heart of Sydney to do some shopping. Many people gathered around the entrance to the seminar room looking at various materials on sale including books that the ancient Rimmon had written. Elijah wondered how Rimmon, a spirit, could write a book. Someone explained the process to him. Marsilla would channel Rimmon who would thus write the books while being channelled. Elijah casually browsed the books, DVDs, and audio tapes on the kiosk but decided not to purchase anything. It was not long until the seminar was scheduled to begin.

Elijah found a seat near the back, just as he did at church, because he felt more comfortable sitting at the back of events. Out of sight out of mind, he thought. Loud music started booming through the P.A. speaker and the crowd erupted in applause as Marsilla came through a door towards the back of the seminar room surrounded by a coterie of large male bodyguards. Once on the stage she said, "Greetings, Earthlings." Elijah pondered that greeting and wondered what it meant.

The presentation was well done, and Elijah was quite taken in at the exercises and displays. In one exercise, they had each member of the audience pair up with another member. One person would draw a picture and the other was instructed to draw what he or she believed the other person was drawing. At the end of the exercise, they asked people to share what they did. Those who got similar results were asked to stand up. About 30 of the 300 people there stood up and showed simple pictures of stars or other common objects. Elijah quickly did the maths and considered that coincidence probably had more to with that than psychic ability.

Marsilla, or Rimmon, depending on who Elijah believed was speaking at the time, had some interesting things to say, but some of it bothered Elijah. At one point Rimmon stated that everyone is a god, that we are all gods. Then he declared that there is no grand God as the church would like you to believe. Then she or he would curse God using vile language. Elijah wondered why Marsilla or Rimmon would feel the need to curse a God who just moments before they claimed did not exist. When Rimmon said this, some people stood up and left the room. Elijah considered leaving as well, but stayed.

Marsilla ran a school in the United States based on the teachings of Rimmon. The course cost several thousand dollars for a weekend and required you to stay at the school. People would attend in hopes that they would obtain some sort of supernatural power. Such powers included the ability to see inside a closed box without opening it, reading other people's minds, and moving objects merely with thoughts. Elijah considered that all these things might be possible, but he was not sure about the source and the way it was being taught. Marsilla even claimed that the CIA had used her services.

Given the performance, Elijah believed that Marsilla was probably channelling, but the real burning question was—just what was she was channelling? How would she know whether what she was channelling was actually good? It had caused her marriage to break down, which made Elijah wonder.

* * *

Castiel and Elijah were standing at the back of the seminar room after entering late from their time-jump. Elijah had already presumed what to expect and, sure enough, he was right. The room was infested with Shadow Figures and Shadow Scavengers scouring the floors. A new type of Shadow Figure that Elijah had not seen before was here. This one looked like a knight protected by some sort of armour. He wielded a large glowing red sword in one hand and raised a shield in the other. The outline of its black shape was wavering like a reflection in water.

"Castiel, what is that Shadow Figure—the one that looks like a knight?"

"We call them Shadow Knights. They are a level up from Shadow Figures and highly trained in warfare. They gather around people who delve into the occult and manipulate them by providing them with certain bits of information for their own gain."

"Is that what she is channelling?"

"Yes, one of many. It's not always the same one. They mess with her. Marsilla believes she is channelling some sort of god, some sort of divine wisdom, but all she is doing is channelling a spirit that was condemned centuries ago. The Shadow Knights grant her certain powers by providing answers to questions she would not otherwise know. She thinks she is doing the right thing, but she has been conned and is aiding the Shadow Knights to con others to do their bidding."

"Do all people who channel spirits channel Shadows?"

"No. The problem is that most of the people channelling have no way of knowing who they are talking to. Think of it as talking to someone in an Internet chatroom whom you have never met in person. You have to rely on that person to tell you the truth, but you have no way of validating it. There have been many cases in which people have pretended to be someone they're not to con people. In some cases, it has ended in death."

"I never considered that, Castiel." Elijah looked at Marsilla aided and abetted by that Shadow Knight. "The only difference here is that it's not across the Internet but across Spiritual Realms, which is open to all sorts of abuse."

"Unfortunately it is, Elijah. There are warnings about talking to strangers in Internet chatrooms, just as there are warnings in the Bible about consorting with psychics and mediums. Speaking of mediums, I think that is our next stop, Elijah. You ready?"

Elijah replied, "Yes, I am interested to find out what happened there."

That said, they left.

* * *

The seminar left Elijah with more questions than answers. As he sat outside the Hilton waiting for Juliana to return he tried to make sense of what had just happened.

After being picked up by Juliana she asked, "How did it go, Elijah?"

"It was interesting. I'm just not sure it answered any of my questions."

"Was she faking it, or could she really channel a spirit?"

"To me, it looked like she was channelling someone or something," he said. "If it was a show, she did it well. The change in her voice and body language was quite distinct when she said she was channelling."

"Good actors can do that, though, can't they, Elijah?"

"I suppose they could. She seemed to have a lot of wisdom about different things, but then again it's nothing you could not read in some New Age books. Those books tend to feed off each other and rehash the same old things."

Juliana nodded. "They do."

"I'm not sure, Juliana. I think I might go and see a private medium and see if we can channel Michael?"

"Do you think that's a good idea, Elijah?"

"I take it that you don't?"

"Well, they might scam you into believing a lie." She lay her hand on his. "How would you know what they say is really truthful or if they are just making stuff up?"

"Maybe I wouldn't," Elijah said, fidgeting a bit. "But I would like to try it."

Juliana's driving became slightly more aggressive. Elijah could tell the thought of delving into the afterlife, channelling, and mediums, made her uncomfortable. Although Juliana did not attend church regularly, she had Christian beliefs from her childhood. Elijah knew that she wished he shared those beliefs, but she never tried to push her beliefs on him. She was supportive of Elijah in his search and hoped—and she sometimes prayed—that his search would help him heal his wounds and find what he was looking for.

Chapter 25 - Medium

Elijah pulled his car to a stop outside an average looking house. He was not sure what to expect on arriving at the medium's house or what type of place it would be. Elijah spent some time searching for the right medium—one he thought was more legitimate and had reliable references. Of all the dozen he researched, she was the one he determined was the best. The only downside was that she was a three-hour drive away.

A large bell was to the left of the front door. Elijah gave the rope hanging from it a tug and waited. A woman in her late 40s opened the door and greeted him. She introduced herself as Ailsa. Elijah recognised her voice and realised it was the same woman he had spoken to on the phone. He had expected her to be a younger woman, but he actually liked the idea that she was older because he associated age with wisdom.

Ailsa led Elijah into a room and showed him to a corner lounge. She sat down on the end of the lounge suite opposite Elijah. He was surprised the room was as regular as it was. In his mind, he had pictured a small room with a table in the middle with two chairs on opposite sides and a crystal ball in the middle.

"Do you mind the smell, Elijah?"

The mild scent of burning incense hung in the air.

"No, it's fine," He said.

"Based on our phone call, Elijah, I'm presuming you still want to try to contact Michael who passed over about seven months ago?"

Elijah hesitated before finally replying: "Yes."

Ailsa repositioned herself so she was sitting in a more relaxed state. She moved closer to Elijah and held out her hands. "I need you to take hold of my hands, Elijah."

Elijah gently took Ailsa hands as she closed her eyes. Elijah's temperature rose and he began to sweat slightly under his arms and on his chest. He was glad he was wearing a singlet under his shirt. Ailsa started to shake slightly, which made Elijah more uncomfortable, and he wondered if his palms were getting sweaty.

"I'm sensing someone around us, Elijah."

After pausing for several seconds she continued, "It is someone who has passed over recently and wants to be here. It is possible that it is Michael."

Elijah sat there thinking *this is not very convincing.*

Ailsa's head shook from side to side and then she said, "Yes, it is a male. Did Michael have children, Elijah?"

"Yes."

"And I'm getting the feeling they were quite young when he died."

"They were," Elijah replied, his interest sparked.

* * *

Elijah and Castiel entered the room and stood beside the couch watching both Elijah and Ailsa.

Elijah looked around the room. "I can't see anybody here but me and Ailsa, Castiel. Whom is she talking to?"

"Ailsa is not actually talking to anyone. She is tuning into your memories and thoughts. They believe they are sensing spirits, but all they are really doing is a form of mind reading."

"So mediums don't actually talk to the Spiritual Realm?"

"Some do."

Ailsa spoke again, "I'm sensing that Michael had two daughters and one son."

Elijah sat up straighter and his pupils dilated. He was beginning to believe she was indeed talking to Michael and replied, "Yes, he did. Twin daughters and a son."

Elijah looked at Castiel and cocked his head. "So the way she knew that Michael had two young daughters and a son was by reading my thoughts and memories about Michael?"

"Exactly. Mediums typically do not tell people anything they do not already know. The thing that catches most people out is that they do not understand how the medium could know so much about Aunt Victoria or Uncle Dave or whoever it is they are hired to encounter. If they thought about it and realised that some people can read other people's thoughts and memories, they would understand that's all they are really doing."

Ailsa paused between sentences. "Michael says he is missing his children and friends. He is sad that he left them so quickly."

The emotion in Ailsa's voice was convincing evidence that she was communicating with someone.

"How did Michael die, Elijah?"

"Heart failure from a rare condition."

"Oh, that must be why I'm sensing so much pain and a sudden death."

"I guess," Elijah muttered.

Ailsa tightened her grip on Elijah's hands and her body jerked a little and she opened her eyes and looked up at the ceiling for a moment before closing them again and returning to a more relaxed state.

"Elijah, Michael wants you to know he is okay."

A strange sense of relief ran through Elijah when he heard that.

"And he is happy where he is."

Elijah remained silent.

"He says he needs to go now but asks that you tell his wife that he loves her."

Elijah looked up as his interest sparked again and he wondered how she knew Michael was married. He realised that she knew he had children and that would be the most likely conclusion but not definite. With a slight crackle in his voice, Elijah responded, "I will."

Ailsa slowly released Elijah's hands, opened her eyes, and resumed a more casual posture.

"Well, Castiel," Elijah said, "this wasn't what I was expecting. I thought Michael might have actually been here, but now it makes sense. You're right. She did not actually tell me anything I didn't already know."

Ailsa asked, "How are you feeling, Elijah?"

"All right, I guess," Elijah said. "Is it normal for the spirits to rush off like that?"

"Sometimes."

"I see."

Ailsa continued to discuss spirits in general with Elijah. She asked Elijah if he had any questions, but he was still trying to process what had just happened and said, "No." They continued chatting for several minutes until Ailsa subtly let Elijah know that the session time was up.

Elijah stood up, pulled out a hundred-dollar note, handed it to Ailsa, and thanked her.

"I hope it helped, Elijah," she said. "Take care of yourself."

Elijah squinted and tried to get a better look at his younger self. "Castiel, are those cracks appearing in my body. I hadn't noticed them before."

"Yes, Elijah. Delving into the spirit world like you were doing was beginning to take a toll on your body and cracks started to form."

"What about Sophia? Why isn't she protecting me?"

"She cannot protect you from your own choices because that would infringe on your free will."

A realisation was just beginning to hit Elijah when Castiel said, "It's time for you to see the consequences of your actions, Elijah. Let's go."

As Elijah made his way back to his car, he wondered whether the experience with the medium had helped him ... or not.

Chapter 26 - From Bad to Worse

Michael's death was taking a heavy toll on Elijah. His very foundation was shaking, which caused cracks to form in the walls he had erected to protect himself. Long-buried emotions were not just seeping now but beginning to stream through the cracks. No longer just bubbles here and there, but they were a constant flow of negative emotions. They manifested as round-the-clock nausea and a general uneasiness. Elijah had no idea what was happening. All he knew was that he felt ill and was getting worse.

He called his doctor, Gary, and made an appointment. Gary was a good doctor whom he had known for more than a decade. Elijah had seldom needed to see Gary because he was generally in good health. Gary ran some routine tests and informed Elijah that his symptoms were consistent with the stomach flu. Elijah did not understand how it could last so long, but Gary told him that it was unlikely to be anything else. Elijah left somewhat perturbed but relieved that it was nothing more serious than a case of the flu.

When he was still suffering the same symptoms two months later, Elijah returned to his doctor. Same diagnosis: stomach flu. Elijah began to suspect then that he must have been causing his own symptoms, that somehow his past had caught up with him. Elijah had read books on psychosomatic dis-ease and how buried emotions can manifest as physical symptoms. So, he made an appointment with a psychiatrist.

On arriving at the psychiatrist's office, Elijah sat in the waiting room and looked at the other patients. He wondered what their problems were. He could hear mumblings through the wall as the current patient conversed with the psychiatrist, but he could not make out the words.

The psychiatrist came out and showed him back to the consulting room. The room was quite small and had various framed diplomas and certificates on the wall, demonstrating the doctor's qualifications, and a bookshelf full of books on psychiatry. Elijah wondered whether the man had read them all or put them out merely for show.

After a general greeting, Elijah gave the psychiatrist a brief run-down of his history in hopes that the man would dispense some general advice on how to cure him of the physical and mental symptoms he was experiencing. At the end of the session the doctor offered him a script for anti-depressants, which Elijah refused. He was seeking answers not pills. Elijah left feeling somewhat jaded by the experience and felt alone and lonely—the same abandoned lonely feeling he had in Thailand.

He had Juliana, sure, but a breach was forming between them—a breach of Elijah's own making. He was hurting and just wanted the world to go away. He turned to the one thing that had always given him comfort, his computer. He started playing online computer games that let him escape into virtual worlds and leave the real world behind.

The virtual worlds were so much better, so much safer. He could be a knight and slay dragons and go on quests with other characters. It empowered him and distracted his mind, which provided relief from his symptoms. Elijah stayed up playing until the early hours of the morning and only went to bed when he was completely exhausted.

He formed friendships with other players in the virtual world. On the surface this seemed great, but then the virtual world started to become reality as they began carrying on real-life discussions in the virtual worlds. Elijah got to know the people he was playing with in the virtual worlds on a more personal level. Then one day the fiancé of one of the players he knew emailed him with the news that her fiancé had died of a brain aneurism while playing the game. They found him dead with his head on his computer keyboard.

This shook up Elijah and again called into question his own mortality. He thought he had escaped reality in the virtual world, but reality had managed to find him even there in that safe place. He felt trapped.

Elijah's father contacted him via email and said he (and his young Thai girlfriend) wanted to come for a visit from Thailand. More than 16 years had passed since Elijah last saw his father and he thought it might be a chance for him and his father to reconcile. His father requested a statement from Elijah that he believed that his father's girlfriend would leave the country at the conclusion of the visit. This was required so that she could obtain a temporary visa. Elijah considered the ramifications of making this statement and wondered what would happen if she did not in fact leave the country. He did not know her, so how could he trust her? In the end he decided to do it, at the expense of making a false statement to the governing authorities.

Elijah picked up his father and his girlfriend from the airport. His stomach was churning like a washing machine on the spin cycle. He felt sick, very sick. His mind was whirling and he was sweating. He had never felt so uncomfortable. This was worse even than when he stood and watched Michael die. His father's young Thai girlfriend, who was at least 30 years younger than his father, reminded him of the prostitutes who hung out at the Pink Panther in Bangkok's red-light district. What were the chances this girl really loved his father and was not just using him? Elijah decided the chance was nil.

On arriving home, Elijah introduced his father to Juliana, who as always was gracious and pleasant and tried to make him feel as welcome as possible. When it came to his young Thai girlfriend, however, Juliana was uneasy and uncomfortable with the situation.

They sat around the kitchen table for a while and made general chit-chat. Elijah decided to take the three of them for lunch in the city, where his father was also to meet up with Claricia later in the afternoon. Elijah was not handling the situation well. His emotional walls were quaking now, which caused his mind and body to behave erratically. He could not put his finger on exactly what he was feeling. The best he could think of was that he wanted to escape—to run away and be as far away from the present situation as possible.

The day passed slowly and Elijah was not sure how he was going to get through it. While having drinks at a café in the city, Elijah formulated an escape plan to end it as quickly as possible. He rang Claricia to see if she and her husband could come join them. He figured this would give him and Juliana an out, and they could leave earlier and head back home.

Claricia turned up within the hour and they all had lunch together. Elijah felt a little relief as there were more people around and he felt less pressured to make conversation. But, he still wanted out. He wanted to get away. His moment came at the end of lunch and he said his farewells.

He was relieved, but the visit had taken its toll. Those fortress walls were now leaking like floodgates on a dam. He felt numb most of the time, but then the feelings would break through and manifest as all sorts of mental and physical symptoms. Elijah was in a world of hurt. The pain was all-consuming, sucking every bit of joy from his body and replacing it with a deep and abiding sadness.

It had begun to seem as though wherever Elijah turned some disaster would follow—adding to his pain. He started to wish it was all over and even, once again, contemplated ending it all.

Then came the night that would change Elijah's world forever.

Chapter 27 - Fear

Castiel and Elijah stood inside Elijah's bedroom and watched Elijah and Juliana sleep. The digital clock on the bedside table displayed 1:29 a.m.

"Should something be here, Castiel?"

"Just wait for it."

Several black portals began to appear around the room, and Shadow Figures hurried through them and gathered around the bed. Then a larger black portal opened and a Shadow Knight stepped through holding one of those glowing green snake-like creatures. The Shadow Figures moved aside to allow the Shadow Knight to walk up to the end of the bed.

A few seconds later two white portals appeared. Sophia charged through the first one with her glistening swords at the ready, and Castiel came through the second one.

"You were here, Castiel?"

"Yes. But I don't think you are going to like what I do next."

Castiel squared off against Sophia and looked her in the face. "No. You can't interfere, Sophia. This is the way it has to be."

"But we can't let this happen, Castiel," she said, pleading. "Please let me stop them."

Castiel stepped closer to Sophia and replied in a sincere, concerned voice: "We *must* let this happen."

Sophia scowled but sheathed her swords and moved towards the back of the room. The Shadow Figures did not seem to care about the discussion Sophia and Castiel were having. They simply ignored them.

Elijah asked, "Why are the Shadows ignoring you and Sophia?"

"They have been waiting a very long time for this moment, Elijah, and they were given the okay to do it by higher authority."

The Shadow Knight placed the green glowing snake-like creature on the end of the bed as the Shadow Figures began chanting in unison in a deep lifeless voice: "Om Ma Kahn."

Sophia's eyes welled up with tears. She knew what was going to happen next. It pained her to see Elijah, whom she had protected for so long, go through what he was about to. Against all her instincts she stood there still and silent, stricken with anger, disappointment, and concern.

The snake-like creature slithered its way up to Elijah's face and entered his body through his nose. Elijah lay motionless as his eyelids glowed green as the creature passed behind his eyes and into his skull. The glow proceeded to go down his throat into his chest and wrap itself around Elijah's soul.

"You don't seem surprised, Elijah."

"I lived through it, Castiel," Elijah said, shaking his head. "I assumed something like this had happened. Now I know it was real. Why did you stop Sophia?"

"It wasn't my choice, Elijah. Higher authorities made a deal with the Shadows to allow this to happen. You wanted answers, and sometimes the best way to find them is to live through situations that force you to find them."

One by one, the Shadows turned and exited through the portals they had come through, with the Shadow Knight bringing up the rear.

Castiel and Sophia stood beside the bed and looked down at Elijah. Sophia asked, "Will he be all right?"

"I'm not sure, Sophia. I hope so."

Elijah glanced at the clock and noticed it was still 1:29 a.m.

"How come the time hasn't changed, Castiel?"

"The whole scene you just witnessed occurred within a few milliseconds of earth time."

Castiel and Sophia exited through the portals they had come through.

"How come we don't need portals to get around, Castiel?"

"You only need them to pass between the Human Realm and the Spiritual Realm. Some shadows lurk in the Human Realm and simply teleport from place to place. I don't think you need to see anything more here, Elijah."

Elijah said, "If what is about to happen is how I remember it you are right, Castiel. I don't need to go through that again."

They departed with a time-jump to a future date.

*   *   *

The clock flicked over to 1:30 a.m. as Elijah woke up grimacing in pain clutching his left arm. He stumbled out of bed and made his way to the bathroom while gripping his shoulder. The pain was excruciating. Elijah drank some cool water from the basin faucet and splashed some on his face. It was not helping. The pain was getting worse, and he felt as though he was going to pass out. He fumbled his way through the darkness into the kitchen, flicked on the light, and searched for some painkillers. *Am I having a heart attack?* His pulse quickened and he started to sweat and then came the nausea. He raced to the toilet while doing his best to hold back the convulsions that carried vomit to his mouth. Once there he shuddered and let the convulsions carry forth the fluids and bits of food from his stomach.

The pain in his arm started to ease up. Elijah continued to feel nauseated, but his sweating and heart rate returned to normal. He slowly made his way back to the kitchen, collected some painkillers, and took them with a small sip of water. He crawled back into bed wondering what had just happened. Juliana woke up and asked him if he was okay. He said yes. He did not want to worry her and he had no idea what had just happened.

He lay there for half an hour with many worrisome thoughts racing through his mind until he started to feel drowsy from the painkillers and drifted off to sleep.

The next day the events of the previous night were on Elijah's mind. He felt unsteady and the nausea he had been experiencing for the last several months had intensified, accompanied by diarrhoea. He made an appointment to see his doctor, Gary, for later that the same day, which relieved him somewhat.

He was beginning to think that something was wrong with his heart. He had seen enough TV shows and read enough to know that severe pain in your left arm could indicate a heart condition. Memories of Michael's sudden death also plagued his mind.

It did not take the doctor long to make a diagnosis. He told Elijah that he had experienced a panic attack. Elijah had heard of panic attacks before in movies such as *Analyse This* in which Robert DeNiro plays a mobster. Apart from that he had no idea what they were. Gary explained the nausea and diarrhoea was most likely caused by anxiety and stress. Elijah left feeling bewildered, anxious, and worried—and not convinced that Gary had made a proper diagnosis.

Elijah went home but couldn't shake the idea that something was wrong with his heart. This caused his stress and anxiety levels to increase, resulting in more physical symptoms. The electric shock sensations that shot across his chest fuelled his belief that something was wrong with his heart and triggered more panic attacks. It was a downward spiral.

He made another visit to the doctor, then another, and kept receiving the same diagnosis: panic attacks. Crippled with fear, Elijah could not venture outside his house. Terrifying thoughts raced through his mind: What if he had a heart attack and the ambulance did not make it to him in time? His mind played out hundreds of different nightmarish scenarios in which something tragic would happen. The fear was driving him crazy, literally, to the point where suicide looked like the only option to stop it. He realised he was afraid of death, and yet dying seemed like the only way to fix it. It made no sense to him and caused even more fear. Consumed by fear he felt abandoned by God. What faith he once possessed had dwindled to nothing.

On his fourth doctor visit, Gary offered him some medication, a type of sedative that assisted with panic attacks. Elijah accepted the drugs and they seemed to work. The panic attacks subsided, and Elijah felt better than he had in a while. It dulled his racing mind and gave him a strange kind of peace.

The peace allowed him to think rationally again. He considered his options for helping himself. The Internet was his first course of action. He Googled "Panic Attacks" and found a wealth of information. Many of the "articles" were clearly Internet swindles for quick fixes that were unlikely to work. He turned to searching for books on Amazon and purchased several that seemed interesting. He quickly realised that he may need the help of a professional psychologist and so made an appointment with one.

He researched the medication he had been taking and found that it was for short-term use only because it was addictive. This strengthened his resolve to rectify whatever was happening to him as quickly as possible, or at least get to a stage where he did not need the medication simply to function.

Chapter 28 - Psychology

"So tell me, Elijah, why are you here?" the psychologist asked.

The psychologist, Jeff, was in his late 30s, and had receding black hair with a little grey creeping in. He wore glasses and had a clean-cut professional appearance.

"I've started having panic attacks and my mind races all day ... full of crazy thoughts."

"Do you have any idea what is causing them?"

Jeff listened attentively as Elijah gave a summarised version of his history, which took around 20 minutes. A brief pause followed as Jeff finished writing his notes on what Elijah had just shared. Elijah took the time to glance around the room and noticed a bookshelf full of books. Most were on psychology but his eye landed on a black edition of the Holy Bible. He thought it was a little odd that a psychologist would have a Bible on display.

"Jeff, do you believe in God?" Elijah queried.

Jeff cocked his head and said, "I believe that faith plays an important part in life and I do attend a local church. Tell me, Elijah, what are you mainly thinking when the fear consumes you?"

"It's more visualising my own death and whether help will arrive in time or not. Other times I sit worrying whether I should call an ambulance based on the psychical pains I'm experiencing."

"What sorts of pains?"

"All sorts really: muscle pains, muscle twitches, numbness, nausea, chest pains, electric shock sensations, dizziness. It is quite random and they are neverending."

"I recommend that you read a couple of books, Elijah."

Jeff wrote the book titles down on a piece of paper and passed it to Elijah. The paper read "How to Stop Worrying and Start Living – Dale Carnegie" and "The Road Less Travelled – Dr. M. Scott Peck."

"Thank you," Elijah said. "So, do you think I should stay on the medication?"

"I can't give advice on medication, Elijah. I'm not qualified in that area. You need to discuss that with your physician."

Elijah felt a little disappointed that he did not get an answer.

The session wound up, and Elijah left feeling a little more upbeat than usual.

Elijah continued with the psychologist for several weeks and, during that time, he came off the medication. It was not easy, but Elijah was learning Cognitive Behaviour Therapy skills to help control his worrying thoughts. This prevented the panic attacks from taking control of his body. He still had minor panic attacks and would wake up in the middle of the night with bad stomach cramps and diarrhoea. They were almost like miniature flu outbreaks with hot flushes. The anxiety and depression hung around along with the deep-seated emptiness that was forever growing.

Elijah took a course in psychology to increase his understanding of what was going on in his mind. He also saw a psychotherapist over a 12-month period. All the new skills he was acquiring enabled him to begin filling in the cracks in the walls that kept his darkest emotions from escaping. This reduced the emotional leakage to its earlier state—the odd bubble here and there.

Meditation, exercise, and a better diet helped Elijah pull himself together, except for the emptiness. When his anxiety and depression reached acceptable levels, he resumed his search for ways to fill the void. He studied many different theories on the origin of life and would debate Christians on the validity of their beliefs. He had a deep-seated hostility toward Christianity and quite often criticised the Bible, a book that he had never read to any degree. There were very few Christians in Elijah's life.

He did not know where his anti-Christian thoughts were coming from or why he had so much contempt for Jesus, someone he had never met. But he had them all the same and with a passion he could not explain. Rumour and innuendo fuelled his justifications for his beliefs and that was enough for Elijah.

A fellow named Jim, who ran an anxiety website that Elijah visited, challenged Elijah to read the Bible and find fault with it. Elijah took the challenge and expected the task to be quite simple. He went out and purchased a New International Version Study Bible. Jim suggested that he start in the New Testament, which he did.

Elijah got to know who Jesus was and what he taught. Each day he would read a bit more, trying to find fault. Over time, and thought, he realised what Jesus taught was basically what his psychologists and psychotherapists had been teaching him on how to overcome everyday life issues as well as complex issues, such as forgiveness, trust, giving, happiness, fear, and worry.

This prompted Elijah to start asking himself questions such as: How did this one man know so much more than 2,000 years ago? There was no Internet for him to research all these topics and come up with such simple, yet effective approaches for dealing with such complex issues. Elijah continued studying and found that the more he applied what Jesus taught to his life, the better his life became. He could not find fault in anything that Jesus taught. It was all positive and it all fell in line with modern-day psychology practice.

Gradually his contempt towards Jesus began to change. He could not help but feel compassion for a man who did so much for others and eventually even gave his own life for others. Jesus wanted for nothing and gave all he had, including his very life. Elijah struggled with how a man could ask God to forgive those who had just nailed him to the cross and knew that his life would end as he hung there. In time that taught Elijah what it meant to forgive and he was able to start forgiving those who had hurt him many years ago.

Still being critical and trying to find fault, Elijah continued reading the Bible, New and Old testaments, but discovered more wisdom on how to live a joyful life. He could not find fault with the teachings of the Bible. He started challenging others to find fault in it, look for a loophole, some escape, something to prove the Bible wrong. Nobody came up with anything reasonable and convincing. It was easy if you took things out of context without logically looking at how those same conditions corresponded with today's society. Read in context the teachings made more sense and became proactive for providing a positive lifestyle.

Then Elijah looked back on his life and saw God as the cornerstone of everything positive in his life—how God had answered his prayers when he was having nightmares as a child; the crucifix scribbled on that 50-dollar note that Lester's colleague had given him for food when he was broke; how John befriended him and helped him move out of the caravan behind his mother's house; the strange incident of finding that same 50-dollar note after giving away his last five dollars. On and on it went: the blessing of Maryanne and Michael who were such wonderful and supportive friends and introduced him to Juliana who became his wife and stuck by him even during the hardest and most difficult of times. Then there was the first psychologist he went to who was a Christian who helped him overcome the panic attacks; and all the random Christians he would debate, who attempted to help him, even though he was quite dismissive towards them.

He kept looking back and kept seeing God in all the positive moments. It was as if something dawned on him and he suddenly realised that the book he was holding was not just a book, but the truth, inspired by God.

The snake-like creature that had wrapped itself around Elijah's soul was not pleased with the thoughts that Elijah was now entertaining. It tried to cloud his thoughts with darkness, but to no avail. The light that was now radiating from Elijah's soul stunned the creature into submission. It had made a mistake by allowing Elijah to acquire a Bible and underestimated Elijah's resolve to find fault, which inevitably and ironically led him to find the truth.

Later that evening Elijah made a choice that would penetrate to the very core of his soul.

Chapter 29 - Salvation

Castiel smiled and said, "Elijah, this is the moment we were all hoping for."

Castiel and Elijah appeared in Elijah's home office where he had spent many a day programming for his clients.

Elijah was sitting at his desk staring at the computer screen, but he seemed distracted. Sophia and Castiel entered together from the hallway. They were in the Spiritual Realm and had come to watch Elijah. It was no secret what Elijah was contemplating. Word quickly spread to Castiel and Sophia and they wouldn't have missed the moment for the world.

Elijah stood up, stepped away from his desk, fell to his knees, looked up toward the heavens, and started to pray.

"God, I give in. I believe. Take away my pain. Heal me. Take control of my life. I surrender to You. I believe Jesus was Your Son who died for my sins—and I have sinned. I have sinned and I'm sorry, really sorry. I'm sorry for the things I said about the Bible. I'm sorry for the things I said about Jesus. I'm sorry for all the wrongs I have done in my life. Please, Jesus, take control of my life, be my guide, come into my life, and fill me with the Holy Spirit."

As he was praying Elijah started to cry—not just cry, but weep, deeply. He surrendered himself totally before God.

In the Spiritual Realm Castiel, Elijah, and Sophia witnessed a strong beam of white light streaking down from the sky and surrounding Elijah. The snake-like creature inside Elijah was screaming in agony but it held on. It knew its time was short and knew it had been defeated.

The white light spread into Elijah's body flowing like a fast-rushing river through his veins, skin, cells, and mind. The light crashed through the fortress walls of his mind as if they were made of glass. They shattered into a thousand pieces, releasing the emotions carrying red energy that had been dammed up behind them to come bursting into the white light. The white light consumed the red energy in a dazzling display that surrounded Elijah in an aura of light beams and red energy until only the white light was visible.

Elijah continued to pray, expressing his deepest sorrow for moving away from God and going his own way. The emotions gushed out of him through tears of sadness that quickly turned into tears of refreshment. The last time he felt emotions this strong was in Thailand more than 18 years before—the day he became "comfortably numb." Overcome with emotion and struggling to speak Elijah fell to the floor and just lay there.

The white light continued to stream from the sky into his body for several minutes. When it stopped, a white light remained inside of Elijah, surrounding the glowing green snake creature that appeared to be in mortal distress.

Elijah felt relief as he had never felt before. He was feeling things he had not felt since childhood. Good things such as love and trust were starting to flow through him. No longer comfortably numb, he was becoming comfortably alive, alive with his emotions.

Sophia looked delighted. She said to Castiel, "I told you he would be fine."

"You did not," he said, chuckling. "You were worried, admit it."

"Never," she said. "He was always a fighter. I knew he would make it through."

"Did not."

Sophia quickly echoed, "Did too," and gave Castiel a nudge and they both smiled as they turned and left.

Elijah said, "It's good to see you and Sophia getting on well back then, Castiel."

Castiel just grinned and replied. "You don't seem surprised at what actually happened, Elijah, when you gave your life to God."

"Oh, Castiel, trust me when I say that I felt it, every last bit of it. I pictured something like this happening in my mind. It doesn't surprise me that it did. This makes perfect sense when taken in context with the dream I had later that night and everything you have shown me."

"Fair enough," Castiel said. "I guess it would. It's time for you to make your decision now, Elijah, and for me to answer some of your questions."

"About time," Elijah said as they left.

*　*　*

Later that night Elijah woke in the middle of the night from what he presumed was a dream. Everything was black and white and slightly fuzzy and out of focus. He jumped out of bed as if something had just startled him. The smell of sulphur hung in the air. Looking up at the ceiling, he saw a glowing green snake-like creature wrapped around the ceiling fan. It quickly scurried away passing through the ceiling. Elijah felt a sense of calmness as it departed and fear left Elijah that very day.

In the months that followed Elijah spent time rectifying any lies he had told by owning up to them. He took responsibility for any wrongs he had done in the past and asked the people concerned for forgiveness. He also forgave all those who had wronged him in the past. He was feeling great joy as he had never felt before, and the emptiness he had spent a lifetime trying to fill was gone.

Sophia came to him in person during this time. Elijah believed he had made her up, that she was nothing more than an imaginary friend. He had mentioned her to Juliana and a friend. Both probably thought he was crazy, but they took it in stride and were oddly supportive. Sophia would fly beside him when he went on a mountain bike ride, run beside him when he went jogging, sit in his office and make jokes and do funny things to lift his spirits while he was working and feeling down. She became his constant companion as Elijah adjusted to feeling emotions that he had pushed away for decades.

Elijah became a new man, free from past hurts. His marriage thrived. Juliana and Elijah welcomed their first child, Reece, into the world. Shortly after that, Elijah decided to ask his cousin who was a pastor to baptise him in his backyard pool. His cousin travelled half a day to lead the service. Many of Elijah's friends came to witness the baptism, including his sister Claricia. Elijah had invited his mother and Jack but they didn't come. When Elijah told his father about his intention to be baptised he was not supportive. His father spoke about Christianity the way Elijah used to speak about it before he took Jim's fault-finding challenge. At the baptismal service, Elijah pledged his life to God, to serve God, and showed everyone that was exactly what he intended to do.

Juliana and Elijah had their second child, Kaley. Elijah felt such love for his wife and children as he had never imagined possible. They were a solid unit, and Elijah was at peace with himself, God, and the world.

Chapter 30 - Elysium

Elijah and Castiel stood before a large stone archway with the word "Elysium" etched in it. Two large, well-armed men stood on either side of the archway. Their armaments consisted of a helmet, breastplate, belt, sword, shield, and boots, all of which had a faint white glow. They looked like knights who had walked straight in from medieval times. Horizontal beams of glowing white light streamed across the arch from top to bottom no more than a hands width apart.

"Follow me, Elijah," Castiel said as he passed through the archway.

They quickly approached a sign that pointed to three destinations: left was to "General Admissions," right was to "Heofon," and straight ahead was to "Discussion Rooms." Castiel headed towards the Discussion Rooms and Elijah followed.

"Castiel, why are we walking? Can't we just zip about?"

"No, in Elysium teleporting and other means of travel besides physical methods is forbidden and prevented. The only way out of here is through a doorway. The only way in for residents is through the archway that we just passed through. Newcomers appear directly in the Waiting Room. It keeps the place secure."

"Secure from what?"

"Shadows."

All of the buildings in Elysium looked as if they were right out of the Middle Ages. The walls were constructed of large stones and most entranceways were embellished with grand pillars made of marble. Stain-glass windows adorned the building with rainbow light, and the panes of glass changed from time to time to form new images such as landscapes, people, battle scenes, and buildings. The pathway they were walking on was fashioned of some sort of stone but it felt strangely soft under Elijah's feet. He looked back and saw that their footsteps left light imprints for a brief time—like memory foam—before fading as the surface became flat again.

Though the architecture and fashion of the place looked medieval, there were technological elements Elijah had not seen before. The lighting appeared to come out of nowhere, with no identifiable source. It seemed almost as though the building materials used for the structures were actually light sources.

They entered a building with several corridors leading off in different directions. Castiel appeared to know exactly where he was going and soon stopped outside a room with an open door. The room was perfectly square and had no windows and only a single doorway. As they passed through the entrance to the room, it sealed behind them. The walls and floor were smooth, white in colour and had no discernible joins or seams. Elijah could not even see where the entrance to the room had been. A single white table stood in the middle of the room with one white chair on either side. Castiel sat on one side and gestured for Elijah to sit on the other.

As Elijah sat down, the walls and floor suddenly changed. A majestic landscape now surrounded them. The floor had become vibrant fresh-cut grass. Just to the right of him was a large apple tree with large ruby red apples on it. The tree provided shade from a distant sun high in the sky, which provided cosy warmth that Elijah began to feel. Off in the distance were snow covered mountains on one side and a vast blue ocean on the other. The table and chairs had vanished and Elijah and Castiel were both sitting on the grass.

Astonished, Elijah asked, "What just happened, Castiel?"

"What do you mean, Elijah?"

"The room, it just changed from plain white to this landscape."

"Oh, that," Castiel said, as if it was nothing. "These rooms allow us to change the environment to whatever we want it to be. I set this room to automatic mode so that it automatically calculates a suitable scene that all participants would be comfortable in based on their memories. It is a bit like the 'HoloDeck' in Star Trek. Rumour has it that Gene Dolgoff got his holographic ideas from one of us and then helped Gene Roddenberry recreate the concept for the series. "

"Is Elysium in the Spiritual Realm?"

"No, it's a place in a realm all its own. The Spiritual Realm itself is like the 'gap' between places, but it does not actually take up space."

"When we took that boat ride the day we were eating hot chips in the park, was that in one of these rooms?"

"It was a creation of our collaborated minds. In the Spiritual Realm, we can create our own environments or visit existing environments like the Human Realm at any point in history."

Castiel stood up and said, "Let's walk and talk. I always enjoy a good walk, Elijah."

Elijah stood up and walked alongside Castiel.

"Elijah, when people die in the Human Realm they end up in the Waiting Rooms here in Elysium. They are processed and sent to interrogation. Interrogation allows the Shadow Leaders to gather evidence for the prosecution. The prosecution uses it in the person's trial referred to as 'The Last Judgement.' The trials are held in the same building. The prosecution presents the evidence they collected during interrogation to try to convince a panel of twelve jurors that the person should be sent to the underworld. I call it the underworld. Some refer to it as Hades, others Hell. It has many names. The panel is convened by what you call God."

Elijah nodded and continued walking alongside Castiel.

"The file they use for interrogation contains everything a person has ever done wrong." Castiel stopped walking and turned to Elijah. "The letter I gave Stolas indicated that Jesus would be your defence attorney during the trial. When you asked Jesus into your life, He became your lawyer. The Shadow Leaders do not even bother taking the case to the prosecution when that happens because nobody has ever beaten Jesus in a trial. He is the best defence attorney in the business. Back when He died on the cross in the earth realm, He caught the Shadows off guard and provided an opportunity for humankind to avoid trial. When Jesus stood at 'The Last Judgement', His file was empty because He resisted all temptation to sin. Jesus felt all the suffering and sins of humanity during His experience on earth giving Him defence material that counters any of the prosecution's arguments."

Castiel resumed walking and continued to talk. "If the person is not found guilty during Judgement, he or she goes on to Heofon. Some refer to Heofon as Heaven, Paradise, or Eden. Heofon, like the underworld has many names. It is a place of immortality without suffering. You do not find Red Energy or Shadows there. That is a one-way trip, however, because once you go there, there is no coming back."

Castiel paused and looked at Elijah. "Some who qualify for Heofon are also given an additional choice. It is not an easy choice because you forgo Heofon for a life of service."

Elijah looked at Castiel with a raised eyebrow and cocked head and said, "Go on."

"You have the choice to become an angel, Elijah, like Sophia and myself. It is not an easy road. There is an application process and a lot of training. If you fail, you still go to Heofon. If you pass, you become an angel. Angels are accountable to rules and can be punished. Angels experience pain, anguish, and temptation. It is why only some get the choice. Those who have already defeated temptation in the earth realm are less likely to fall to temptation as angels—it is not, however, unheard of. Some angels do fall from grace."

Castiel and Elijah stopped walking and looked to the sky as it turned to night lit by vibrant twinkling stars and a bright moon.

"Angels can also die, Elijah. They call it the spiritual death. When that occurs, nobody knows where they go as they are never seen again."

Elijah looked at Castiel with an expression of concern. "How do they die?"

"In the earth realm angels have powers that transcend those of humans, but they are bound to the physical laws of the realm. If they sustain fatal injuries in the Human Realm they die a spiritual death."

"So that's the decision I have to make?"

"Yes. That is your choice, Elijah."

Chapter 31 - Decisions

Elijah gazed at the stars wondering where to start. So many questions were racing through his head.

Castiel said, "I know it is a big decision, Elijah. We are recruiting because darkness is spreading across the earth realm at an ever-increasing pace. People are turning away from God's ways, bent on doing things their own way—like sheep gone astray. Shadows are convincing people to do their bidding, which ultimately creates more red energy for them to feed on. We need more angels to help fight them."

"Given the number of Shadows I saw, Castiel, how can angels compete with them, beings that don't die?"

"By changing the hearts of human beings. You see, although angels protect humans from Shadows through combat, they also attempt to change their hearts by creating situations. The more hearts we change, the less red energy is produced and the harder it becomes for the Shadows to feed. Our task is to create a famine of evil. If they cannot feed, the Shadows starve and must return to the underworld. They cannot survive in the Human Realm without red energy to feed on."

Castiel started walking towards a park with a set of swings in the middle of an open field illuminated by a single light hovering just above it under the night sky.

"How do angels 'create situations'?"

"Through coincidence, mainly. We influence people to do something or be somewhere at a certain time. This results in something happening for someone else, which seems to him or her like a coincidence. Over time, such coincidences add up and the person may look at them collectively and interpret it as someone or something looking out for them. This can trigger a spiritual search in the person, a search for the greater meaning or purpose to life. If they let God take control of their life, as you did, they become filled with white energy or, as some refer to it, the Holy Spirit. If that happens, their life changes for the better in many ways."

Elijah nodded. "I can certainly testify to that from my own experience, Castiel."

Castiel and Elijah casually sat on the swings and continued their conversation.

"Can I see my wife and children if I become an angel?"

"Yes," Castiel told him. "That is allowed but ... they can't see you. You can also influence and protect them. One reason—perhaps the most common reason—angel candidates choose to become angels is that they love their families so much and want to protect them. They sacrifice Heofon because they want to ensure their families are protected and make it to Heofon."

"Well, then, it's not much of a choice for someone like me, Castiel."

"No, I guess it's not, Elijah. Protocol mandates that we ask and explain everything—give full disclosure so that, in legal terms, the candidate can give 'informed consent.' On the odd occasion, some people decide against becoming an angel. Others fail the application process or training. The selection of candidates is based on whether we suspect that they will accept the offer."

The swingset that Elijah and Castiel were seated on transformed into a lounge suite situated in the centre of an average sized room in front of a big-screen display. On the screen was a strange symbol that looked like two large feathers overlapping.

"Any chance I could just be resurrected and go back and be with my family?"

"I'm afraid not, Elijah."

Then it hit him full-force, the realisation that he would never again be with his family. Tears welled in his eyes and spilled onto his cheeks. He cleared his throat and dabbed at his eyes. "How do angels know where to go and who to influence?"

"People call out for God or pray. That creates a case file. Angels get to look through those files and decide whom they want to help. Resources are limited, and we cannot answer everyone's request, but we try our best. Some angels believe that God takes care of the cases we do not address in His own way. All we can do is work within our means and with what we are given. Being an angel is very rewarding. You would know that from those times in your life on earth when you helped someone out of a difficult situation and fostered his or her spirituality. When you saw the person become filled with joy and make positive life changes, it was nothing short of wonderful."

"Yes, it was," Elijah agreed. "I just wanted them to feel free from the everyday burdens of life, to live in grace, and to feel their soul filled with joy."

The big screen displayed the faces of the many people Elijah had helped. Elijah saw the people he had helped enjoying life. It also showed before-and-after scenes, showing the polar opposites of who they were and who they had become in a short span of time.

"I'm sure there are many more people you can influence, Elijah. As an angel you can give to them what you have given to all of these people. It is a cascade effect, Elijah: The numerous people you influenced are likely to go on and influence other people. Those will go on to influence still others and so on and on. It spreads the white energy. The downside is the Shadows are doing the opposite of what you did. You created love and gave people faith. They create fear and fill people with hate."

"Why doesn't God just create angels, Castiel."

"That's an interesting question, Elijah," Castiel admitted. "Of course, I cannot speak for God, but my take on it is that a person who has been through certain hardships can see into the hearts of others who are facing similar challenges. They are in a better position to be able to help and understand them."

"Makes sense," Elijah said. "Can people who end up in the underworld be saved?"

"I don't know, Elijah. I have lost friends to the underworld. The best we can do is try to make sure they don't end up there to begin with."

The display screen changed back to the logo of the two overlapping feathers.

"So what do you think, Elijah? Do you want to give Angel School a try?"

Elijah stared at the screen as he pondered the choice. Deep down he knew that he never really had a choice. This was his destiny.

Chapter 32 - Application

On entering the General Admissions building Castiel and Elijah were greeted by a man named Uriel. Elijah said, "Aren't you the same person who greeted me in the Waiting Room when I first came here."

"Yes, that would be me. They move me around a bit. It helps keep my job interesting. Follow me this way, please."

Uriel led them down a few corridors until they came to a room with a sign reading "Applications" on the door. It was a large circular room with a rectangular oak wood desk in the middle with two chairs on one side a single chair on the other. Uriel moved around to the far side of the desk and asked Castiel and Elijah to take a seat on the opposite side.

The walls of the room were stone and the room itself had an ambient light with no visible source. As with the buildings outside it seemed as though the walls and objects provided their own light—the way bioluminescent plants do. On the desk lay a tablet-based computer no thicker than a sheet of paper. Uriel picked it up and made hand gestures that the tablet responded to—without any physical contact.

"You have been the talk around here for some days, Elijah. You are one of a few who managed to rid himself of an Andromalius parasite without assistance."

Castiel interrupted, "That was the green snake-like creature that took up residence inside you."

"Oh, *that*," Elijah said, shifting around uncomfortably on his chair.

Uriel looked up from the computer and peered directly into Elijah's eyes and asked joyfully, "So you want to become an angel?"

"I guess so," Elijah responded.

"Good. Then we just have to run through some questions to make sure everything checks out and then you can go through to induction."

Uriel looked back at his tablet, made a few hand gestures as though he was entering information. "I'm presuming that you are his sponsor, Castiel."

"Yes, I am."

"Okay, okay. Good. This should not take long, Elijah. I'm just going to ask you a few questions, and I need a simple Yes or No answer."

"Have you been told that angels can suffer a spiritual death?"

"Yes."

"Have you been extended an offer to go on to Heofon?"

"Yes."

"Were you told that if you go to Heofon it is a one-way trip?"

"Yes"

Castiel drummed his fingers on the desk and Uriel quickly glanced at him and quibbled, "It's not that I don't think you are perfectly competent, Castiel, in preparing recruits. You know that I am required to ask these questions."

Elijah chuckled at the interaction between them.

"Bureaucrats," Castiel said with a roll of his eyes.

"Somebody's got to do it," Uriel said. He turned back to Elijah. "Have you been informed that angels feel pain, can suffer, and are open to temptation?"

"Yes."

"Were you given a free pizza?"

"Umm, no, I didn't get any pizza."

"He's just messing with you," Castiel said, "with me, actually. There is no free pizza."

Uriel smiled. "Okay, then, it looks as though Castiel did his job preparing you for the 'Yes' and 'No' questions." He paused before saying, "Elijah, did Castiel or anyone else put any undue pressure on you to become an angel?"

"No, not at all. Castiel has made the options very clear. It is my choice, and I feel this is where I should be."

"Good to hear, Elijah. Now for the fun stuff." Uriel cleared his throat. "Do you want to keep your current identity or receive a new one?"

"What do you mean?"

"You have the option of changing your name and appearance if you wish, Elijah."

Elijah looked at Castiel, then back at Uriel. "Why would I want to do that?"

"There are many reasons people choose to do so. Castiel did."

Curious, Elijah looked at Castiel. "You did? Why?"

"It was necessary for me to be the one to show you your life after you die and offer you the choice of becoming an angel. While I did not know when or if I would be able to, there was a chance. I did not expect it to be this soon, though."

Uriel looked at Castiel and raised an eyebrow. Then he turned to Elijah and said, "You didn't recognise him as Michael?"

Elijah, taken back, looked hard at Castiel with narrowed eyes. Sure enough, he could see that Castiel was Michael. "M-M-Michael…Michael!" Elijah and Castiel stood up and embraced each other tightly.

"I'm sorry I couldn't tell you earlier, Elijah. I wanted to."

Elated, Elijah responded, "Man I should have guessed. I felt as though I had known you for years, but I just dismissed it due to all the 'strange' things that were happening."

Uriel shook his head. "Well, well. It seems you didn't know, Elijah. That is good thing because if you had known that may have presented a problem as it would have influenced your decision." He turned to Castiel. "Fine work, Castiel."

"Why thank you, Uriel. Coming from you, that means something."

Castiel and Elijah sat back down.

Elijah asked, "Can you change back to Michael?"

"I could, yes," Castiel said. "But there is a process to go through and I've grown fond of this look over the years."

Elijah was feeling much more comfortable with his decision knowing that he was sitting beside his old friend.

"So, Elijah," Uriel said, "do you want to keep your appearance or choose another one?"

"I think I will keep my current appearance, Uriel. I have no reason to change. I'm presuming I can at a later date?"

"Yes, that is possible, Elijah, for the right reasons."

Uriel looked down at the tablet computer and made a few verbal noises along the way as if he was questioning what he was reading.

"Hmmm… Elijah, all seems good. I have arranged accommodations for you in Wing C of the Haamiah building. Room twenty-seven."

With a little excitement in his voice, Elijah said, "We get a room?"

Castiel winked at him. "We sure do, and they are not like any room you have ever seen before. Wait until you see it, Elijah. It's pretty close to my room. We'll be neighbours."

Uriel stood up. "You fellows should now go through to Induction where Elijah will get a run-down on what will happen over the coming months and a tour of the facilities."

"Thanks, Uriel," Castiel said as he and Elijah stood up. "This way Elijah. It's not far."

Chapter 33 - Induction

"Welcome to Induction, Elijah. I am Dina. How are you?"

"I'm doing well, thank you, Dina."

Dina was standing behind a waist-high counter dressed in a shimmering yellow dress. Her blonde hair, which flowed down to her shoulders, accentuated her slender pretty face and vibrant blue eyes.

Dina added, "And you, Castiel?"

Castiel replied cheerfully, "Terrific, as always."

Dina reached under the counter and pulled out one of those flat tablet computers. "This is your EVE device, Elijah. Please hold out your left hand."

Elijah held out his hand and Dina brushed the EVE device against it. Elijah shuddered slightly as it made contact with his hand.

Castiel said, "That was just the device attaching itself to you, Elijah."

"It's all yours now, Elijah," Dina said as she handed the device to Elijah. "EVE is your constant companion. It contains a wealth of knowledge on every subject specified for your access level."

Elijah could not believe how thin the EVE device was. It seemed impossible that EVE, which was as thin as a sheet of paper, could be solid as a rock. There were no buttons on the device, which was just a display screen. The back was pure black while the front currently displayed the prompt "Please register your name with EVE" under that logo consisting of two overlapping feathers.

"To operate EVE you simply hold your hand in front of the display screen and think about what you want to do. Some people gesture with their hand, but it is not necessary to do so. For example, Elijah,

EVE is currently asking you to register your name. Hold your hand in front of the display and then think about entering your name into EVE."

Elijah held EVE in his right hand and placed his left hand in front of the screen. He then thought about entering his name into the space provided. "Elijah Hael" appeared in the space provided followed by an acceptance message. EVE then went blank.

"Impressive," Elijah said. "And I thought touch-screen technology was amazing."

Dina nodded. "To send your EVE device to eSpace simply drop it. If you set EVE down and leave it unattended, it will go to eSpace. To retrieve EVE from eSpace simply hold out your left hand and either think or say aloud 'EVE.' It will hover in front of you for a short period where you can simply take it. If you don't take it, it will automatically return to eSpace."

Elijah considered asking what eSpace was, but decided against it. He figured he could ask EVE later to avoid looking like such a newbie.

"Castiel, why did Uriel use what appeared to be a normal tablet computer when I arrived? And why did Stolas have that hardcopy file on me rather than a digital version in EVE?"

"They try to keep the waiting and interrogation processes appear as normal as possible to new arrivals."

Elijah nodded.

Dina said, "Try asking EVE something, Elijah."

Elijah moved his left hand over EVE and thought about "Who is Elijah Hael?" EVE quickly responded by presenting him with a complete dossier on who he was, accompanied by photos and short video clips of various signature events in his life. It continued and displayed his whole family tree spanning back thousands of generations to a single starting point that said A & E—presumably, he thought, for Adam and Eve.

"Well done, Elijah. Just give me a few seconds here."

Dina appeared to be operating a device behind the counter.

"There," she said. "All done. I have downloaded your itinerary to your EVE. When you want to see your schedule just ask EVE."

"Schedule?"

"Yes, you will be attending various classes including Angel Theory, Blessings, Combat, and Flying. It is all in your EVE. You have free time now for two sectons."

Elijah was puzzled.

Castiel saw Elijah's puzzlement and informed him, "A secton is a unit of time measurement. It is what is used to measure time in Elysium. One secton is roughly six earth hours."

Dina asked, "Do you have any questions, Elijah?"

"Many, but I wouldn't know where to start."

"Everyone does at this point," she said. "Remember that you can always just ask EVE or come back and see me anytime. We are all done, Elijah."

"Thanks, Dina," he said, smiling. "I really appreciate all your help."

Castiel tapped Elijah on the shoulder. "Come this way, Elijah, I want to show you something."

Elijah followed Castiel through a hallway to what looked like an entranceway. It seemed somewhat strange to be seeing an entrance within a building. The architecture was different. The styling was futuristic, which Elijah had not seen before. The colours were vibrant and the surfaces were smooth.

The door opened upwards as Castiel moved towards it. Elijah quickly followed.

They were standing on a balcony high above the ground looking out on a vast futuristic city with what looked like flying cars whizzing about. The large buildings were ultra-modern but had an assortment of vegetation intertwined with the materials they were constructed of. Nature appeared to animate within them making them appear as though they were alive. The cloudless sky was bright blue and there was no visible sign of a sun. A river weaved its way around smaller buildings. Some sort of high-tech boats were moving up and down the river.

"Is this a hologram, Castiel?"

"No, this is all real. This is the 'real' Elysium."

Elijah stared in amazement. "Wow. So much life is happening here, but everything seems so synchronised and balanced."

"Yes," Castiel said. He patted Elijah on the back. "Let's go to your room, my friend."

They walked along the balcony they were on until they came to a door marked "Transport Point."

The door opened as Castiel approached and they both stepped into a small room no bigger than an average elevator car. A display panel on the wall said, "Waiting...." Castiel held his hand up to it and then the display changed to "Destination set to Haamiah, C wing." The door closed. The display updated to "Transporting" and within a few moments it updated to "Haamiah, C Wing" and the door opened.

They walked through a short corridor with numbered doors on both sides. They kept going until they came to the one with 27 on it. "This is your room, Elijah."

"How do I open it?"

"Simply walk up to it," Castiel said. "It will recognise you and open."

As Elijah approached the door, it vanished. Elijah looked through where the door used to be into a small square room no larger than a motel room with a white floor and walls. The room was completely empty. "Hey, Castiel, you were right. This is certainly not like any room I have seen before. I admit I was expecting something a bit, uh, fancier from the way you talked about it earlier."

"Step inside, Elijah," Castiel said, smiling. "You will see."

As they stepped inside, they were no longer in the white room but inside a cozy log cabin with a fireplace burning brightly on the far wall. A window in the cabin overlooked a lake with snow-covered mountains off in the distance. There was a chill in the air, but the fire provided nice warmth. On the floor in front of the fireplace lay a nice rug made from lamb's wool surrounded by beanbags and a few pillows. On the left side of the cabin was a small cooking area and a table and chairs. On the right side was a door to a bedroom with a queen-size bed covered with an artistic quilt also made from lamb's wool. The bedroom window provided a view into a lush forest.

"Nice, Elijah. You do create the most wonderful places with your mind."

"I created this?"

"Yes. The room automatically works out where you would like to be, what sort of dwelling you would like to live in, and creates it for you."

"Does it change?"

"Only if your concept of what type of dwelling you prefer changes."

Elijah gazed around the room and realised that it was his "dream house." He used to dream about living in a cabin situated on the shore of a lake surrounded by a vibrant forest. The chill in the air would require a log fire burning with a very peaceful roar punctuated with pops and crackles.

"Amazing."

"Anything you want, Elijah, is just a thought away. Just imagine it and it will appear. If you prefer to cook, think of the raw ingredients and make a meal. If you want to skip the cooking just think of the meal and it will appear. For now, though, you should probably get some sleep. You have a big day ahead of you tomorrow."

"I am feeling tired," Elijah said. "Why is that? I thought being a spiritual being I wouldn't need sleep."

"You're an angel, Elijah. You have an angel body that behaves pretty much like a human body with a few differences. Angel bodies do not get sick, but they can be damaged. Damage typically fully repairs within a secton—unless it is fatal. Angels age, but you can obtain a new body when it becomes too old. You can obtain a younger version of the same body or a completely different design. Your body will feel pain and emotions. That is why angels are susceptible to temptation. You will feel emotions similar to what you felt when you were in the Human Realm. You do not require food, but it is pleasurable to eat. Angel bodies get their energy from white energy. In Elysium white energy is plentiful, so your body will heal and rejuvenate very fast. God created us in His image as He did humans. We are not very different. We are just more, shall we say 'evolved.'"

Elijah walked around the cabin, still adjusting to the realisation that everything around him was created by his own mind. He theorised it was similar to when you are in a dream. Your mind creates the reality around you and it appears real. Unlike a dream, however, he was in control of it.

Castiel rocked back on his heels, looking very pleased. "Anyway, Elijah, I'll leave you to it. I'll come back before your first class tomorrow. It's theory. I think you will find it quite interesting. Your EVE will automatically wake you before appointments so do not worry about oversleeping. It can't happen in Elysium."

"Hey, Castiel, if I had gone to Heofon, what sort of body would I have there?"

"Nobody really knows, Elijah, because nobody has ever come back to talk about it. There are theories, like the ones you heard on Earth. As angels, though, we are none the wiser in that area. I tried asking EVE but she replies: 'Restricted Information.'"

Elijah walked up to Castiel and gave him a quick hug. "Thanks for everything, Castiel."

"No problem, Elijah. I'm glad I could be here for you. Till tomorrow…" Castiel said as he turned and saw himself out the front door of the cabin.

Elijah thought about cooking something but was feeling rather tired. It had been a long journey to this point and suddenly it all caught up to him. He guessed he had been running on adrenalin, which keeps you going until you stop to rest and then the exhaustion just hits you. He made his way to the bedroom, collapsed on the bed, and fell asleep almost instantly.

Chapter 34 - Theory

Elijah awoke to see his EVE floating above him making a loud beeping sound. The display read: "You have an incoming call from Castiel." A live view of Castiel was beneath the text. Elijah thought "Accept it" and immediately Castiel appeared full screen.

"Time to get moving, Elijah."

Feeling refreshed Elijah responded, "I don't think I've ever slept so well and so deeply."

"You sleep better in Elysium because of the absence of Shadows. Your soul knows so it is less on guard. I am waiting just outside your door. To exit your room just think about leaving, but don't forget to think about what you want to wear first." Castiel laughed. "We don't want any streakers running around Elysium."

Elijah laughed the comment off as EVE returned to eSpace when Castiel ended the call. He realised he was still dressed in what he had been wearing since he first arrived in Elysium—an average everyday trench coat, khaki slacks, and a button-down shirt. He found it comfortable and decided to continue wearing it. So he just thought about it being refreshed, ironed and clean. And it was.

Castiel and Elijah made their way to the Suriel building where the theory classes were held. Castiel explained that the building was named after Suriel, an angel who was renowned as a great educator. The Suriel building had the same futuristic style and building materials intertwined with vegetation living in harmony. Inside, the building had a very modern, functional layout.

"Your first lecture is in room A4 today, Elijah, and Suriel himself is the lecturer. It will be a treat. He doesn't lecture much these days, but occasionally you spot him teaching the new inductees the basics of Angel Laws."

Room A4 was a typical lecture hall with theatre seating arranged in a semi-circle around the staged area with a large display screen at the back. It was about half full. Elijah quickly tallied 34 heads.

"I'm not alone then, Castiel?"

"No, angels are recruited at a fairly constant pace. Only about ten percent graduate."

"Why so few?"

"Angels are held to a very high standard, Elijah. It is not an easy road. Think about it—the choice is between everlasting peace and no suffering in Heofon or being part of an everlasting war against evil. It's not for everyone and during the rigors of training the option of Heofon seems more appealing to some than others and they opt out."

Elijah looked at Castiel and wondered if he thought Elijah would make it through.

As if reading his face, if not his mind, Castiel said, "You'll be fine, Elijah. Take a seat. I'll come back later after class." Castiel left and Elijah made his way toward the front and found a vacant seat. He realised he was sitting closer to the front than he normally would at these sorts of gatherings but felt comfortable in doing so.

Suriel entered from a door to the left of the stage and, as he did, everyone stood up and clapped. Elijah stood up as well and clapped lightly, not really understanding why he should be clapping.

"Take a seat." Suriel's voice resonated around the lecture hall. His voice seemed amplified, but there was no sign of a microphone anywhere.

Everyone sat back down.

"Today we start with the three main laws of being an angel. You can call them the Three Commandments, if you like," Suriel said with a smile.

Elijah glanced around at the other students and noticed that all were watching attentively.

 "No angel shall interfere with the free will of a human."

The commandment appeared on the large display screen behind Suriel as he spoke it.

"No angel shall make himself or herself visible to a human."

Elijah thought: *Sophia broke that one.*

"Unless it is approved."

Pondering that for a moment, Elijah wondered if Sophia had secured approval and, if so, from whom.

"No angel shall inflict physical harm on a human, whether through inaction or directly."

"These simple rules are the foundation of all the other rules an angel is required to abide by. If you are ever in doubt about a particular action you wish to take, consult your EVE device. Are there any questions?"

No hands were raised.

Suriel continued. "You may be wondering how we can change the course of events without affecting a human's free will. Let me give you an example."

Elijah considered a few ways based on his own experience but was eager to hear Suriel's example.

"You become aware that a robbery is about to take place at a service station and you also know that the human you are protecting is about to leave home to go to that same service station. Delay tactics are quite common. Here are some examples: move their keys, flatten their car battery, puncture their car tire, or influence someone to call them. These things do not affect their free will. They can result in delay of action or require them to make a different choice."

Elijah thought about all the times when he had misplaced his keys and wondered if he really had or whether Sophia was using a delay tactic.

"Thought injection is useful if you want a person to carry out a certain action that may help himself or someone else. The way to do this is to inject a thought into his or her mind that he or she believes is their own. The person will still have the free will to accept or reject the thought. Some examples of injecting thoughts are to call a certain friend when the friend is in need; ask someone a particular question, a question they have to think about; or inspiration to achieve a particular task."

Suriel went on to explain many other ways angels can influence a person without overriding free will. The creativity of some of the examples was ingenious. Elijah quickly considered numerous coincidences from his life that were probably orchestrated for one reason or another.

"The most important thing to keep in mind is that while angels can carry out things like Delay Tactics and Thought Injection, so can Shadows. Shadows do not, however, obey the three commandments. It is a constant battle of good versus evil intentions. Our job is to help humanity see the power of good and to protect them the best we can."

In a louder, more stern voice Suriel continued. "Ultimately each human will make his or her own choices and we must never feel responsible for negative outcomes. I have seen angels take it to heart when they lose the person they are protecting to the Shadows and it can literally destroy them. So consider yourself forewarned."

Suriel concluded by asking if anyone had questions. Castiel turned back up after the question-and-answer session just as Suriel left the stage.

"How did it go, Elijah?"

"It was very informative and has given me some wonderful ideas on how I might help people."

"You'll need those ideas when it comes to examination time."

"There is an examination?"

"Yes, on both theory and practice. You get one shot at it. If you do not pass, it is off to Heofon for eternity. If you pass, you graduate and become an angel. You have much more to learn before that, though. For now, let me show you some more of Elysium."

Chapter 35 - Gethsemane

As he stepped onto the futuristic boat, Elijah was in awe of the technology. The boat hovered slightly above the water without actually disturbing it. Elijah likened it to a silent hovercraft. As the boat started to move there was no noise other than people talking and the sound of the water flowing in the river beneath it.

"Where does this river come from, Castiel?"

"From the mountains on the western side of Elysium, referred to as the Elysium Divide. It is rumoured that the river is formed and fed by the tears of humanity—tears shed of sadness, hope, joy, and grace. Those who have trekked there and returned never speak of it."

Elijah gazed into the clear sky-blue water below. He could see large creatures swimming in the depths that looked like large fish but moved intelligently and seemed to be interacting with each other.

"Those creatures," Castiel said, "are called Pterophyllum. They transport resources around the river and creek systems to feed the vegetation that grows in Elysium."

The boat continued up the river a ways before coming to a stop. Castiel and Elijah disembarked. After a short walk they came to an entrance with a sign above it: "Gethsemane." The doors of the entry slid upwards as they approached. Stepping through Elijah saw that the dimensions inside the building seemed infinite. He tried to make sense of how the building could be much larger on the inside than the outside and quickly drew comparisons to the "Tardis" on the TV series "Dr. Who."

"Castiel, I'm presuming this isn't a hologram. But how is this possible?"

"The entrance provides a gateway to a place in eSpace called Gethsemane."

Castiel walked over to a cabinet and retrieved two pairs of dark glasses. He handed a pair to Elijah. "Put these on."

As Elijah put on the glasses, his breath left his lungs. What appeared before him was the most wondrous, beautiful sight he had ever seen. Spheres of energy of every size and colour were everywhere. As some vanished, new ones would appear. Some were small while others were quite large. He observed some actually merging and growing in the process. Others would shrink for no apparent reason. As they overlapped and merged, the colours blended through their transparency and produced magnificent colours he had never seen.

Elijah caught his breath and looked at Castiel in awe. "What are they?"

"Prayers from humanity. Every prayer currently being offered on Earth is appearing before you. The smallest ones are prayers of individuals. The larger ones are the prayers of people praying about the same topic. The colours represent the type of prayer. Green ones represent prayers of grace; blue ones, prayers of intercession; yellow ones, prayers of help. Red ones are prayers of urgency and white ones are prayers of salvation. Merged colours represent combination prayers. EVE creates a case file and catalogues them for every prayer that arrives here."

Still amazed, Elijah responded, "Why do some vanish?"

"When a prayer is said, what is registered is what is in the person's heart. When the situation the person is in changes or the prayer is answered or the person simply stops believing in what they prayed for, the prayer spheres vanish."

Elijah was mesmerized as he watched the prayers dance around the vast space.

Castiel passed Elijah a small ear bud device and said, "Put it in your ear, Elijah, and then focus on any prayer."

Elijah fitted the device in his ear and focused on a prayer. He could hear what the prayer was saying. When he focused on larger prayers he could hear many voices asking for the same thing in harmony. He scanned the room and listened in on hundreds of different prayers. He noticed that he was beginning to feel the emotions of the people asking the prayer—he could feel their deepest desires, their sadness, their joy and grace. Before long he became consumed with listening in on the prayers and removed the device from his ear.

"Wow!" Elijah exclaimed.

"It can be exhausting, Elijah," Castiel said. "Hence, it is easier to review prayers via EVE. When reviewing through EVE you don't feel the emotions. But, if you really want to *feel* what humanity is praying for at any given time, this is the place. "

Elijah turned to Castiel and said, "The urgent prayers were the hardest to listen to—hearing and feeling all the desperation in the people's voices."

"Those are monitored closely, Elijah, as they typically require a prompt response. Quite often, they are assigned to angels for immediate attention. This room allows us to obtain a general feel of the state of mankind. When a worldwide tragic event occurs, this room quickly reflects it by showing us what people are praying for. Natural disasters, terrorist attacks, even global economic calamities cause this room to fill up with a sea of red prayers."

"This is incredible, Castiel, that all the prayers of humanity are in this room for us to see, hear, and feel."

Elijah sauntered around the room and looked at the prayers from different angles. He was astonished at the dynamic nature of how the prayers were changing. Though it was like a giant work of art, he realised that these were people's innermost thoughts and heartfelt feelings.

"I could spend all day here, Castiel, just watching the patterns. It is hypnotic."

"Indeed," Elijah said, lost in the moment.

"You're welcome to come here any time, Elijah. Just be cautious when using the earpiece for any length of time. As you have seen, the emotions can be overwhelming. Try to balance out the prayers for help you listen to with prayers of salvation and grace. At times, I just come here and listen to prayers of grace. It reminds me why we do what we do."

"Thanks, Castiel, for showing me this."

"No worries," Castiel said. "I will be on assignment for several sectons so you will not see me around for a while. If you need me just call me on EVE. Use EVE to find your way around and to check your schedule. Stay here as long as you like."

Elijah gave Castiel a hug and thanked him again before saying goodbye. Though he knew he would miss Castiel, Elijah was confident that he would be all right by himself.

Tired from seeing, hearing, and feeling prayers for a considerable time, Elijah decided to make his way back to his room. He had no trouble following EVE's directions for where to go and what transport to use.

As he lay on his bed, Elijah asked EVE to show him Reece Hael, his son. EVE quickly started showing video and photos of Reece. Some of them showed scenes of Reece with his sister and mother. Elijah was joyful to see that his family was doing okay, but at the same time he felt a bit uncomfortable and even felt a bit of nostalgia because he missed them. One of the options at the bottom of EVE's display was that Elijah could see Reece's recent prayers. Elijah chose this option and saw a list of Reece's recent prayers colour-coded to match the prayers in Gethsemane. Elijah's heart sank when he read Reece's last prayer: "God, can you please let Daddy come home."

Elijah put down EVE and closed his eyes. He drifted off to sleep thinking back on all the wonderful times he had enjoyed with his family.

Chapter 36 - Combat Training

As he arrived at the combat training building, Elijah thought about how much he was looking forward to something different from angel theory lessons. While he had learnt a lot from Suriel, who was indeed a master educator, and considered it extremely beneficial, it was time for something different.

He peered through the doorway to the room EVE was telling him to enter and saw that it was empty. He thought his instructor must have been running late. He ventured forth into the room. As he passed through the threshold, he felt something like a cricket bat hit him across the back of his head. Stunned and dizzy, he fell face-first onto the floor and grasped the back of his head. He rolled over moaning from the pain radiating from the base of his skull. He looked up and saw a man standing over him.

"Welcome, Elijah. I am Nemamiah and I'm here to teach you how to fight. That was your first lesson. Always be on guard when venturing forth into unknown territory."

Nemamiah held out his hand, which Elijah grabbed, and Nemamiah pulled him up onto his feet. "Your head will stop aching soon, Elijah. Our angel bodies heal quickly."

Elijah noticed the large two-metre metal pole-arm that Nemamiah was holding and realised that's what whacked him. "That's some welcome."

"We don't muck about here, Elijah," the man said, his tone serious. "First things first: Are you proficient with any sort of weapon?"

"Um … no," Elijah responded.

"Do you have a weapon preference?"

"I've never really considered it. In video games, I tend to go for more of a ranger configuration. You know—sword, shield, bow and arrow."

Nemamiah laughed. "Video games, eh? Well, this is a little more real than video games. Nonetheless, what you learnt in them may actually help. You see, we do not require years of combat skills training, nor do we need to build up physical attributes or muscle memory. We simply have to imagine what we want to do and our bodies will carry out the action. If you can imagine it, your body will do it—within the physics of the realm."

Elijah just nodded.

"Hit me, Elijah."

After a moment's hesitation, Elijah threw a punch. The punch landed softly on Nemamiah's chest and did not even cause him to blink.

"Right," Nemamiah said. "See there, you imagined hitting me, but with the limitations of what you remember from your life on earth. Don't try to do something; rather, imagine it the way you want it to be. Pretend you are Superman, and hit me the way Superman would hit someone."

Elijah conjured up an image in his mind of Superman hitting someone in the chest, causing the person to fly across the room. A moment later, he hit Nemamiah again. His punch landed squarely in the centre of Nemamiah's chest with such force that it sent him flying clear across to the other side of the room where he slammed into the wall and sunk to the floor dropping his pole-arm.

"Are you all right, Nemamiah?"

Nemamiah scrambled to his feet. "I see you're a fast learner, Elijah. I was not expecting you to pick that up so quickly. Now the hard part is doing that with speed while taking into account your environment and incoming attacks. There is no point in throwing a punch if your opponent is going to block it and then trip you up. Battles are won and lost in the mind. You have to out-think your opponents."

"Like video games?"

Nemamiah smiled. "Yes, I suppose so, but with many more variables. Let us start with just hand-to-hand combat in this room. As you can see, apart from the pole-arm sitting on the floor, the room is empty."

Elijah and Nemamiah moved to the centre of the room. "When you are ready, Elijah, start your attack."

Elijah considered what sort of hand-to-hand combat he could think of that his body would follow swiftly. He recalled the many Bruce Lee and Jackie Chan movies he had watched over the years. He opened by running toward Nemamiah, but instead of attacking, he leapt upwards over Nemamiah's head and flowed into a somersault followed by a twist and landed behind him. Nemamiah was quick to respond to the leap and spun around just as Elijah's left foot landed hard on his right jaw. The impact sent Nemamiah spinning to his right. He quickly recovered and responded by sweeping his legs out in front of him to fend off Elijah's approaching attack. Caught off guard, Elijah's legs were swept from under him causing him to fall heavily to the ground.

Nemamiah leapt back onto his feet before Elijah could regain his composure and kicked him in the face. Elijah tumbled backwards with the stream of blood from his nose leaving a red trail in his wake. Elijah turned the tumble into a controlled backwards roll and emerged in a standing position. Nemamiah was running towards him, and Elijah contemplated what to do next. He recalled the "Crane" stance from the original *Karate Kid* movie. Elijah positioned himself like a crane: He stood on his left foot with his right foot off the ground and both hands hovering below his arched arms at his sides Nemamiah continued his forward approach and was met by Elijah's right foot colliding with his chin, sending him flying backwards into the wall.

Nemamiah gradually stood up. "Well done, Elijah. You learn quickly, and it seems like you have a vast array of knowledge to draw from."

Elijah blew the remaining blood from his nose. "Thanks."

"Now let's look at how to interact with the environment." Nemamiah held his hand out towards his pole-arm and it hovered over to where he could grasp it. "To do that, Elijah, requires that you believe you can do it. Think about the result you want. The result will then happen, but you really have to believe you can do it."

Nemamiah threw the pole-arm to the ground. "Try it, Elijah."

Elijah looked at the pole-arm, held out his hand, and imagined it coming to him. He stood there, hand outstretched, thinking intensively as the moments passed. The pole-arm trembled but didn't rise and, defeated, Elijah said, "I can't."

"That is why you fail, Elijah, because you believe that you can't. When you believe that you can, without any doubt you will."

Nemamiah walked over to a wall and seemed to press a button. A cabinet containing an assortment of armaments appeared. He retrieved a handful of Chinese throwing stars. "I'm going to start throwing these at you, Elijah, and if you don't manage to get that pole-arm, each will hit you—and trust me, they hurt!"

Elijah held out his hand again and willed the pole-arm to come to him. It fluttered slightly. Nemamiah flung a throwing star towards, Elijah. Elijah saw it coming towards him in slow motion. He moved slightly to dodge it, but like a heat-seeking missile, the throwing star adjusted its path and lodged in Elijah's left shoulder. Elijah recoiled from the impact. Nemamiah readied to throw another star and Elijah concentrated on the pole-arm. This time, the star lodged in his left shin causing Elijah to sink to his left knee. Nemamiah took three stars and threw them simultaneously, each headed for a different part of Elijah's body. In pain, Elijah gave up *wanting* the pole-arm to come to him. He *needed* it to come to him. That change of mind caused his doubt about whether it was possible to leave him, and the pole-arm came swiftly to his hand. He clenched it with both hands and quickly fended off the three throwing stars heading towards him.

Elijah winced as he pulled the throwing stars out of his shoulder and left shin. The wounds healed before his eyes.

"Very good, Elijah. Bravo! Physics governs what we can and cannot do, but we can use it to our advantage. We can manipulate the atoms that make up objects either to attract or repel."

"Can humans do that as well?"

"Some did. If you look back through history there are reports that Moses parted the RedSea and Jesus walked on water. Jesus told the people around him at the time 'If you had faith even as small as a mustard seed, you could say to this mountain, move from here to there, and it would move. Nothing would be impossible.'"

Elijah recalled a time back on earth when he believed he manipulated an object through sheer will. As he was putting a four-pack of soda bottles into the fridge, the packaging broke and two fell towards the tiled floor. In that moment he willed, wished, and prayed there would not be a mess. One bottle bounced and the other smashed into several pieces. The soft drink inside the bottle should have spilled across the floor, but it had vanished. He picked up the broken glass fragments and realised at that moment he had physically changed something merely with faith. Doubt always crept into his mind when he tried to repeat it. Looking back, he realised that in that moment of desperation he had overcome his doubt and performed a feat that was deemed "impossible."

"Keep in mind that manipulating the environment consumes energy. The larger the object, the more atoms you are trying to manipulate, and the more it will mentally fatigue you. Your mind is your weapon; when it tires it can leave you vulnerable."

Suddenly, the walls of the room and floor transformed into an empty football stadium with Nemamiah and Elijah standing in the middle of it.

Nemamiah said, "It's easy to fight one opponent at a time, Elijah. When there are hundreds, well, it's not so easy. Let us see how you handle this situation. I will fight with you to defeat the oncoming simulated Shadows. I must warn you: Though they are only simulations, they will hurt you if they get past your defences."

Elijah scanned the entire stadium. It appeared empty.

"Before we get started, arm yourself with your preferred weapons. Just think them up, Elijah, and they will appear in this simulation. In the Human Realm, however, you have to ensure you are well-armed before entering any situation in which you may need to attack or defend."

Elijah thought of a bow, a quiver of arrows, and a sword. A quiver of arrows appeared strapped to his back along with a bow. On his side, a sword was in a sheath suspended from a belt around his waist. He took the bow, armed it with an arrow, and drew it back to full draw.

Shadows began to appear from the different entrances into the stadium. Elijah targeted one and let the arrow fly. As the arrow was leaving the bow, he quickly armed another arrow so quickly that his arm appeared not to move. He targeted a second Shadow, then repeated, and targeted a third. By the time he repeated this several times the first arrow had hit its target, then the second, then the third, and so on. Elijah took it up a notch by using three arrows at once and targeting three separate Shadows with a single shot. The arrows left the bow and splintered off and hit their intended targets. Shadows were falling in every direction as Elijah continued to use his exceptional bow skills. Before long, the sheer number of the Shadows soon became too many to handle. They began to surround Elijah and Nemamiah and trap them in a circle growing ever smaller.

Nemamiah readied his pole-arm and Elijah threw his bow to the ground and unsheathed his sword. They stood back to back and each scanned 180 degrees in the direction they were facing. As the shadows closed in, Nemamiah belted the shadows sending them flying as his pole-arm connected with them and Elijah sliced through the shadows with his sword. Back to back, they spun slowly while fighting in unison. They were dancing the fight of their lives. They leapt simultaneously in the air, still back to back, while spinning around and taking out several Shadows in one movement.

As they landed they separated by leaping over the shadows that now surrounded them and attacked them from their rear. Nemamiah and Elijah were now on either side of a large circle of Shadows. Just a moment before they were in the centre of danger, and now the Shadows realised that *they* were in the centre of danger as Elijah and Nemamiah circled around them destroying them one by one as the circle of Shadows grew smaller and smaller. With only a few Shadows left, Nemamiah and Elijah threw down their weapons and defeated them with hand-to-hand combat.

When the last of the Shadows vanished to defeat, the room changed back to normal. Nemamiah said, "I must say, Elijah, I've had many students come through here, but never have I seen anyone pickup skills as quickly as you."

"That was exhilarating, Nemamiah."

"Well there's a lot more 'exhilaration' in store for you in the coming training sessions."

Elijah and Nemamiah continued with the present training session until Nemamiah bought it to a close. "I really enjoyed teaching you,

Elijah. It's been a pleasure. I am looking forward to our next session. At the rate you are picking things up, something tells me *you* will be teaching *me* soon."

Elijah thanked Nemamiah and made his way back to his room. He considered exploring some of the entertainment areas in Elysium but thought he had better get some rest. The combat training had sapped quite a bit of his energy. Before going to bed, he looked at his schedule. Flight training was next. He was really looking forward to that. His days of flying planes on Earth left him with so many fond memories of soaring through the air. He tried to imagine what it would be like to fly without a plane surrounding you.

Chapter 37 - Flying

Elijah arrived at the flying training centre and entered the wing fitting room. Raphael explained the process as quite simple and moderately painless. Raphael said, "Okay, Elijah, stand inside the white circle with your arms by your side and your feet together."

Elijah walked over and stood inside the circle as instructed.

Raphael continued. "Your first set of wings is what we call 'beginner wings,' Elijah. They will provide you with basic flight capabilities. While not as nimble as the higher-level wings, they are a good place to start. Please stand still."

The circle Elijah was standing on began to rise leaving a cylinder of blue light surrounding him as it rose from the floor. He stood still and watched the circle rise until it was above his head.

"Take a deep breath and hold it in, Elijah, until I say you can breathe again."

Elijah took a deep breath to prepare himself for what was about to happen. The blue cylinder surrounding him started pulsating. Suddenly, a white light completely encased him. It was so bright his eyes involuntary closed. A moderate painful sensation shot down his back with such force that his legs became weak and he fell to the floor as the cylinder vanished.

"Okay," Raphael said. "You can breathe now, Elijah."

Elijah gasped for air, trying to recover his lost breath. Out of the corner of his left eye, he could see the top of a wing made of feathers jutting above his left shoulder. He reached behind him, touched it, and followed it to where it connected to his back near his shoulder blade.

"Try to move them, Elijah. They're new to you so it may take a moment or two for your mind to connect with them."

Elijah tried to move the wings, but it was as if they were not there. The feeling made him feel queasy and he felt like he might be sick. He slowly rose to his feet and again tried to move them. This time his mind connected with them. They spanned outward, then inward and folded behind him.

"That's the way, Elijah. It takes a moment for your mind to acknowledge your new limbs."

"How do they detach, Raphael?"

"They don't detach, Elijah. Once you are fitted with angel wings they are permanent until removed by a similar process. When they are not being used, they will fold back so they are streamlined with your back. In that position, they become transparent. They take some getting used to, but once you get used to them you will hardly notice they are there. Your clothes will automatically alter to allow the extrusions between your shoulder blades to extend through your shirts."

Elijah spread his wings so they were parallel to the ground and held them there for a few moments before folding them back in. "They feel a little weird."

"That feeling will pass, Elijah," Raphael assured him. "Just give it time."

"How do I get them upgraded from beginner wings?"

"Once you have been through flight training we will upgrade them to standard wings. As you become more competent, we will upgrade them to higher-level wings with more features that will give you more abilities, which we will discuss when you qualify for the upgrades."

"Sounds good," Elijah said.

"But first things first," Raphael said. "For now, Elijah, please proceed down the corridor to the flight training room."

Elijah soaked in the various sensations from the newly fitted wings as he stepped into the flight training room, eager to learn how to fly.

"Hello, Elijah, I'm Isis. I am your assigned flight training instructor. How do you feel about testing out those new wings?"

"Nervous, but excited."

"Good on both counts," Isis said. "In my review of your profile, I see that you have flown planes."

"Yes."

"That's a plus," she said. "Angel flying is a little different—a lot different in fact—but the physics are the same. Your wings serve the same functions as the wings on an aircraft. They control your pitch, roll, and yaw. There are two ways to gain altitude when flying. One is to flap your wings, and the other is to look for thermals that will carry you upwards."

Elijah nodded. "I see."

"Unlike an airplane, however, your left and right wings work independently of each other. This allows for some very fast manoeuvres. Your beginner wings have the left and right wings synchronised to a degree, which makes flying a little easier. What that means is that when you extend your right wing your left wing will extend the same amount. Higher-level wings have reduced synchronisation to the point that they become completely independent. You are vulnerable to G-forces determined by the physics of the realm. If you pull too many G's you will black out, which of course can have fatal consequences."

Looking a little concerned, Elijah responded, "Fair enough."

Isis operated a control panel on the wall. "Our first training ground will be in territory familiar to you—Earth's physics and environment. Although similar to Elysium, it is slightly different. This way, Elijah." Isis motioned towards a doorway that opened at the back of the room. Elijah proceeded to pass through it into a small corridor with a door at the far end. Upon entering the corridor, Elijah felt somewhat heavier.

"That extra weight you are feeling is a gravity adjustment that simulates Earth's gravitational pull."

"Ah, so I didn't just put on twenty kilograms," Elijah said with a smile.

Isis chuckled. "No, you're just as fit and trim as when you were before entering the corridor. In Elysium, the gravitational pull is weaker—not by much, but once you become accustomed to it you will feel the difference when stepping back into Earth's gravitational field."

Elijah continued down the corridor to the far door. Behind it was a sheet of bright light. "Pass through it, Elijah," Isis instructed.

Blinded by the white light, he felt as though he was being teleported similar to when he time jumped with Castiel. When he recovered his sight, he discovered that he was standing on the edge of a high cliff. He looked down and squinted. He could make out a river winding among some trees far below at the very bottom of the cliff-face, barely visible from such height.

He turned around to see a white portal behind him and Isis stepping through it.

"This isn't a virtual environment, Isis?"

"No, we are actually on Earth, in a desolate part of Arizona. That corridor you come through allows for a gravity adjustment before the portal jump. It serves a purpose similar to a decompression chamber that divers use."

Realising that he was actually back on Earth, Elijah felt a little nervous as he looked down at the drop in front of him. He recalled that injuries could be fatal, causing spiritual death. Those old feelings of just jumping and being able fly came back to him, along with that old fear that had caused him acrophobia.

"When you are ready, Elijah, jump and try to fly."

"I, uh, I'm not sure about this, Isis," he responded, feeling quite nervous. "What if it doesn't go well?"

"You'll be fine," she said.

Elijah stalled. "I'm really not so certain. I don't think my wings are quite ready."

Isis moved up next to him and whispered "Trust me, Elijah, you'll do just fine" and gave him a push causing Elijah to lose his footing and tumble forward off the cliff's edge.

Fear gripped Elijah as the ground rushed towards him. Forgetting he had wings, he flapped his arms and legs as he fell in an attempt to fly—to no avail. He was falling ever faster. He focussed and attempted to extend his wings. The left wing slightly extended and the right followed, but slightly behind it, causing him to go into a spiral dive that disoriented him. The ground was fast approaching. In seconds he would either hit the river or crash into the trees. As he started to lose consciousness from the disorientation caused by the spinning spiral dive, he tried to retract his wings. They retracted and the spinning slowed, and just before he hit the treetops, something grabbed him under his armpits. It was Isis. She had flown down behind him ready to assist if something went wrong. Isis quickly turned the downward dive into an upward climb and then levelled out to a slow climb as she carried Elijah back to the top of the cliff.

"Not bad for a first attempt, Elijah. Shall we try again?"

Elijah responded in a disgruntled tone: "No." He was still feeling disoriented from the spinning. "And don't push me." He took several steps back from the edge of the cliff.

Isis walked over to Elijah and said, "You did well for your first attempt."

"I did?"

"Yes, you did. Most don't even move their wings. When you are ready, fully extend your wings and then jump. It will stop you from going into a spin. After you jump and have picked up a bit of speed from the descent tilt them upwards slightly. They will generate lift due to your speed and you will climb."

Elijah moved towards the edge of the cliff and extended his wings. "You'll catch me again if I fall, right?"

"Of course I will," Isis assured him. "I only dropped a person once and she landed in the trees and recovered."

"That's encouraging. I bet she was impressed."

"It was Sophia. Even though her wing was broken at the time, she just got back up and tried again. She impressed us all as she supported the break in her right wing with her arm as she flew."

Elijah already had great respect for Sophia, but hearing about those heroics made him grow just a little more fond of her.

Elijah peered over the edge of the cliff and contemplated how he should leap off. He decided to dive the way he would dive into a swimming pool. He dived and started descending. With his wings outstretched, he was stable and quickly picking up speed. He tilted his wings up slightly and they generated lift and he started to slow his descent and then began to climb. He was gliding and it felt amazing!

His speed was dropping as he climbed and he realised if his speed got below a certain point he would stall like a plane and fall. He tilted his wings down slightly and started to descend and pick up speed. Feeling a little adventurous, he tilted his left wing slightly upwards and turned towards the right in a slow arc. Straightening his wings, he continued downward in a shallow glide. It was a wonderful feeling. He was flying. He had never felt so free. The only noise he could hear was the wind rushing past his ears. He decided it was time to try climbing and attempted to flap his wings. He raised both wings, ready to push them downwards, but he raised one at a slightly different speed causing a steep bank to the left. He recovered and attempted to do it again, but this time he kept his wings together while raising them. He then pushed them down fast, which caused him to gain upwards momentum and speed.

Elijah continued this for some time, experimenting more and more, taking a few more risks. Sometimes he went too far, causing a spin or stalling, but he recovered confidently. His aircraft flight training jibed with the way his wings worked, and he soon became competent at flying.

He saw Isis standing at the cliff's edge and flew back over to her. He contemplated how he would land. Moving his wings into position to allow a shallow glide, he positioned himself so his descent would land him near Isis. He figured he would be able to extend his legs while performing a stall at the final minute, similar to how a plane engages its landing gear. As he approached the ground he tilted his wings to slow his descent and speed until he practically came to a stall position just over the ground and he … fell. It was only a foot and he landed relatively softly. Not as good as he would have liked, but he knew he would get better at it with a little more flight time.

"Congratulations, Elijah, you do learn quickly," Isis said. "Nemamiah told me that you were a quick study. Your pilot training must have helped."

"Thanks, Isis."

Isis continued to instruct Elijah on how to use his wings and perform different manoeuvres for some time. When the training session was over, Elijah decided that being able to fly was the best part of being an angel. He just loved it. He loved the feeling of freedom it gave him. Flying! It was something he had always dreamed of being able to do.

Elijah and Isis returned to the flight training room through the portal.

"One last thing, Elijah," she said. "You are not allowed to use your wings in Elysium except in virtual environments."

Elijah felt a little disappointed about the restriction but said, "No problem."

"Oh, and don't forget to get your wings upgraded."

That was Elijah's first stop. He wanted his standard wings as soon as possible, so he returned to Raphael for his upgrade.

After the relatively simple upgrade procedure, he received an incoming call from Castiel on EVE.

"Long time, no see, Castiel. When are you coming back?"

"I've been on assignment working on something," Castiel said. "It's time for you to come and see. Meet me at departure point R1 in the Bezetha building. Use EVE to show you the way." Castiel disconnected before Elijah could ask any additional questions.

Elijah, curious to see what Castiel had been working on, followed EVE's directions to the Bezetha building.

Chapter 38 - Justice

Castiel greeted Elijah with a hug, "Good to see you again, Elijah."

"You too, Castiel. Where are we going?"

"Spiritual Realm on Earth to watch something that you will be interested in. But we have to hurry because it is about to start."

Elijah and Castiel exited the doorway at the departure point. They appeared standing in the upper balcony of what appeared to be a courthouse. Elijah looked around and noticed that it was the Supreme Court of New South Wales. Looking below he could see his family—wife Juliana, son Reece, and daughter Kaley—sitting at the back of the courthouse. In the defence area was a lawyer and a man he vaguely recognised.

"Who is he, Castiel?"

"Remember the day you lost control of your bicycle because someone startled you and you careened down the hill to your death?"

Elijah cocked his head and raised an eyebrow. "Yes." He had recalled an image from deep in his subconscious of the face looking back at him from the side-view mirror of the car, which the passenger had yelled. Elijah figured he must have caught a glimpse of him after being startled. It was the same face of the man standing by the lawyer in the defence area below. A sense of anger came over him.

Castiel said, "Let it go, Elijah."

Elijah considered Castiel's comment. He took a deep breath and let the anger flow out of him. He looked at the man on trial and realised that he probably never thought that his actions, however reckless, would lead to Elijah's death.

The judge began to speak. "Jeremy Spark, you stand accused today of manslaughter in the second degree of Elijah Hael. How do you plead?"

Jeremy Spark responded, "Guilty."

"He's pleading guilty, Castiel?"

"Yes, against his lawyer's wishes," Elijah. "They really have no evidence on him."

"Why is he pleading guilty then?"

"His conscience got the better of him. Or you could say *Cas*tiel got the better of him."

The judge continued. "Jeremy, do you wish to address the court with a statement?"

"Yes I do, your honour."

"Very well," the judge said, "please proceed then."

"It is with great regret that I stand here. Although my actions were not intended to cause physical harm, they were inexcusable. My actions have caused two children to grow up without their father and a wife to spend her days without a husband."

Jeremy struggled to hold his composure and tears flowed down his cheeks as he spoke. "This day I stand before you and take full responsibility for those actions and accept any punishment that this court deems suitable and just. Regardless of that punishment, for the rest of my days I will carry the burden of knowing I have taken a life through foolish behaviour. I would like to caution everyone that while a simple prank may seem harmless, it might end up taking a life, a debt you will always bear and can never repay."

Jeremy turned and looked at Juliana. "Mrs. Hael, Reece and Kaley, I hope in time you will be able to forgive me for what I have taken from you." He wiped his eyes and took his seat.

The judge turned to Jeremy's lawyer and asked, "Do you have anything to add, Counsellor?"

The lawyer stood up and said, "Given the young age of my client and his genuine remorse I ask the court for leniency in the sentencing."

The judge turned to the prosecuting attorney and asked, "Do you have anything to add?"

The prosecuting attorney rose. "While the defendant's remorse appears genuine, I would like to stress to the court that his actions resulted in the loss of life. I ask the court to consider this and impose the maximum sentence allowed by law."

"Would the defendant please stand?"

Jeremy and his lawyer both stood up.

"Given the nature of the crime and the circumstances surrounding it," the judge said, "I am tempted to impose a more lenient sentence. However, given the tragic outcome of your actions, which resulted in the loss of life, I have no choice but to uphold the law."

Jeremy nodded.

"Jeremy Spark, I hereby sentence you to five years in prison with a minimum term of two years for manslaughter in the second degree."

Juliana stood up. "Your honour, may I please address the court?"

The judge said, "You may. Mrs. Hael, please come forward and stand beside the prosecution."

Juliana made her way to the front of the court and stood in the prosecution area. Looking at the judge she said, "My children and I will suffer the loss of Elijah for the rest of our lives. Sentencing Jeremy to prison, however, will not bring Elijah back or ease our pain. I understand that Jeremy voluntarily surrendered himself to the police for his actions after the police failed to find the person responsible for Elijah's death. I have, after giving this matter deep consideration, managed to forgive Jeremy for his actions. I ask the court to consider probation and a sentence of community service."

Elijah was puzzled. "Castiel, why is Juliana asking for a lighter sentence for Jeremy?"

"It is better to forgive than to live with a vengeful heart, Elijah. Forgiveness brings peace. Lewis Smedes once wrote: 'To forgive is to set a prisoner free and discover that prisoner was you.'"

Jeremy listened to Juliana's plea for clemency with an expression of shock on his face. His eyes seemed to be fixed on her necklace—a crucifix on a chain.

Juliana walked slowly back to her seat next to her children, careful to avoid eye contact with Jeremy on her way.

The judge considered Juliana's statement and responded, "While your appeal is warming, Juliana, my sentence will stand. Please take the defendant into custody."

Two police officers escorted Jeremy through a side exit and took him to the holding cells pending transfer to prison.

Castiel and Elijah stood watching as the courtroom slowly emptied. The last to leave were the defence attorney, the prosecution attorney, and Juliana and her children. The defence attorney approached Juliana and thanked her for her statement, saying, "Your statement no doubt touched my client. He is genuinely remorseful about what happened."

Juliana replied, "I sensed that. Thank you." She then turned to the prosecuting attorney and thanked him.

He said, "I know you wanted a lighter sentence, Juliana, but it's important to get the message across to others who behave in a similar way that their actions can lead to severe penalties."

Juliana nodded and thanked him again as they left the courthouse.

"Castiel, why did Jeremy confess?"

"It's a long story, Elijah. Let's go back to Elysium and I'll tell you all about it."

Chapter 39 - May 24, 2012, Jeremy

It was slow going in the peak-hour traffic, and Jeremy was restless. He told the driver: "Joe, drive as close as you can to that cyclist. Let's see if we can give him a scare."

Joe nodded and eased the car almost onto the shoulder of the road so they could pass as close to the cyclist as possible without hitting him.

Just as the car pulled alongside the cyclist, Jeremy yelled out "Wanker!" through the passenger window of the car. Startled, the cyclist began losing control of his bicycle. Laughing, Jeremy and Joe watched through the vehicle mirrors as the cyclist tried to regain control of his bicycle before crashing into a tree.

Jeremy said, "What a dweeb. If he can't ride his bike better than that he shouldn't be on the road in the first place. He should have training wheels on it. That'll teach him a lesson he won't soon forget."

Joe replied, "True, right. Lycra-wearing pansies have no place on the roads."

"So how long until we get to the hospital, Jeremy?"

"About another thirty minutes in this traffic."

On arriving at the hospital, Joe dropped Jeremy off at the main entrance and told Jeremy he would be back to pick him in around 30 minutes.

Jeremy made his way to the admissions desk and got his mother's room number and headed down the corridor. Jeremy had been in class at the university when the police came and got him and delivered the news that his mother had been taken to the hospital by ambulance following a domestic violence incident with his dad. Jeremy was startled but not surprised. His mum and dad were fighting more than usual lately since his father lost his job and finances were tight. They were struggling to pay the mortgage. His father had turned to alcohol for stress-relief, and when he drank, he became a violent monster. The police had also told Jeremy that his father was in custody and awaiting a court appearance pending bail.

Before entering his mother's hospital room Jeremy took a deep breath, expecting the worst. "Mum," he said as he approached her bed. Her left eye was barely visible, black and swollen to the point she could not open it. A row of stitches ran down the side of her face from above her left cheek to the corner of her mouth.

"Are you okay, Mum?" Jeremy said, as he took his mother's hand and stroked it.

"I'll be okay, son," she said in a small voice. "Don't you worry about me."

Jeremy could never understand his mother's optimism in such terrible situations. She had developed a strong faith in Jesus Christ after she had some sort of "religious" experience several years earlier. Jeremy didn't really go for the whole religion trip, but if it worked for her so be it. He always wondered why, if Jesus was so great, his mother was always the one who ended up battered on the floor after being beaten. He acknowledged that it gave her some sort of hope and he did not want her to lose that because it kept her strong. Thus, he never attacked her belief. His father did enough of that.

"Apparently my kidneys are failing, Jeremy," she said. She closed her eyes, which forced a forming tear to cascade down over her left temple. "They say I need a transplant." She breathed in deeply. "He hit me so hard, Jeremy, that it caused blood clots which damaged them."

Jeremy squeezed her hand, partly in anger towards his father and partly in concern for his mother. He did not know how to reply and so he kept quiet.

"I'm not scared Jeremy. I'm okay."

Nodding his head, Jeremy tried to understand how she could not possibly be scared.

"Jesus is with me," she whispered. "I feel His presence."

He felt like replying, "So where was this Jesus when you were beaten—was he with you then, too?" But he kept quiet, allowing the rage to build inside.

They sat together for a while in silence before Jeremy said his goodbyes and told his mum he would visit her daily. He left and swiftly made his way back to entrance where he knew Joe would be waiting.

A woman rushing past knocked into Jeremy causing both of them to stumble. Jeremy's focus landed on a cross hanging from a necklace around the women's neck. That irked him more than the fact that the woman had run into him and knocked him down and without even looking at her face, agitated and hateful, he said, "Stupid bitch, watch where you are going."

"I'm sorry," she replied, and hurried off.

Jeremy went outside and looked for Joe but couldn't find him. He sat for a while and then saw a person selling some flowers from a little mobile flower stall. He walked up and looked over the different combinations on sale. He purchased a bunch of red and white roses.

He made his way back to his mother's room. As he waited for the elevator he heard a woman's voice yell, "No, it can't be." He looked down the hallway and saw a doctor standing in front of a woman. He wondered if she was the woman who had run into him but could not quite see her or even recall what the woman looked like. All he could remember was that cross necklace. The woman turned away from the doctor with one hand on her mouth and one on her stomach and then vomited on the floor. The doctor called out to a few nurses who came running and helped the woman into a side room. He shrugged his shoulders, wondered what her problem was, and entered the elevator.

His mother was sleeping so he quietly filled a glass from the side table with water and put the flowers in it and fanned them out.

Back outside the hospital's main entrance he saw Joe just then rolling up in the car. "Where have you been, Joe?"

"I got back a little early and was waiting here but was forced to move on when an ambulance arrived. They said I was blocking the drive to the Emergency Room or something. Since then I have just been driving by every ten minutes looking for you."

"Let's go to the watch house, Joe. I have to see my father."

"You sure you want to see him?"

"No, not really, but I don't think he is getting out any time soon."

"How's your mum?"

"I don't want to talk about it, Joe. Just drive."

They drove through the traffic to the watch house in silence.

Joe parked the car in a visitor space and asked if Jeremy wanted him to go with him. Jeremy said, "No thanks, I'll be fine."

The front reception desk at the watch house was unattended. Jeremy gave the little bell on the counter a whack, which sounded a shrill ding. The place seemed deserted. He wondered what was going on. An old man sitting on a chair said, "There has been a fatal accident involving an officer's brother. The officers excused themselves and went to console her."

Jeremy said, "I see. Hope they don't take too long. We all have our own problems."

The man returned to the magazine he was reading. Jeremy gave the bell another whack and then took a seat. A few minutes later, a police officer came to the front desk. "Who is next?" The man who was waiting before Jeremy gestured for him to go first.

Jeremy asked the officer to take him to see his father. The officer informed him that another officer would arrive in a few minutes to accompany him and asked him to take a seat.

The old man stood up and spoke to the officer at the reception desk. Jeremy grabbed a magazine from the rack and glanced through it. Before long, an officer came to get Jeremy.

On the way to the meeting area, Jeremy asked the officer, "What happened to the officer's brother?"

"Unfortunately he passed away after sustaining fatal injuries in a cycling accident."

Jeremy's gut flip-flopped as he considered his earlier actions that caused that cyclist to lose control. He suddenly felt like he was a gazelle in a lion's den about to be eaten. The officer looked at him and asked, "Are you okay, man? You have gone all white."

Jeremy tried to maintain his composure. "Sure, I'm fine, just a bit shocked that you can die in a cycling accident. How did it happen?"

"We are not sure yet. Officers are on the scene taking witness statements. They will check the traffic cameras later and hopefully get some footage that will help determine what happened."

Jeremy's heart started racing. He considered asking more questions about where the accident occurred but stayed quiet.

"Take a seat, Jeremy," the officer instructed. "Your father will be here shortly."

His father appeared through a side door and sat opposite him separated by a see-through acrylic divider.

Looking remorseful his father started, "Son, I'm sorry, so sorry. I lost it, lost it again. I—"

"This time you have gone too far," Jeremy interrupted. "We are not going to able to afford your bail, nor do I want to bail you out this time."

His father rubbed his face with his hands and replied, "I understand. They will take me to the Long Bay Correctional Centre in the morning until the court appearance."

"Why were you drinking? What happened to Alcoholics Anonymous?"

"I thought I was on top of it," he said, hanging his head. "Your mum and I got in a fight over the mortgage. I just lost it. I don't know what happened. Is she all right?"

"No," Jeremy said, feeling the anger rising in his gut. "No, she's not all right. Her kidneys are shutting down due to a blood clot. She is going to need a transplant."

His father cupped his face in his hands and started to whimper.

"I don't think you're going to get out this time, Dad. You'll likely serve time—some length of time at that—as you were already on probation from last time you just 'lost it.'"

He removed his hands from his face revealing red swollen eyes. "It's what I deserve."

"Damn right you deserve it!" Jeremy said, slamming his fist on the desk in front of him.

The supervising police officer urged Jeremy to tone it down. Jeremy nodded.

"I've tried, son. The alcohol—it just seems to get the better of me."

"I don't care anymore, Dad. You have had enough chances. For all I care you can rot in this stink hole."

Jeremy stood up, walked out, and made his way back out to Joe's car.

A few kilometres down the road, Jeremy said, "I think we might be in trouble, Joe."

Joe turned to Jeremy and said, "Trouble? What do you mean?"

"An officer's brother just died in a cycling accident. It may have been the cyclist I yelled out to. I'm not sure. They're taking witness statements and analysing traffic camera footage."

Joe slowed the car and kept it to the limit. "It couldn't have been, Jeremy. The guy just fell off his bike after hitting that tree. He looked okay. He couldn't have died.... Could he?"

Jeremy gazed out the passenger window. "I'm not sure, Joe. It seems like a bit of a coincidence, doesn't it?"

"Well, I guess people die in cycling accidents all the time.... No, they don't," he said, thinking better of it. "If he was the cop's brother, Jeremy, they're going to hunt us down."

"I know, Joe. I know."

They remained silent until they arrived at Jeremy's place.

"Don't discuss the accident with anyone, Joe."

"Okay."

"And don't talk about it on the phone. If we are going to discuss it we have to do it in person."

Joe looked at Jeremy, "I think you are getting a little paranoid."

"Cautious, Joe, just cautious."

Chapter 40 - Café Babylon

"Now that we're back in Elysium, Elijah, let me take you to a café in the entertainment district. We can discuss Jeremy Spark there."

Elijah smiled. "There are cafés in Elysium?"

"There sure are. Elysium has quite a few entertainment areas to keep us occupied between assignments. While we have the virtual environments, the real thing is still better. The quickest way to get there is via the flying cars. We call them Ancars, short for angel cars."

"I like it," Elijah said.

Ancar terminals are a short walk from just about any place in Elysium. Elijah and Castiel followed EVE's directions to the closest one. On the way Elijah asked Castiel, "Why does Elysium have a no-fly policy? Wouldn't it be easier if we could just fly about?"

"It's all about safety, Elijah. Imagine thousands of angels all trying to leave an event at the same time. When you bump into someone on the ground, worst-case scenario is you fall over and possibly break a bone. In the air, it can lead to death. The Ancars are fully automated with safety devices to ensure there can't be collisions."

"I see," Elijah said. "Flying cars are good enough for me."

The Ancar terminal was a white pole with a sign attached "Ancar Terminal" and a number. Castiel held his hand up to the pole and it responded by glowing green. A few moments later an Ancar approached and hovered just in front of them. The doors opened upward to reveal several empty seats. Elijah and Castiel climbed in and took a seat.

A voice came from the Ancar: "Destination, please?"

Castiel responded, "Café Babylon."

The doors closed and the Ancar started to move. The ride was so smooth that it felt to Elijah as though the vehicle was not moving at all.

"How come it feels like we are not even moving, Castiel, yet I can see us going up and down and moving forward quite quickly."

"Inertial dampers."

"Could have used a set of those on my car on Earth," Elijah said, gazing out the windows of the Ancar as it glided through the air.

Café Babylon was buzzing with people sitting at round tables engaged in spirited conversation. Different size tables accommodated different size groups. Castiel and Elijah found a table for two.

"Is it always this busy, Castiel?"

"It's a popular spot and one of the better cafés in Elysium."

The table in front of them had a shiny surface, which was itself a display screen. On the right side was a menu. Elijah glanced through the options then touched one, which opened a sub menu of options. He touched a menu item and a holographic representation of the selection appeared before him showing what it looked like. The meal rotated slowly giving Elijah a 360-degree view of it.

"Make your selection, Elijah, and then place your order through the menu options."

After reviewing the holographic representations of various meals and drink choices, Elijah chose an egg salad and a chocolate milkshake.

"I've ordered, Castiel."

"Me, too. It shouldn't take long for our meals to arrive."

"I'm confused, Castiel. Why eat here and not in a virtual environment?"

"Virtual environments are like eating in a dream. Here it is for real. While your angel body does not need food or drink to sustain itself in Elysium, it is still enjoyable to partake in a real meal occasionally. The eating process generates white energy, which saves your angel body from having to draw it from the surroundings. In situations in which there is no white energy around, eating is necessary to sustain to your angel body."

The table's display had changed and was displaying various news reports on events occurring on Earth.

As they waited for their meals to arrive Castiel discussed Jeremy Spark's situation, including the domestic violence incident between his mother and father up to the point where Jeremy left the police station after seeing his father.

The waiter put Elijah's and Castiel's meals on the table. "Can I be of any further assistance, gentlemen?"

"No, were fine, thanks," Castiel replied.

After the waiter left, Elijah asked, "Is he an angel?"

"Yes."

"Why would he be a waiter?"

"Fighting a war requires all kinds of trades, here as on Earth. Just as not everyone who enlists in the Air Force, Navy, or Army on Earth serves on the front lines, not every angel serves on the frontlines of spiritual warfare. We are one large group of angels assembled to protect humanity the best we can. In the great spiritual war between good and evil we all work together for good."

They stopped talking long enough to eat their meals. When he had finished eating, Castiel continued. "Jeremy started to get very anxious at the thought of the police identifying him and Joe from traffic camera footage or an eyewitness testimony."

Elijah said, "And did it turn out that the police got any evidence of their involvement?"

"No," Castiel said. "The police could not get any clear video footage from the traffic cameras. Nor did any witnesses see what caused you to lose control of your bicycle. The police considered that it may have been 'rider error' due to the poor road conditions and failing light. Without any evidence they didn't have anything to go on."

"Then why did Jeremy confess?"

Castiel proceeded to select options on the table display and then placed his EVE device on the table. His EVE device displayed a message: "Searching for connection...." Moments later the message changed to: "Connected to Café Babylon Table 23 Holographic Display."

"I've recorded various scenes on my EVE," Elijah. "I'll take you through them by playing them back through the table for a better view."

The table went dark and then a holographic image started to appear on the centre of the table. The hologram was clear and solid. Castiel instructed Elijah to use the table controls on his right to rotate the image and zoom in and out. Elijah quickly adapted to using the controls to gain the best perspective to view the scenes Castiel was displaying.

The hologram displayed a hospital room with a woman lying in a bed, Jeremy sitting beside her, and Castiel standing at the end of the bed.

"The lady is Jeremy's mother, Elijah."

Elijah watched the scene and listened to the discussion playing through some sort of speaker system around the table that created a very impressive surround sound audio signal. He discovered that if he focussed on a particular person he could also hear their thoughts and feel their emotions.

Jeremy's mum said, "Son, they can't find suitable kidneys for me." She paused before continuing, "But I'm not scared.... An angel has been with me and has comforted me during the past month."

Elijah focussed on Jeremy who was thinking that his mother must be delusional from her medication.

"The angel's name is Castiel, Jeremy, and he is here now."

Jeremy replied, "Where?"

She looked directly at Castiel. "Standing at the end of the bed."

"There is nobody there, Mum."

"He is there, son, believe me."

With a curious look Elijah asked Castiel, "How can she see you, Castiel?"

"I allowed her to, just like Sophia allowed you to see her."

"I didn't think that was allowed."

"It isn't without permission, but of course I secured permission before allowing her to see me. I am a stickler for the rules. After someone has accepted Christ, having visions of angels does not affect their free will because they already believe. Permission is easy to obtain in those situations."

"Is that why the son can't see you?"

"Exactly," Castiel told him. "He still has his own choices to make. Allowing him to see me would affect his free will in choosing to believe in God."

Jeremy did not reply. He just held his mother's hand as she drifted off to sleep.

The holographic image faded to black as Castiel continued talking.

"Mrs. Spark died a week later, Elijah. I stayed with her right to the end and afterwards guided her to the portal to Heofon."

"What does the portal to Heofon look like?"

"Like the other portals—a bright white light. Love and peace encase you as you stand before it and draw you towards it. It is difficult not to just go through it, Elijah. Some angels accompanying loved ones to Heofon pass through the portal with them and never return."

Castiel operated his EVE and the hologram displayed a scene with Jeremy in his house.

"Let's continue watching Jeremy's journey, Elijah. I must say, he surprised me in the end."

Chapter 41 - Jack

Jeremy sat at his kitchen table staring at a full bottle of Jack Daniel's Tennessee Whiskey. Jeremy was not a drinker. He knew all too well the monstrous effect it had on his father. Yet the lure of Jack was difficult to resist. He felt the seductive come-on of the brownish-gold liquid in the bottle just begging him to have a taste and promising to take his emotional pain away.

He grabbed the fifth of Jack and poured it into an empty glass clenched in his other hand. He poured so quickly that it overflowed. He slammed Jack back onto the table, causing a spurt of the brownish liquid to erupt from the top.

His hand clenching the glass of Jack was trembling as he drew it to his lips. The smell overwhelmed his senses as the glass passed under his nose. Bottoms-up, he gulped down the liquid accepting Jack's promise to kill all his pain. Quickly he prepared a second glass while his throat still burned from the first. Several glasses later, he was feeling the full effect of the whiskey as it coursed through his bloodstream. Euphoria filled his mind and the emotional pain he was feeling started to vanish. Jack was keeping his promise. Jeremy was continuing to accept it.

A few glasses later and Jack had him. His head fell onto the table as he passed out.

As he observed the scene through the hologram Elijah began to feel empathy for Jeremy. "I guess we all have our own struggles to deal with in different ways."

"Yes we do, Elijah," Castiel responded. He advanced the hologram to important events. Elijah watched intently.

Jeremy's head stirred on the table and then his eyes opened. He rose and staggered towards the bathroom but failed to make it and collapsed on his knees while vomiting. Honey-coloured traces of Jack and the food he had eaten earlier cascaded down his chin and onto his shirt before puddling on the floor. Covered in vomit, Jeremy crawled his way into the bathroom and knelt over the toilet bowl awaiting the next great heave of his body.

Over the next several hours his body continued to expel what it could of Jack, leaving him writhing in pain and wishing death would take him. Between kneeling sessions, he would curl into a ball on the tiled floor of the bathroom and weep.

Some 12 hours later Jeremy scrambled into the shower fully clothed. The cascading water helped dull his throbbing head. After showering and changing into clean dry clothes, he made his way to the kitchen in search of some headache tablets. Jeremy swallowed the tablets with a cup of strong black coffee.

The smell of the coffee and the warm sensation of it flowing down his throat sparked some life back into him and brought his senses back online. His throbbing head slowly dulled, but the ache remained. He searched and finally found the keys to his motor bike and made his way out to the garage.

He turned the key and the engine roared to life. The roar caused his head to throb violently. He put on his helmet and drove aggressively to the Long Bay Correctional Centre.

The first thing Jeremy noticed when his father entered the meeting area was his gaping black eye and swollen lip.

"What happened, Dad?"

"They don't take too kindly to men that hit their wives in here, son."

Jeremy looked around and noticed several guards overseeing the visitors talking to the prisoners.

Jeremy looked at his father, but not straight in the eye, and said, "Mum passed away yesterday as a result of the kidney failure. The police informed me they will be upgrading your charges to manslaughter."

His father nodded. "They informed me this morning, too. I'm sorry, son, I never meant—"

Jeremy interrupted by slamming his hand on the table, drawing the stern glare of the guards. "Don't say it. I don't want to hear it."

His father looked downwards and stayed quiet.

"How many years are you going to get, Dad?"

"Whatever the judge decides. I am pleading guilty."

Jeremy looked his father square in the eye now. "So you should."

"A prison chaplain came to visit me a while back," his father told him. "He offered to discuss things with me if I wanted to. Over time I started to talk to him about the guilt I was carrying over failing as a husband and father...."

"Whatever, Dad."

"He helped me to understand the importance of taking responsibility for what I have done. As I have learned how to do that, my guilt is subsiding. I am no longer angry inside but remorseful."

"I'm really glad that is working out for you," Jeremy responded with bitter sarcasm. "Maybe you can live happily ever after."

Looking directly at Jeremy, his father said, "One day, son, I hope you will forgive me for what I've done."

Jeremy detected a sense of sincerity in the way his father was talking but dismissed it and let the anger he had for the man burn it up. "Don't hold your breath."

His father nodded. "I was reading an article in the newspaper the chaplain brought me the other day. It was about a devoted father, Elijah Hael, who died tragically in a freak accident when the bicycle he was riding struck a tree. He left behind a loving wife and two beautiful children, one five and the other three years old."

Jeremy shifted uncomfortably on his chair.

"They said the daughter, Kaley, didn't really understand, but the son, Reece, is aware that his daddy had gone up into the sky to be with Jesus. They described him as having a good Christian family."

Jeremy asked, "Do they know why he hit the tree?"

"No, the report said the roads were wet and it was near dark, but they didn't really know what had happened other than that he came off his bike."

"Why are you bringing this up, Dad?"

"Because it got me thinking about how lucky I am to be alive. How I have squandered everything good in my life and worried about things that are not important. Family is what is important—the moments we have together. The chaplain said we should be grateful for every moment we have regardless of our circumstances. He used that news report as a way of showing me we never know when it's going to be over."

Castiel paused the hologram display.

Elijah said, "A bit of a coincidence there, Castiel?"

"Well, not really a coincidence at all, Elijah. I did plant that thought in the chaplain to give that particular newspaper report to Jeremy's father. First, because I thought it would help the father, and second, because I wanted to bring your family to Jeremy's awareness—to bring it before his conscience."

Castiel resumed the playback.

Jeremy said, "Gee, Dad, it would have been nice if you had thought about that before you went and killed Mum."

"I know, son," the man said, hanging his head. "It is too late for me. My mistakes are unforgiveable. But it's not too late for you, son."

"What do you mean?"

"The anger you have, I see it, and it will destroy you."

Jeremy did not respond.

The buzzer sounded indicating that visiting time was over. Jeremy's father said goodbye and Jeremy left, shaken up about the newspaper report his father had brought up. He had done his best to forget all about that incident.

Chapter 42 - The Note

The next morning Jeremy heard knocking on his front door. He made his way to the living room and peered out from behind the drapes and saw two police officers—one male and one female—and another man in plain clothes standing on his front porch. His stomach sank and his heart leapt. His first thoughts were: *Did they find a witness? Did the surveillance cameras catch us? Did Joe talk?*

Fully expecting to be arrested he slowly opened the door and just looked out at them.

"Jeremy Spark?" the male officer asked.

"Yes, I'm Jeremy Spark."

"Do you mind if we come in, sir?"

"Uh, what for?"

"There's a matter we need to discuss with you, sir."

Jeremy opened the door and led them into the lounge room. "Have a seat."

The first officer introduced herself. "I'm detective sergeant Claricia, and this is Constable Simon. The gentleman to my left is Chaplain Dave Wall from Long Bay Correctional Centre."

 Elijah scanned his eyes from the hologram to Castiel. "My sister was there, Castiel?"

"Yes. But that wasn't my doing. It just worked out that way. Small world, isn't it?"

"Indeed it is."

Claricia continued. "Unfortunately, Mr. Spark, we have some bad news for you."

Relieved momentarily that they were not there to arrest him, Jeremy suddenly became concerned on a different level. "What sort of bad news?"

"Your father, sir.... He passed away last night at the prison. We are very sorry for your loss."

Deep inside Jeremy felt a wave of sadness come over him. "How did it happen?"

"There was a fight in his cell involving three other inmates. Your father sustained fatal wounds from a shank made out of a toothbrush."

Claricia paused to allow Jeremy a moment to come to terms with what she had just said and then continued. "Chaplain Wall here spoke to your father yesterday evening. Your father gave him a letter to give to you. It appears your father suspected something was going to happen. We have begun an investigation into the matter."

Jeremy blinked rapidly to prevent tears from welling in his eyes. The loss of both his mother and his father started to weigh on him heavily.

"What did the note say?"

"The chaplain wouldn't give it to us," Claricia told him. "He wanted to hand it to you in person. That is why he is here. After you have read it, sir, we will have to take the note with us and enter it into evidence."

The chaplain removed a note from his coat pocket and handed it to Jeremy. "I'm very sorry, Jeremy."

Jeremy opened the note and read it:

"Son, no words will ever be enough to describe the pain I feel for what I have done. I do not deserve your forgiveness or God's. I ask only that one day you will be able to forgive me. Forgiveness will set you free and release the anger in you. I do not ask you to forgive me for me, but for yourself. I have lived a life of bitterness, anger, and hatred. Drinking would let it all out in the most damaging way. I fear I have passed some of that onto you and that is not what I wanted. Tonight I face my jurors and accept my sentence. For me that is likely to be life. I accept that. In many ways, death will be my pardon."

Tears rolled down Jeremy's face. He was not ready to forgive his father—far from it—but under all the hate he loved his father. His last words in this note had chipped away one brick in the wall holding back his forgiveness.

Elijah looked up at Castiel. "You couldn't have stopped the attack on his father?"

"No, unfortunately that was out of our control. Soon after arriving at the prison, he provoked the other inmates in hopes that they would kill him. Suicide by provocation. He finally got that wish, but by then he wished he could have taken it all back."

Jeremy handed the note to Claricia who quickly scanned it and said, "I'm sorry, Mr. Spark. I lost my brother recently to a cycling accident and know that it hurts. It hurts a lot."

Jeremy's heart skipped a few beats and he went white as a ghost. He could not believe he was sitting in front of the sister of the man he had killed. He figured God was haunting him. He focussed on the ground, avoiding eye contact with Claricia. He could not look at her.

Claricia and Simon stood up. "The chaplain will stay here with you for a while, Jeremy. We have to return to the station."

Jeremy continued staring at the ground and did not reply. Chaplain Wall saw Claricia and Simon out. A few moments later the chaplain said, "I'm going to visit you daily for a while if that is okay, Jeremy. Would a particular time suit?"

Jeremy was about to reject the offer, but deep down some of the things his father told him about how the chaplain had helped him stirred him to accept. "I get home from university around five, weekdays. Weekends, it just depends."

"Okay," Chaplain Wall said. "I will come around about six each weekday. We will find a time each Friday that suits us both for the weekends."

Jeremy nodded.

"Is there anything I can do or get for you?"

"No, I'll be okay."

"Do you have any relatives or friends you can call?"

"Yes, my best friend Joe. I will call him later. For now I just want to be alone."

The chaplain slowly rose and said, "Okay, I'll see myself out and I will see you tomorrow."

Jeremy said, "Thank you." He was not sure why he gave thanks. He was not used to people going out of their way for him, and it had caught him off guard.

An hour passed before Jeremy got up and went to the kitchen to prepare his dinner. He ate slowly trying hard not to think of anything in particular. He was hurting, and the less he thought about things the easier it was. It seemed that every thought that came to mind brought him pain. After picking at his food, he went to the medicine cabinet and shook a few sleeping pills from the bottle prescribed to his mother. He set his alarm clock and lay down on the bed. Tomorrow would be easier, he thought, because he could drown himself in a university lecture. He lay on his bed staring at the ceiling until the sleeping pills took effect and he passed into a deep, if fitful, sleep.

Chapter 43 - Coincidences

Jeremy awoke to the alarm clock playing the song "What Love Really Means" by JJ Heller. He roused slowly from his sleep but did not pay much attention to the song's lyrics until the third verse played.

"He's waiting to die as he sits all alone.
He's a man in a cell who regrets what he's done.
He utters a cry from the depths of his soul.
Oh Lord, forgive me. I wanna go home."

He thought of his father and wondered if his father had asked God for forgiveness. The song continued:

"Then he heard a voice somewhere deep inside
And it said 'I know you've murdered
And I know you've lied
And I've watched you suffer all of your life
And now that you'll listen I'll, I'll tell you that I...'"

He wondered why this would be on the hard rock station. He glanced over and saw that somehow the channel he normally listened to had been changed.

"I will love you for you
Not for what you have done or what you will become
I will love you for you
I will give you the love, the love that you never knew."

The words of the song sent a chill down his spine, and he did not quite understand why. It was as if the radio was speaking to him. When the song was over Jeremy realised he was listing to a Christian radio station and quickly changed it back to the hard rock station.

Elijah smiled. "Castiel, I'm guessing you switched the station while he was sleeping?"

"A clever observation, Elijah."

"But how did you know that song would be playing at precisely the moment when the alarm was set to go off?"

"Oh, that involved a bit of thought-injecting at the radio station. It wasn't terribly difficult, though."

Elijah thought about all the times in his past that a particular song had come on the radio that seemed to be just the right song for what he needed at the time. He wondered if it was just a coincidence.

Jeremy showered and got ready for university. Joe was picking him up shortly so he hurried to be ready on time.

The song lyrics kept playing back in his mind: "I know you've murdered and I know you've lied." Over and over it played. Jeremy had no idea how his radio station had changed in the first place, but in the end, he concluded that he must have just bumped it. The news report his father had mentioned—about the dead cyclist's family—was also bugging him. He was experiencing so many coincidences that he began to question whether there was something more to them.

Joe arrived to pick him up on time. "So what's been happening, Jeremy?"

"The police came around last night, Joe."

"Uh-oh," Joe said. "About the cycling accident? What did you tell them?"

"No, no," Jeremy said, swatting the words away. "It's what *they* told *me*. My father died in prison."

"What? Really? How?"

"He was killed in a fight."

"I'm sorry, Jeremy."

"It's okay. In some ways it seems that is what he wanted."

"What do you mean, Jeremy?"

"Doesn't matter." Jeremy shook his head. "Strange, but one of the officers—Claricia—was the sister of the man in the cycling accident."

Joe grimaced. "Really?"

"Yes, really. The weird thing was the day before yesterday my father told me about a newspaper report describing the accident and how the man had a wife and two children. One age five and one age three."

"Ouch," Joe said. "That hurts." He drove toward the university campus in silence for a while. Then he said, "I guess I never thought of the man having a family and young children and a wife."

"I know," Jeremy said. The words of that song continued in Jeremy's mind: "I will love you for you, not for what you have done or what you will become." The thought struck him that there was no one left to love him, but he felt a nagging feeling clawing at his very soul. "I feel awful, Joe."

"Yeah," Joe said, his voice catching in his throat. "It's understandable considering all you have been through."

"It's not that, Joe," Jeremy told him. "It's like something is nagging at me, trying to tell me something. Maybe it is my mother. I dunno. The weirdest thing happened this morning when my alarm went off and the radio started playing a song from a Christian radio station. Do you believe in ghosts?"

"No, Jeremy, I don't," Joe said. "Should I?"

"Well, I just don't understand how it could have happened."

Jeremy gazed out the passenger window and saw a billboard on the side of the road that said, "Will the road you are on get you to my place? – God."

He felt a warmth come over him, and in that moment Jeremy Spark decided to change the road he was on and, when he did, he was instantly rewarded with a peace he had never felt before.

"Joe, take me to the police station. The one my father was held at."

"What about class? Lecture starts in twenty minutes."

"No."

"You serious? What are you going to do?"

"I can't live like this, Joe. I am going to confess to what I did. Don't worry: I won't mention you."

Joe's tone was angry. "I'm not doing that. You're nuts, Jeremy. It's just because your dad passed away. You'll be fine in a couple of days."

"Then stop the car, Joe. Stop it now."

"No."

Jeremy removed his seatbelt and opened the passenger door.

"Are you crazy, Jeremy? What are you going to do, jump?"

Jump he did. He hit the pavement and started rolling. Over and over he rolled while clutching his head to avoid it hitting anything. Jeremy saw the world spinning around and around as he rolled wondering when and if it would ever stop. Slowly, he came to a stop with only skinned knees and elbows. He stood up as people all around looked at him.

Joe slammed on the brakes, brought the car to a stop at the side of the road, exited the car and quickly ran back to Jeremy.

"Are you okay, man? What are you trying to do, get killed? Get back in the car and we can talk about it, Jeremy."

"No, Joe, I'm going." He started walking in the direction of the police station.

"You can't walk from here, Jeremy. It's hours away on foot."

"I don't care. I'll get there sooner or later."

Joe followed for a while, trying to persuade Jeremy to turn around. Nothing he said had the slightest effect on Jeremy's decision. Finally, Joe gave up and returned to his car.

A few hours later Jeremy arrived at the police station and asked for Claricia.

Claricia came out and immediately recognised him. "Jeremy Spark, how are you doing? How can I help you?"

"I have something to tell you."

"Sure, sure," she said. "Come right this way. We can talk in here."

Jeremy proceeded to tell Claricia what he did in the late afternoon on May 24. Tears rolled down his cheeks as he asked for forgiveness.

Chapter 44 - Assignment

Castiel's and Elijah's EVE devices simultaneously displayed incoming calls from Araton.

"This must be important, Elijah," Castiel said. "Araton handles angel assignments."

Castiel and Elijah both answered the incoming call.

"Castiel, Elijah: We have an urgent issue that needs to be taken care of immediately. Please report to the assignment briefing room at once." The call ended.

"That's in the Megiddo building, Elijah," Castiel said. "It's a short Ancar ride from here. We better get moving."

At the assignment briefing, Araton asked Elijah and Castiel to approach the table in the centre of the room. Araton stood on one side of the table and Elijah and Castiel stood side by side on the other. Moments later, a large semi-transparent holographic sphere appeared and floated above the table. The sphere was a virtual globe that represented all the landmasses and oceans of Earth.

Araton began. "We have a situation in the Dandenong Ranges in Melbourne, Australia. Sophia and her team were dispatched there a secton ago and have failed to report back. They were investigating the reasons behind a cluster of suicides, murders, and accidents, in the area. Since they were dispatched, a serious car accident has occurred close to where they last reported. We have sent angels to the scene to take care of those injured and dying."

Castiel asked, "Did any of the angels at the accident scene see any signs of Sophia or her team?"

"No, none at all," Araton replied, "and that is what has us concerned. Accidents always take immediate priority. Sophia and her team should have attended to the accident due to its close proximity to her assignment."

The sphere zoomed in to the Dandenong Ranges in Melbourne, highlighting the region that Araton was discussing.

"Castiel, I want you and Elijah to go into the Earth Realm and attend those at the accident scene and investigate. Elijah, I know you are due for your practical examination, but given the exigent circumstances we are going to send you on this assignment under the care of Castiel instead."

Castiel looked at Elijah, then back to Araton, and replied, "Not a problem, Araton. Elijah will do just fine."

"See that he does," Araton said. "Your first task will be to check around the accident site for a cause. See if it is a result of Shadow activity. Then I want you to go and investigate the string of tragedies that we sent Sophia to examine."

The sphere zoomed in to show a closer picture of the Dandenong Ranges. "This is the area Sophia and her team were dispatched to. It appears there may be an extensive underground cave system here. Our sensors are unable to detect anything living in the area, including animal life."

"Is something blocking them, Araton?" Castiel asked.

"Most likely. We have received reports of Shumans in the area, and they will be able to see you, so be careful."

"Shumans?" Elijah asked.

"Shumans are humans under the complete control of a Shadow," Castiel explained.

Araton added, "You can tell them by their black eyes. If you engage in combat with them, try not to destroy the body. Subdue, evict the Shadow, and then heal the human body if necessary."

Elijah said, "What happens if they die?"

Araton said, "It happens. While we have a directive to not inflict harm on a human through action or inaction, Shumans create a difficult situation. Inaction can cause them harm or harm to others. For a human to become a Shuman means he must have made a choice to sell his soul to the Shadows."

"Why would a person sell his soul?"

"Typically for personal gain of some sort," Araton said. "Humans typically refer to is as cutting a 'deal with the devil.' Look it up on EVE when you get a chance."

"Can we save them?"

"Sometimes. After evicting or killing the Shadow, you can perform a cleansing blessing. Castiel can show you how."

"Have you ever seen a Shuman, Castiel?"

"Yes, and so have you," Castiel told him, "on more than one occasion on Earth. You don't really think a human would simply pick up an assault rifle and start shooting people randomly, do you?"

"Wouldn't the police notice their black eyes?"

"Only angels and Shadows see that, Elijah."

"So you are saying people who go on shooting sprees are Shumans?"

"I am not sure about all of them. But, it certainly fits the Shadows' MO. If you look at the court transcripts of the ones who don't self-terminate you will see that, when charged, they do things such as laugh hysterically at the judge or make outlandish speeches. It is something Shadows typically do—inflict maximum damage, create as much red energy as possible, and be proud of it. Of course, they never come through with their end of the deal that the human sold their soul for. It's all just a con to gain control."

Araton interrupted. "Sorry to interrupt, but time is of the essence. Grab some armaments and port to Earth."

Elijah and Castiel made their way to the armaments area in the lower lever of the Megiddo building. "Hey, Castiel, why can't we just zip into the Spiritual Realm and search for Sophia there?"

"Whatever is blocking the sensors would also block us from seeing what is really going on. The sensors work through the Spiritual Realm."

Nemamiah greeted Castiel and Elijah as they walked into the armaments room. "You want your usual, Castiel?"

"Yes, thanks."

Nemamiah handed Castiel a couple of 9mm Uzis. "Araton informed me that Shumans are in the area you are reporting to. So I loaded the 9mm clips with Angel Light bullets. They are highly concentrated white energy that will penetrate a Shuman and wound a Shadow inside without damaging the human body."

As Castiel mounted the Uzis on his back under his wings he said, "I call these the 'Judgement Twins,' Elijah."

"Must say they do look pretty cool, Castiel."

Nemamiah turned to Elijah and said, "For you, I have a Bow of Sentencing. This bow shoots Angel Light arrows, which work the same as the Angel Light bullets. All you do is draw back the string and an arrow will auto-form. Then you fire it as you would any arrow. It eliminates the need for a quiver."

The bow glowed with a faint white light and had inscriptions engraved in its woodwork. It was a beautiful piece of workmanship.

"This is very nice," Elijah said, "but how come I don't get a set of guns?"

"Given the way you shoot arrows, Elijah, why would you want a gun?" Nemamiah asked. "Besides, arrows are silent."

"Good point!" Elijah mounted the bow on his back.

"I also have the Sword of the Spirit for you, Elijah, in case you get engaged in close combat. It is one of a kind and used by only a few angels. It was constructed many sectons ago by an Archangel."

Nemamiah handed Elijah the Sword of the Spirit. The sword was about the length of Elijah's arm not including the hilt. The blade was pure silver and glowed with a white aura. It looked heavy but was quite light. The hilt was gold and had three gems mounted in it. Elijah swung the sword a few times and noticed it was extremely well balanced.

"Here is the sheath, Elijah." Elijah mounted the sheath around his waist under his trench coat and sheathed the sword in it.

"You putting me away already? Ha! That wasn't much of a play."

Elijah looked around to see where the voice had come from.

"Down here, you nincompoop."

Elijah looked down at the sword.

"Yes, that's right, I can talk."

Nemamiah said, "Its name is Gunthor."

"The sword has a name?"

"Yes, *I* have a name."

"Why?"

Elijah shook his head, trying to make sense of a talking sword.

"So you can talk to me, of course."

Elijah looked at Castiel, who just smiled. "My guns don't talk. You're lucky. Although I hear Gunthor has a bit of an attitude."

"I do not," Gunthor replied whimsically.

"Sure you don't," Nemamiah said. "Elijah, Castiel, Gunthor, you are all ready to go. The doorway at the end of the corridor will take you to a port door that has been pre-set to your destination."

Castiel and Elijah thanked Nemamiah.

As they left Nemamiah said, "Godspeed, guys."

Chapter 45 - The Crash Scene

An ambulance, a fire engine, and a few police cars were already on the scene of the accident involving two vehicles and a motorcycle. The motorcyclist lay under a blanket.

Castiel and Elijah stepped through a portal a few hundred meters up the road and advanced toward the scene.

"This is likely to be where the accident started, Elijah," Castiel said, pointing down at the pavement. "See the skid marks?"

Elijah looked at the skid marks from one of the cars that began on the left side of the road and crossed the median strip into oncoming traffic. A little farther down the road off to the left he could see a red sedan wrapped around a tree. On the right side of the road a white Ute had somehow flipped and was lying upside down in the middle of the right lane. Several fire fighters were using the Jaws of Life to cut open the driver door of the Ute. A motor bike was on the left side of the road wedged in the guardrail.

Elijah shook his head as he surveyed the devastation. "What on earth do you think caused this mess, Castiel?"

"I'm not sure. Let's go stand near the police officers and see if we can pick up anything from their conversation."

As they made their way towards the police officers, Elijah noticed three angels. One had positioned himself in the Ute holding the hand of the man trapped behind the driver's wheel. The second angel was comforting a female on the side of the road who appeared to have been thrown from the red sedan. Ambulance paramedics were also attending to her. The third angel was standing beside the red vehicle as close as possible to the driver trapped inside.

Elijah was moved. "It is comforting to see angels caring for the injured and dying in such tragic circumstances, Castiel."

"As we approach the officers, Elijah, remember not to stand too close. While they cannot see us, nearly all humans will sense our presence. Our presence is much stronger when we are in the Earth Realm."

Elijah and Castiel stood close enough to overhear the officer's conversation.

The police officer on the left said, "It appears the red sedan braked suddenly to avoid something, lost control, and veered into the path of the Ute coming down the other side of the road. They collided head-on, flipping the Ute over, and sending the red sedan into the trees. The motorbike was following close behind the red sedan and was unable to avoid colliding with the Ute. The motorbike rider was thrown into the centre of the road and sustained fatal injuries. He was pronounced dead on the scene. From the skid marks it appears he tried to stop the bike suddenly, overusing the brake and causing a highside."

The police officer on the right nodded. "I concur with your assessment. Wrap this up and pass this theory onto the crash scene investigation team when they arrive. Their ETA is a few hours. In the short term, we need to clear the road so we can get it reopened and get traffic flowing again." He paused and cocked his head, then said, "The only puzzling part is what that red sedan braked so suddenly to avoid."

"It may have been an animal. Plenty of wildlife run across the road here."

"True. I guess that makes as much sense as anything else."

The police officers then parted and walked off in different directions to attend different areas of the crash scene.

"Do *you* think it was an animal, Castiel?" asked Elijah.

"Not sure. It could have been."

Castiel pulled out his EVE device and worked it deftly to call up a video of the current location minutes before the accident took place. He started the playback. As the red sedan approached, the playback display grew so fuzzy that nothing could be seen until a full minute after the accident occurred.

"Something is blocking the playback, Elijah. Based on that, I don't think it was an animal. It was more likely caused by Shadows."

Castiel rewound the video to the first frame that could be seen clearly towards the end of the accident. He manipulated the video so he could view it from all angles and different vantage points. The EVE device let him control the camera zoom, location, and angle while viewing the resulting picture.

"Look here, Elijah." Castiel pointed to a bush on the side of the road in the video. "You can see that this bush is disturbed as though something had run off into it. Let's find that bush."

They located the bush in question and found that some of the brush leading away from the crash site and into the bush did show signs that it had been trampled.

"Castiel, the *tracks* seem to be heading in the same direction as the caves that Araton said Sophia was investigating."

They decided to follow the disturbed brush to track whatever had caused it.

"Not too far from here, Elijah, two teenage girls hung themselves a few years back. They used a single rope with dual nooses, tied it onto a branch overhanging a small ledge, and jumped."

"Why?"

"I'm not sure. Suicides are handled in a special victim's area in Elysium. The case files are sealed due to the extenuating circumstances surrounding them."

Castiel and Elijah continued their trek keeping a close eye on the trail they were tracking.

"Several other events have also occurred in the area, Elijah, which has set off some alarms. Six men were arrested and charged with the murder of an African man who was stabbed to death. A mother of two was shot twice in the face then dumped in the bushlands. In 1983 there were the notorious Ash Wednesday fires. A few years back the so-called Black Saturday fires swept through the ranges. Nobody actually died here in the ranges, but the fires that passed through claimed over a hundred lives in different areas."

"Do you think it's all connected, Castiel?"

"It's difficult to know for sure. Gethsemane has shown an increase in urgent prayers in the area. There is certainly unrest in these parts. Unrest creates red energy. The red energy draws the Shadows. The Shadows fuel unrest. It's a vicious cycle."

Elijah and Castiel followed the trail until they came to a small opening at the juncture of stones in a large rock formation.

"This looks like the entrance to the cave system," Castiel said.

Elijah nodded. "And where whatever we are tracking went."

Chapter 46 - Caves

Castiel and Elijah entered the opening between the rocks and followed it down into an underground cave system. The only light source was the opening behind them, and it was quickly failing to provide enough light for them to see where they were going.

"We'll need a torch to go much farther, Castiel."

"Pull out Gunthor, Elijah."

Elijah unsheathed Gunthor and held it upwards like a burning torch. "Its light glow isn't providing much light, Castiel."

Castiel looked towards Gunthor and said, "Gunthor, increase your glow to provide light."

In a grumpy voice Gunthor mumbled, "Gunthor do this, Gunthor do that. That is all I ever hear."

Castiel retorted sternly, "Do it, Gunthor, or I'll give you an acid bath."

"You wouldn't."

"Oh wouldn't I?"

At once Gunthor's glow was bright enough to illuminate the cave walls around them. Gunthor mumbled something that neither Elijah nor Castiel could make out.

Elijah said, "You were right, Castiel. Our dear Gunthor does have a bit of an attitude." He proceeded through the cave to what appeared to be a passage on the far side.

The passage was quite narrow—too narrow to accommodate them walking abreast—so Elijah led the way and Castiel followed close behind. The cave echoed with a screeching noise and startled, Elijah, muttered "I hate bats" as a colony of the creatures flapped over their heads and headed out of the cave.

They continued down the passageway until it opened into a large cavern with a smouldering campfire by a little rock-shelf. "Do you think this is Sophia's work, Castiel?"

"It might be, Elijah. Her team may have rested here."

Castiel explored the far side of the cavern and discovered two passageways—one that led upwards and to the left, and one that led straight ahead and slightly downwards. There was no sign that either passage had been used recently.

Castiel peered into the upward passage and said, "Let's head this way, Elijah."

After a short walk, the passage terminated in a ledge overlooking a large cavern. It was too dark to make out the size of the cavern. Castiel looked around for any signs of activity and then said, "Gunthor, increase the light."

Gunthor responded by glowing even brighter, illuminating the far walls of the cavern. They were on a ledge about two stories above the floor of a cavern about the size of a basketball court. Then she caught their eye. Castiel and Elijah simultaneously spotted Sophia, in a dusky corner of the cavern, bound by rope around her wrists with her arms stretched along the crossbeam of a wooden cross. Another rope around her ankles secured her legs to the vertical beam. The cross itself stood in the middle of a circled pentagram painted on the cavern floor in a reddish liquid the colour of blood. Sophia's head tilted downwards with her eyes closed indicating that she was, at best, unconscious.

"We've got to do something, Castiel," Elijah said.

"The first thing we have to do is be careful, Elijah," Castiel cautioned.

Elijah nodded. "What is that symbol under the cross, Castiel?"

"It's dark magic that the Shadows use. It is a binding spell, which keeps Sophia from leaving the inner pentagon of the circled pentagram so long as it stays intact."

Elijah surveyed the room and could see no sign of Shadows or Shumans. He wondered why they would leave Sophia unguarded. On the far side of the cavern were three entrances. One high, opening onto a ledge like the one they were standing on, and two lower ones that entered on the floor level of the cavern. Darkness shrouded the far corners of the ceiling and Elijah couldn't see if there were additional entrances to and from the cavern.

"Gunthor, can you go any brighter?" Elijah asked.

"Nope," Gunthor replied.

"This looks like a trap, Castiel."

Castiel examined the area a bit before responding. "No doubt."

"Why can't we just fly down and release her, Castiel?"

"That would be a suicide mission. Chances are Shadows and possibly Shumans are lurking in the far passages just waiting to ambush us.... Gunthor, can your scan pickup any activity in the area?"

"None. Scan isn't working."

Elijah raised his eyebrows, surprised at Gunthor's many abilities.

"How good are you with that bow, Elijah?"

"I can hit an apple a football field away."

Castiel turned towards Elijah. "I think our best bet will be to try to release Sophia from here and hope she wakes up to defend herself. We can provide cover for her if something attacks."

"How?"

"First we need to release either of her hands so she can untie herself. Then we need to break that circled pentagram to quash the binding spell."

Elijah looked at the rope binding Sophia's wrist. "I'll shoot an arrow to cut through the rope binding her left wrist. That may wake her up so she can untie her other hand and legs. I'm not sure how we can break the circled pentagram, though."

"I'll have to do that from below," Elijah. "I'll enter the cavern through the lower passage, make my way to the circled pentagram, and break it. By then, if all goes well, Sophia will have untied herself. You'll be busy holding off any attackers from here."

In a grumpy voice Gunthor asked, "And what do I get to do?"

Castiel retorted, "You get to provide the light."

Elijah stood Gunthor up against the cavern wall and readied his bow.

"I'll yell when I'm in position down below, Elijah, and then you shoot your arrow."

"Wait, wait," Elijah said, feeling a little uneasy about the mission. "Will the Angel Light arrow cut through rope, Castiel?"

"Yes, Angel Light armaments have the same effect as normal weapons on all matter other than human flesh and bones."

"Okay, then." Elijah drew back the string on the bow and an arrow appeared just as Nemamiah said it would. He aimed it and stood at the ready for Castiel's call.

Castiel hurriedly moved back down the passage. The light Gunthor was providing quickly faded forcing him to navigate using his hands to feel his way through the passage. When he got to the intersection where they had originally gone upwards he stared down the alternative passage. At the end of the passage, he could see a faint light, which he concluded had to be coming from the cavern. Without hesitation, he made his way towards the light until he was at the lower entrance.

He grabbed both of his 9mm Uzis and prepared himself for what was about to happen next....

Chapter 47 - Rescue

Castiel yelled, "Now, Elijah!"

Elijah steadied his aim and fired an arrow towards the rope binding Sophia's left wrist to the crossbeam of the wooden cross. The arrow streamed through the air leaving a white trail of energy in its wake and sliced through the top part of the rope, severing it and allowing Sophia's left arm to fall to her side. Sophia's eyes opened and her head tilted upward. She had regained consciousness!

Sophia looked over and saw Castiel approaching. She raised her head and spotted Elijah up on the higher ledge and seemed at once to realize her predicament. She reached over to the rope on her right wrist and began untying it with her free hand.

Elijah kept a keen watch for any movement and before long, as expected, several Shumans appeared in the lower passages and one in the higher. Armed with AK-47 assault rifles they moved out of the darkness and took aim at Sophia. Castiel targeted one of his 9mm Uzis at the Shumans appearing in the left passage and targeted the other at the ones entering through the right passage. Simultaneously he pulled both triggers firing in two directions while moving forwards towards Sophia.

Elijah kept an eye on Castiel in his peripheral vision and took aim at the Shuman on the higher ledge. He drew back the string to full draw and let the arrow fly. He watched as the arrow pierced the Shuman through the chest causing a brief puff of blackness around the Shuman as it toppled off the ledge and plunged to the ground. Likewise, Castiel's Angel bullets intercepted the Shumans emerging from the lower passages and caused them to fall to the ground shrouded in a puff of blackness as the Shadows possessing them disintegrated.

Sophia had untied her right wrist and was now working on untying her legs as Castiel made his way to the circled pentagram. Once there, he began rubbing at the circle with his foot to force a gap in the circle. The liquid was, as both Elijah and Castiel suspected, human blood.

Kicking off the final rope securing her to the cross, Sophia looked around then glanced upwards and saw Shadow Knights descending from the ceiling. She yelled, "Look up!"

Elijah glanced upwards and counted seven Shadow Knights emerging from the dark recesses of the ceiling and rappelling down black ropes. Elijah took aim and fired several arrows. The Shadow Knights used their shields to fend off Elijah's arrows. Elijah took aim at the top of the ropes they were rappelling down and released arrows towards them. One after another they connected with a rope, severing it and sending the knights free falling towards the ground. Two did not get up but disappeared in a cloud of blackness. The other five scrambled to their feet and readied their swords and shields. Two charged towards Sophia and three towards Castiel, who continued to rub away at the circle.

The circle had broken and Castiel shouted to Sophia, "You're free!"

She had no weapons to defend herself with, just her considerable martial arts skills. She stood still waiting for the Shadow Knights to come closer. Castiel took aim at the Shadow Knights approaching him with his 9mm's Uzis and let loose a flurry of Angel bullets only to have them bounce off their shields. "Elijah, were going to need Gunthor!" he shouted.

Elijah put away his bow, grabbed Gunthor, leapt off the ledge, and spread his wings and entered a shallow glide. He positioned himself right behind one of the Shadow Knights and sliced through its back. Caught off guard by his stealthy approach, the Shadow Knight disintegrated outwards from the point where Gunthor had cut it in two.

Gunthor squealed in delight. "Yeah, *now* we're talking."

Elijah landed and ran towards the back of the second Shadow Knight approaching Castiel. The Shadow Knight readied its shield and turned to defend itself against Elijah's advance. Elijah dived into a forward roll and then slid forwards and sliced across the Shadow Knights legs just below its knees causing it to fall face down on the floor. Elijah rolled to his left, sprung upwards, and plunged Gunthor into the Shadow Knight's back.

Sophia had engaged two Shadow Knights and was dodging their sword strikes. She had one Shadow Knight on either side of her as they closed in. She leapt on top of the crossbeam of the cross and waited for them to come closer.

Elijah, seeing that Sophia had no weapon to defend herself with, flung Gunthor towards Sophia. He yelled, "Catch!"

Sophia saw it coming and caught Gunthor by the hilt. She spun around the top of the cross while extending Gunthor out at full arm's length and decapitated both Shadow Knights with a single sweep, sending them back to the underworld.

The last Shadow Knight was staring down Castiel who was dodging his blade strikes while shooting his 9mm Uzis. The Shadow Knight's shield easily deflected his Angel Bullets but it was the best Castiel could do to fend off the attack. Elijah readied his bow and pulled back the drawstring, causing an arrow to appear. He aimed for the back of the head of the last Shadow Knight and released the string. The arrow hit its mark on the back of the Shadow Knight's head and caused it to disintegrate as it fell to the floor.

Sophia walked over to Elijah and handed Gunthor back to him. Castiel put away his 9mm Uzis and made his way over to Sophia and Elijah.

Elijah gazed at Sophia. It was the first time Elijah had ever seen her knowing that she was not merely a figment of his imagination. He did not know where to begin, to thank her for everything she had done for him. He stuttered "I, uh, I…."

Sophia moved forward and grabbed Elijah in a tight embrace and Elijah embraced her back. Interrupting, she whispered, "I know, it's okay, you don't need to say anything." They held each other for some time before Castiel spoke up. "Okay you two, reunion's over. We have to keep moving."

Elijah released Sophia from his embrace. "Where are your weapons, Sophia?"

"I don't know. They took them from me before tying me to the cross. I suspect they are close by." She pointed to the passage on the far side of the cavern. "They took my team and weapons down that way."

"Then that's the way we are going," Castiel responded, "after we attend to the Shuman who fell."

Sophia hurried over to the Shuman, now a human without the presence of a Shadow. She checked him over for damage and discovered a broken arm and a few broken ribs. She placed her hands over his body and they started to glow. White energy flowed from them into the human's body, mending the broken bones and repairing the flesh damaged from the fall. Sophia said quietly, "He'll be okay."

Castiel had proceeded to round up the other two humans and placed them beside the one Sophia was working on. Castiel said, "They will wake up with a nasty headache. We'll move them outside the cavern on our way back."

Chapter 48 - Deeper

Continuing farther into the caverns the trio of Elijah, Castiel, and Sophia found themselves in a small cavern carved out of the surrounding rock. Castiel glanced around then said, "It looks like we have come to a dead end."

In a sarcastic voice Gunthor said, "Really, Sherlock? How did you arrive at such a brilliant deduction? The wall is blocking our way forward?"

Elijah let out a small chuckle.

"Think I was kidding about that acid bath, Gunthor?" Castiel shook his head and continued examining the walls of the cavern. He felt there was something unusual about them.

Elijah called out. "There are some markings on the wall over here."

Castiel and Sophia made their way over to Elijah. Sophia said, "They're not random markings. It's Sumerian, one of the first written languages on earth."

Castiel added, "Yes, sometimes Shadows use it to communicate with each other. Can you translate it, Sophia?"

"Give me a minute or two."

Elijah and Castiel continued to search the cavern for any other information they might turn up to help in their effort to defeat the dark forces.

Sophia muttered, "It seems to be instructions on how to operate a doorway." She continued deciphering the Sumerian script. "I've got it! If I press here...then here...and finally here...."

A shuddering noise boomed through the cavern and then a section of the wall next to the writings sunk inward and then slid sideways revealing a passage.

The trio ventured into the passage. Castiel led the way, followed by Elijah and then Sophia. The passage was so narrow it allowed only single-file traffic. The walls were damp with moisture. Castiel said, "Must be seepage from underground springs."

Like the rest of the caverns the passage was a mixture of limestone and sandstone. Castiel whispered, "Careful, the floor is becoming slippery from the water." The passage continued forward 50 metres or so and then descended sharply with steps carved from the rock to prevent sliding down. At the bottom of the descent, the passage opened into a rectangular room with a small hole in the floor that masked the top of a long shaft with a rope ladder leading down into it. Castiel looked down the shaft but could not see the bottom through the darkness. Castiel picked up a pebble and dropped it down the shaft and counted as it fell— one-one thousand, two-one thousand—until he heard the thud. "That's quite a drop!" he said.

The shaft was too small for them to fly down using their wings. Their only choice was to use the rope ladder. Castiel looked at Elijah and Sophia, "Who's wants to go first?"

"I will," Elijah said. He walked to the side of the hole. "After all, I've got the light." He sheathed Gunthor, which reduced the amount of light considerably but still provided enough for them to see. "When I get to the bottom I will hold Gunthor up the shaft to provide more light for your descent."

Elijah eased himself down into the shaft and rested his right foot on the first rung. A touch of nerves came over him as he began his descent. Rung by rung he clambered downwards. The light from Gunthor provided enough light for him to see around him but did little to penetrate the darkness below. He heard Sophia's voice, "Are you okay?" and replied, "Yep" in a cautious but confident voice.

The floor below finally became visible and he increased his pace to get to it. He let go of the rope ladder and dropped about two metres onto the floor. He unsheathed Gunthor to light up the surrounding cavern and noted immediately that it was man-made. The walls and ceiling were smooth and flat and several corridors carved out of the surrounding rock led off in various directions. He held Gunthor up the shaft he had just descended and shouted, "Okay, next! Come on down."

Castiel was next followed by Sophia. The light at the top of the shaft was minimal, but Elijah was visible standing at the bottom holding Gunthor, which made for a quick, easy descent.

They peered into the different corridors. Sophia asked, "Which way should we go?"

"Let's see if any corridor has more signs of activity than the others," Castiel said. "Ah, this one looks promising. Let's go this way."

The corridor opened to a large room subdivided into a series of small cells with vertical bars of red energy over the openings. Two of the cells held Sophia's team members. "Hang in there, guys," Sophia told them. "We'll get you out of there. Just be patient.", then she turned and scurried to scout the other cells leaving Castiel and Elijah behind.

Sophia's teammates moved towards the bars. One said, "Glad you guys came to rescue us. I thought we might be in here for some time." Elijah replied, "Glad to help." and stayed with them while Castiel went further down the corridor.

Sophia searching another cell, which had no bars on it, found her team's gear. She retrieved her equipment—a torch, backpack of supplies, her cross necklace, and swords—then returned to her teammates.

Elijah asked Sophia's teammate, "Any idea how to shut off the bars?"

"No, they threw us in here under guard and then the bars just appeared. I suspect the controls are close by, though."

Just then Castiel shouted out, "Found them." He pressed a button and the bars disappeared.

Both staggered out of their cells and fetched their equipment. Sophia said, "You guys have been tortured? 'Yes.' You're in no condition to carry on this mission. You need to return to Elysium and recover." Sophia instructed them to return to the entrance of the caverns and carry out the three humans they came across whom the trio had left behind on the way in. She reminded them to wipe their short-term memory so they would have no recollection of recent events and then return to Elysium. They nodded and went on their way as directed.

Castiel said, "Right, one last thing to do—find out what is causing the sensor interference." Elijah took the lead and proceeded down the corridor they came through to get to the cells. Back in the room below the shaft, Elijah had a 50-50 choice between which corridor to take, and for no particular reason he chose the one on the right.

Gunthor started whistling a slow, depressing tune. Castiel looked at Gunthor and said, "Gunthor, enough already."

"But I'm so bored."

"That acid bath should help bring some excitement back in to your life."

"It always comes down to the acid bath," Gunthor said. He let out a final defiant whistle and then went quiet.

The corridor was long and narrow and the limestone walls were damp with droplets of water. The floor was wet and slippery. Elijah moved cautiously forward. They came to a large spacious open area.

In the centre floated a large black irregular-shaped void about two stories wide and one story high. Flashes of blue lightning were streaking across it. The edges were jagged and moved irregularly inwards and outwards distorting the shape while maintaining its overall size.

Elijah gazed at the void, astonished at its size. He wondered how it had become so large. "What is it?" he asked.

Castiel responded. "A rift, Elijah, a gateway between the Earth Realm and the Underworld. They are not usually this big."

Sophia nodded. "It's a rift, all right. Explains the interference to the sensors and the unusual activity around these parts. Thousands of Shadows can come and go as they please."

Elijah looked towards Sophia and Castiel, "So, how do we close it?"

"There's only one way," Sophia responded: "From the inside."

Chapter 49 - The Rift

The rift was a chilling, ominous site—a doorway to a different world. A world where screams of pain and suffering were the norm and happiness was nowhere to be found.

Castiel, Elijah, and Sophia stood before the rift considering what to do. Castiel said, "It's going to be a one-way journey." Sophia nodded.

Elijah, feeling confident, sensed an adventure.

Sophia said, "I'll go in." She cleared her throat and took a deep breath and held it. "It's the only way to close it. If we don't close it now, by the time we get back here with reinforcements they may have sent an army of Shadows through."

"I'll come, too," Elijah said.

Castiel shook his head. "It's a one-way trip, Elijah."

"And what does that mean, Castiel?"

"It means when you close it, you cannot come back the same way as you went. You would need an army of angels to fight the hordes of Shadows that will attack. They have to be held off long enough to close the rift and establish a portal back to the Earth Realm."

Elijah looked at Sophia, admiring her commitment to protect humanity from the Shadows even if it cost her own existence. "You're brave, Sophia."

"I'm scared to death, but that's okay." Sophia prepared herself. "Okay, well I guess this is it. Wish me luck."

Castiel raised his hands and said, "Wait, I have an idea." He looked around at the walls of the cavern and saw they too were dripping with water and the slick floor was pocked with puddles of water. "Sophia, do you have any T1 explosives in your backpack?"

"Yes, a few, Castiel."

"Great!" he said. "So let's place them alongside the left wall of this cavern, set them for ten minutes, and retreat out of here."

Sophia cocked her head and looked puzzled. "How would that work? Collapsing the cavern will not close the rift. It might buy some time, but not much, because the shadows would clear it quickly."

Castiel nodded. "But I suspect there is an underground water source surrounding this place. If we blow the wall, there's a very good chance that water will flood this cavern and enter the rift. The Shadows would have no choice but to close it, as they would not appreciate tons of water flooding through it."

Sophia nodded. "That would work."

Sophia took out the T1 explosives and handed one to Elijah and one to Castiel. She took the other one and leaned it against the lower left wall. Castiel and Elijah promptly placed their T1s in line with Sophia's. Standing in front of their T1s Castiel said, "Synchronise the timers to ten minutes on my count." He paused and then counted "5, 4, 3, 2, 1, *now*." The T1s simultaneously emitted a loud beep.

Elijah said, "Time to get out of here."

They made their way back down the corridor. Back at the rope ladder, Elijah sheathed Gunthor and was first to begin his ascent through the long shaft. Once at the top he unsheathed Gunthor and did his best to provide light for Sophia and Castiel as they climbed up.

Gunthor alerted, "I'm sensing a squad of Shadow Knights assembling in the cavern after coming through the rift. For each Shadow Knight there appears to be ten Shadows accompanying them. It's a small but significant strike force making its way into the Earth Realm."

Castiel tried to regain his breath after a fast climb up the rope ladder. "One minute until detonation. We have to pick up our pace to make a safe distance."

They huffed and puffed as they hurried up the long steep climb, assisted by the small steps. Between breaths Elijah stated, "It was much easier coming down this path!"

The Shadow Knights followed closely by the Shadows started moving down the corridor to the cavern with the shaft, in an orderly fashion.

"T-minus ten seconds and counting," Castiel said. He began counting down from ten, as they were half way up the stairs. Elijah, Castiel, and Sophia all turned as they heard the large explosion and gripped the walls as the passage they were in shook violently. The sound of water rushing through an opening followed the deep rumbling sound of rocks falling. After the shaking stopped the trio resumed their climb—at an even faster pace.

* * *

Water came cascading down the corridor to the cavern containing the shaft. Shadows and Shadow Knights scrambled to outrun it, some climbing the ladder, others running down the corridor. The rushing water caught the ones running, picked them up as if they were weightless, and carried them way. The water rapidly caught up to the few Shadows Knights that managed to start ascending the shaft and spurted them out the top like champagne well-shaken and uncorked. Pounded into the walls or succumbing to the watery depths, the Shadows and Shadow Knights one by one started to disintegrate.

* * *

Hearing the sound of mighty rushing water swiftly approaching, Sophia looked behind and saw the tide advancing up the corridor they were ascending. She shouted, "Run!"

"I am!" Elijah responded, and he did manage to pick up his pace slightly.

They made it to the room where they had opened the hidden door just as the water started rushing around their feet. A moment later the water had risen to shin-level, making it difficult to run. But, it was rising much slower now and had almost stopped.

Out of breath, Castiel said, "It must have reached the same level as the surrounding water source, an underground lake perhaps."

Sophia's EVE appeared in front of her and said, "Message Received." She read it aloud: "We are back in Elysium after moving the two humans outside and wiping their memory. We thought you said there were three, but we only found two."

Castiel said, "That's odd. I wouldn't have expected any of them to wake up for some time. Keep a look out for him, just in case he wandered off the beaten path. On the bright side, since EVE is receiving messages we know that the sensors are back up, meaning the rift closed."

Elijah pumped his fist in the air. "We did it."

They trudged through the shin-high water until they came to the cavern where Sophia had been held hostage. The water flooded the cavern, but the passage leading out was up a slight incline. It wasn't long before they were out of the shallow water. When they reached the room where the campfire was, they took a break to regain their stamina.

"How does a rift like that open, Castiel?" Elijah asked.

"It takes two elements. The first requires humans to get involved in some sort of occult practices such as human and animal sacrifices, black magic, and other dark rites. At some point they typically try to raise the dead, pledge their allegiance to dark forces, or call for the Underworld creatures to come forth. The second element is that the Shadows create the rift on their side. When enough red energy flows from the Earth Realm to where they are trying to establish the rift, it opens."

Sophia added, "That will be our next task—finding the source of the human involvement and stopping it so they don't re-open another one."

Elijah spun around at the sound of a crazed voice shouting, "You'll never stop us."

He saw several bullets cruising through the air. He calculated their trajectory and realised they were headed directly for Sophia. He lunged to his side, spinning in mid-air, and put his back to the bullets as he seized Sophia, wrapping his wings around her, and continued falling sideways. The first bullet pierced his back between his shoulder blades; the second bullet hit a little lower down his back; and the third hit his left kidney as he fell. Plumes of blood spurted out of the bullet holes, spraying out and staining his wings red.

Castiel had turned to see the gunman and willed the AK-47 from his hands, sending it flying. He ran towards the gunman and bounded into a double flying sidekick that landed both his feet directly on the human's chest and sent him flying backwards into the cavern wall. The human hit the wall with a loud thud and fell to the floor limp as a rag doll. Moments later the blue soul of the human left his body and entered the Spirit Realm. Shadows appeared and surrounded the soul and dragged it off into darkness as it struggled to get free.

Castiel then rushed over to where Sophia and Elijah had landed and knelt down. Sophia was sitting on the floor holding Elijah in her arms. She looked up at Castiel and said, "His wounds are too many."

Elijah coughed up a little blood while managing to say, "Did I do okay?"

Sophia nodded and with tears welling in her eyes said, "You did great, kid."

Elijah coughed again and more blood came out of his mouth. "Look after Juliana and my children for me, Castiel." Elijah closed his eyes as he took his last breath.

Sophia screamed, "No! It's not fair!" as Elijah disintegrated into dust leaving Sophia holding Elijah's empty clothes.

Chapter 50 - From Dust

Sophia laid Elijah's clothes on the ground and looked up at Castiel. He was clearly in shock and could find no words to express what he was thinking and feeling. He extended his hand and helped Sophia up onto her feet. They stood together in a long moment of silence looking at Elijah's clothes.

"Why do some humans want to cause such pain, Castiel?"

"I have no idea, Sophia," he said, his voice low and raspy. "It is hard to understand why some people, even without Shadow involvement, are evil. Maybe it just comes back to being selfish. They want what is best for themselves without concern for anyone or anything else—no matter the cost."

"What are we going to do, Castiel?"

They stood still and silent again, trying to come to terms with all that had happened. It just did not seem possible that it could all come down to this.

Just then a dust whirlwind began animating Elijah's clothes. Sophia noticed it first. "What's that, Castiel?"

Castiel shook his head and watched as the whirlwind began spiralling up ever wider and higher. Castiel and Sophia took a few steps backwards so as not to be swept up in it. The dust was swirling around like a mini tornado. White light began glowing in the centre of the whirlwind as it reached the height of a man. It was spinning faster and faster.

Sophia and Castiel just looked on in wonder. The whirlwind began changing shape and smaller areas of circling dust started to protrude in the form of arms and legs. The top part of the whirlwind morphed into the shape of a head. White light was now flowing throughout it.

It assumed the appearance of a transparent man made of swirling dust. Sophia and Castiel watched as organs started to form inside the body. The outer layers of the whirlwind started to turn to skin. More and more detail appeared. Hair, eyes, nose, mouth, teeth—all were forming right in front of them.

"It's Elijah!" Sophia exclaimed as they watched him forming from the dust. Moments later, he was standing in front of them, in the flesh, motionless, eyes closed. Then, all of the sudden, his eyes opened and he spoke.

"What are you two looking at? You look like you have just seen a ghost. Is there something on my face or something?"

Castiel and Sophia stood there wide-eyed, at a loss for words.

Elijah looked down and saw that he was naked. He covered his privates with his hands. "Hey, is this some kind of practical joke, Castiel. What did you do?"

Sophia just then realised that Elijah was standing in front of her naked and quickly turned around and looked the other way. "I think you should put your clothes back on, Elijah. We will wait over here for you." She motioned for Castiel to walk over into the far corner of the cavern with her.

Elijah started putting his clothes back on. "You know I'm not sure this is very funny."

Gunthor started cracking rather crude jokes about who was the longest sword.

Over in the corner, Sophia whispered to Castiel, "What just happened?"

"I'm not sure," Castiel said. "He was spiritually dead. I have never seen anyone return from that. For that matter, I've never even heard of it." After pausing for a moment, he continued. "Maybe because he is not actually an angel yet and is still yet to graduate but he is also no longer human. He is in-between places."

Sophia looked over towards Elijah and saw he was still dressing. She looked back to Castiel. "I guess."

"I do know one thing, Sophia. To my knowledge, only God can turn dust to man, as it says in Genesis 2:7: 'Then the Lord God formed the man from the dust of the ground. He breathed the breath of life into the man's nostrils, and the man became a living person.'"

"I think we should keep this to ourselves until we learn more, Castiel."

"I agree," Castiel said. "The other angels will think we have lost it if we tell them this story."

Sophia paused for a moment and then whispered to Castiel, "Do you think he could be the one the legends speak about?"

"I'm not sure, Sophia. I suppose it is possible. If he is, things are going to escalate down here in the Human Realm very quickly."

Elijah finished dressing. "Hey, somebody fill me in. What just happened?"

Castiel said, "Well, I certainly had no desire to see you naked so we can rule that out."

Elijah shook his head and rolled his eyes. "Right. Very funny, Castiel. Seriously, though, what happened?"

Sophia answered. "We're not sure, Elijah. In the process of saving my life, you were wounded very badly and then healed by a radiant white light."

"I remember diving and pulling you to the ground to avoid the bullets, Sophia ... but nothing after that."

Castiel approached him. "Are you okay to continue, Elijah?"

"I feel great, like I'm brand new."

Sophia looked curiously at Elijah. "If we learn more, Elijah, we will let you know."

Elijah nodded. "Please do." He looked at the dead human on the floor. "About the guy who shot at us, what happened to him?"

"Castiel terminated him."

"Isn't that against the rules, Castiel? I thought you were a stickler for the rules."

"There is an exception to every rule, Elijah."

Sophia added, "I can't wait to hear how you explain this to Araton, but I'll stand by you on this one, Castiel. If they are going to punish you, they will have to punish me, too."

"And me," Elijah added.

Castiel smiled. "Thanks, guys."

"Castiel, how could the human see us to begin with?"

"Elijah, when a human has been recently possessed by a Shadow and turned into a Shuman he retains the ability to see angels for a period of time. It is one of the reasons we do the memory wipe, which removes the ability."

Glancing back at the human a final time he said, "I see."

Castiel looking at Elijah and Sophia. "For now, we need to locate the humans who opened the rift on this side. Now that our sensors are back up and running it should not be too difficult to locate where they are operating from."

Chapter 51 - The Search

Castiel operated his EVE device and said, "Nothing obvious is showing on the EVE scans. I think the best way to find the source of the red energy that allowed the rift to open is to do an aerial search."

Sophia looked at Elijah. "What do you say, Elijah, you up for some flying?"

"Sounds good to me."

Castiel looked up at the sky and spread his wings. "We'll have to stay below the clouds."

He took to the sky followed by Sophia and Elijah. They assumed a triangle formation with Castiel in the head position, Elijah on the left, and Sophia on the right. Sophia and Elijah glided easily in the slipstream of Castiel's wake.

"This is amazing." Elijah exclaimed, enjoying his first flight with Castiel and Sophia.

"Over there: *Look*," Castiel said when they were a little way from the caves. "That's a possible source to the red energy."

Elijah and Sophia looked and saw, way off in the distance, a rundown old farmhouse nestled amongst the trees.

They circled over the house for a closer look. The surrounding trees provided camouflage for the house. They could see a large burnt out bonfire situated in the centre of a paddock surrounded by a circle of stones. The trio descended below the tree line and landed at the back of the paddock.

Animal remains were clearly visible in the ashes of the bonfire. Several undernourished live goats grazed around in a gated paddock area. On a concrete patio near the back door of the farmhouse stood a large blood-stained wooden table. Suspended from the eaves of the farmhouse were several decapitated goat heads.

Castiel looked to Sophia. "Animal sacrifices. We're close."

Sophia nodded and grimaced in disgust. Elijah spotted several large barrels with flies buzzing around them and looked inside and discovered the carcasses of several cats that appeared to have been skinned alive, covered in maggots.

Elijah turned away and winced. "What are they doing, Castiel?"

"Most likely using the animal sacrifices to call forth demons. It's an ancient ritual that humans perform to gain power through demons. The sheer evil nature of what they are doing would generate enough red energy to power the rift the Shadows opened. From the looks of that large rock circle I'd say the cult that takes part in the ritual has quite a few members."

Elijah left the barrel and joined Castiel and Sophia at the back door of the farmhouse. The door was open and they all went inside. The farmhouse had several well-used rooms, the one of most interest to the trio was full of semi-automatic weapons, handguns, and other armaments.

In another room, a large project board hung on the wall outlining future rituals. The next one was scheduled for that very night.

The trio continued searching the house—each with a different mission. Castiel noted the possible places from which the cult members would defend themselves if attacked. He said he knew from experience that attempts to stop cults from performing a ritual tended to get ugly fast and quite often resulted in a ferocious shoot-out. Sophia's task was to use her EVE to record all the different weapons in their armoury, including knives, swords, and guns. Castiel and Sophia took copious notes, and it was obvious to Elijah that they were both used to this routine and the planning involved. *Thank God for that*, he thought.

Elijah's task was to scour the house for other evidence about the cult and its dark ritual. He made his way to the kitchen, opened the fridge, and found several Tupperware containers full of animal or human organs. Repulsed at the sight, he quickly slammed the fridge shut and shouted, "Organs in the fridge … in Tupperware containers."

Castiel rushed into the kitchen and looked in the fridge. "They are from the goats. They use them in the rituals."

Elijah shook his head in disgust and walked into the main living area of the farmhouse. He did feel a little relieved to learn that they were animal rather than human organs.

Castiel headed out the door. "I'm going to check the roof, be right back."

Sophia joined Elijah in the living room. "He'll be checking to see if they use the roof as a defence point."

Castiel returned moments later. "It appears they use the roof quite a bit as a vantage point, judging by the number of cigarette butts up there."

They moved into last room to search—the dining room. A large oak table surrounded by 12 chairs was in the centre of the room. The table was set atop a large maroon coloured wool rug.

Castiel noticed pocks on the floor that suggested the table was regularly relocated to another spot in the room. "Gunthor, can you scan under the table, see if anything is under there?"

"Scanning…," replied Gunthor. Moments later, Gunthor said in a proud voice: "I'm sensing two human life forms, in a sleeping state."

"Let's take a look," Castiel said. The trio carefully moved the table and then rolled up the rug to reveal a trapdoor. Slowly they opened the trapdoor and descended a dark old wooden staircase. On the far side of the cellar were two females chained to the wall by their wrists. They were lying on mattresses in nothing but underwear.

Castiel said, "I think we should call Frank, Sophia."

"I agree," Sophia replied.

"Who is Frank?" Elijah asked.

"Frank works for the Australian Federal Police. We cannot involve ourselves in human affairs, but we can tip off the authorities and guide them when they are on scene. We'll show you how when they get here."

They made their way back up the stairs and quietly closed the trap door to avoid waking the sleeping hostages, replaced the rug, and put the oak table back in place.

"What do you think they have been doing with those women, Castiel?" asked Elijah.

"I shudder to think, Elijah."

Castiel contacted Frank at the Australian Federal Police and tipped him off about the ritual that was scheduled to take place at the farm. He provided him with details on the location, armaments, and the hostages bound in the cellar. From the conversation, Elijah gathered that Castiel had a long-standing rapport with Frank.

"Does Frank know you're an angel, Castiel?"

"No, he has never seen me. As far as he is concerned, I am just someone who gives him anonymous tips that pay off. Sometimes Sophia uses Frank as well. As an angel, it will be up to you, Elijah, to choose whom to help to take action against people committing crimes. Word to the wise: It's a good idea to check them out first and ensure they are not corrupt."

"Aren't they suspicious about how you get the tips?"

"Why would they care? All they know is that I'm a credible source of information. They do try to trace the calls on occasion, but our EVE devices are untraceable."

Castiel led Elijah and Sophia out the front door. "Now we wait for Frank to arrive. He will be about two hours. That gives them about two hours to set up before the start of the ritual."

Chapter 52 - The Ritual

Gliding in the sky above the farm, the trio saw three federal police vehicles arriving and parking in the bushlands surrounding the farmhouse to hide their vehicles. Seven officers left their vehicles and assembled around Frank for a briefing. The trio, invisible to the humans, flew down and joined them.

Frank began the briefing by telling the men he suspected there were female hostages inside—perhaps in a cellar under a trapdoor in the dining room although they may have been relocated. He explained the plan: They were going to wait until the ritual was underway before taking any action. Frank explained to the officers that to ensure a proper conviction it was important to catch the perpetrators in the very act of committing the crime. He warned his officers that the cult members were well-armed.

Castiel injected a thought into Frank's mind that cult gunmen might be stationed on the roof. Frank then shared it with his officers in the briefing. One of the officers said, "What makes you think that, sir?" Frank replied, "Just a gut feeling."

The officers spread out to separate posts concealed in the bushland where they had good visuals on the farmhouse. They put in earpieces to stay in radio communication with Frank, the commander, and each other. Three officers covered the front of the house. One went to the left side and one to the right side. Another climbed a nearby tree and found a spot from which he could clearly see the house. Armed with a sniper rifle, he set up a harness to hold him in place.

Frank stayed with the team of three at the front of the farmhouse. All the officers except the sniper in the tree carried shotguns and had side-arms in their belts.

Darkness fell around the house as the sun set. Shortly afterwards several cars started to arrive and park at the front of the farmhouse. Eighteen people from five vehicles arrived within 15 minutes of each other. All were dressed in casual clothes and none appeared armed.

Elijah was inside the house watching the cult members arrive. A few were just teenagers, and the rest were adult men and women of varying ages. They assembled in the main living room and one of the men carried a box of robes out of one of the bedrooms. They put on the gowns and raised their hoods. They now looked the part—all dark and mysterious dressed in long black robes with their faces concealed in the dark shadows cast by the overhanging hoods.

Once Elijah realized that no more members were coming, he exited the front door of the house. Castiel walked over to him. "It will not be long now before they raid the house, Elijah. Most likely there will be a lot of gunfire. Keep in mind that we are only invisible, not invulnerable. Bullets will hurt us. We must stay out of firing lines and avoid colliding with people and objects."

"How does that invisibility work, Castiel?"

"It has to do with light waves. Angels appear out-of-phase, meaning that light waves pass right through us. Matter, however, does not. This allows us to interact with the environment. When we allow a human to see us we give them a temporary ability to see things out of phase."

Elijah was a little puzzled, but he understood the gist of it.

"Now we wait, Elijah, until Frank gives the call to send his men in."

Elijah gazed up at the clear night sky and marvelled at the stars of the Milky Way. He was reminded of his first date with Juliana.

Castiel said, "Beautiful night, isn't it, Elijah?"

"It reminds me of the time Juliana and I got stuck at the top of the Ferris wheel in Luna Park during that blackout. Our first date that you—Michael—and Maryanne set up for us. We saw a falling star and both made a wish."

"What did you wish for, Elijah?"

"It seemed an impossible dream at the time," Elijah said, shaking his head in wonder. "I wished for Juliana to fall in love with me, just as I had fallen in love with her from the moment I first saw her."

A moment later Castiel and Elijah joined Sophia at the rear of the farmhouse. They stood on the far side of the circle of stones and glanced at the remnants of the previous bonfire. Several cult members dressed in black robes came out the back door, proceeded to the side of the house, gathered wood from a nearby woodpile, and carried it to the middle of the circle of stones. They stacked the wood in a pyramid shape, poured on several gallons of gasoline, and then ignited the bottom. It swiftly flamed up into a large bonfire, burning brightly.

They listened in as Frank monitored the radio reports from his team members. The sniper notified Frank that he had his scope trained on a robed man carrying an assault weapon who was standing on the roof near the chimney smoking a cigarette. The two officers on either side of the farmhouse informed Frank they had moved farther back along the sides of the farmhouse to get a better view of what was happening around back. They also let Frank know about the construction and lighting of the bonfire.

His final instructions to his team via radio consisted of telling the sniper to take down the gunman on the roof with a rubber bullet to the head to render him unconscious. Once the gunman was down, the team out front would go in through the front door of the farmhouse. The left officer would flank the rear of the farmhouse from the left while the officer on the right would flank from the right. Frank would join the frontal assault team. Inside, his team would split up and secure the premises one room one at a time. They would all then assemble at the rear of the house. They were to wait until the ceremony began when most of the members would be around the bonfire.

A male cult member came out of the back door of the house and opened the gate to the small fenced paddock and grabbed one of the goats by its ears and dragged it towards the blood-stained table. A second cult member assisted him in placing the goat on the table with its neck dangling slightly over the front edge. The goat struggled but to no avail. A third cult member appeared with a butcher knife in hand, and a fourth member carried a large silver chalice. The fourth cult member held the chalice under the goat's head while the third sliced off the goat's head with a single swing of the knife. Blood spurted from the beast's neck and then slowed to a trickle. The fourth cult member did his best to catch as much blood as possible in the chalice. Several other cult members then came out the back door and gathered around the circle. They began to chant in some unrecognisable dialect.

The two cult members who had sacrificed the goat tossed it onto the bonfire. Then they returned to the table. One picked up the goat's head and placed it on a hook suspended from the roof. Blood dripped down from it onto the pavement below. The other cult member picked up the silver chalice and carried it to the large circle around the bonfire.

The federal officer on the left side reported the events to Frank and informed him that 12 cult members were outside the back of the farmhouse. That meant five members were still inside. The armed cult member was still on the roof. Frank said, "We'll have to go in soon. Await my command."

The cult members passed the chalice and each took a turn drinking from it as they looked down at the bonfire with their hands clasped together in front of them. They continued chanting.

"Look at all that red energy," Sophia said. "It's streaming through the Spiritual Realm coming from the back of the farmhouse and from the circle of cult members around the bonfire." The intensity of the red energy was extremely disturbing.

Castiel said, "That is certainly enough to power the rift opening."

Frank told all his members to prepare to go in on his order.

He seemed to pause for a moment to consider whether there was a better way. But then he said, "Go, Go, Go."

Chapter 53 - The Raid

A loud bang sounded as the sniper pulled the trigger that sent the rubber bullet rocketing towards the armed cult member on the roof. He fell instantly as the rubber bullet collided with the side of his head, dropping his newly lit cigarette.

The sound of the sniper rifle fire and the gunman's fall on the roof sent the cult members who were still inside the farmhouse scrambling to the room with the armaments. They quickly armed themselves and took up defensive positions inside the house.

Frank and his team approached the front door. They split into two teams of two on either side of the door. One officer put a small explosive on the lock of the front door. An officer from each team then removed a flash-bang grenade from his belt, smashed the window closest to him with the butt of their shotgun, and threw the flash-bang grenade through it.

A cult member shouted, "Grenade!" The flash-bangs exploded, creating a blinding light and deafening noise. The explosive on the lock erupted with a quick flash and bang, signalling the teams to run in and take up offensive positions inside the house.

Castiel and Elijah were close behind. Reeling from the flash-bang explosion, the cult members tried to refocus their eyes to no avail and retreated into the rooms of the house to recover their sight. Elijah moved into a room that one cult member had retreated to. Taking into account the cult member's position, he injected thoughts into a nearby officer. The officer came into the room with his shotgun pointed where he thought the cult member would be and had him directly in his sights. Caught off guard, the cult member raised his gun to shoot the officer but was not quick enough to dodge the incoming shotgun blast, which sent the cult member flying against the back wall of the room. He fell to the floor and crumpled over.

Castiel observed two cult members who had moved into a back bedroom. Both had automatic weapons pointed at the open door and their fingers were on the trigger ready for any officers who passed the threshold. Castiel moved back outside the doorway and saw an approaching officer moving up the corridor towards the doorway. Castiel injected a thought into the officer's mind that there were a couple of cult members in the room armed and ready for attack. The officer hesitated, seemingly while accepting Castiel's thoughts, and then he continued to approach the doorway very cautiously. Before coming to the doorway, the officer dropped to his knees, leaned forwards, and slid into the open doorway. The cult members saw him, but their guns were aimed high. Before they could re-aim, shotgun spray had struck them.

Meanwhile, at the back of the farmhouse the two officers on either side had the cult members around the stone circle on their knees with their arms up. Unarmed, the cult members had quickly surrendered to the approaching officers who had their shotguns poised to fire on anyone who dared resist. The officers reported to Frank that the back of the farmhouse was secure. One officer stood guard while the other tied the cult members' hands behind their backs with plastic cable ties.

Elijah moved into the dining room and spotted a male cult member, hood down, climbing up from the cellar, pulling up his pants as he stumbled towards the armaments room. Elijah shook his head and willed the cult member's pants to fall back down, which they did, triggering him to trip and fall. An officer quickly noticed him and whacked him in the head with the butt of his shotgun, knocking him unconscious. The officer dragged him into the kitchen and handcuffed him to a water pipe.

Standing in the rear corridor that led to the back door, a cult member who had managed to elude the officers saw Frank in the distance with his back to him. Seeing that the cult member had Frank in his sights, Sophia injected a thought into Frank's mind: "Duck, behind you." Frank immediately ducked, avoiding the bullet the cult member had just fired. He turned and fired his shotgun, hitting the cult member in the stomach. The cult member arched forwards from the impact while being propelled backwards by the blast and came to a halt at the back door where Sophia had just jumped out of the way.

Frank informed his team that all suspects were down and made his way to the dining room. He radioed for the ambulances that had been stationed nearby on standby to come and tend to the wounded and deceased. He climbed down the cellar stairs and immediately noticed the two women in chains, one curled up and crying in the corner naked, the other sitting on a mattress in her underwear. Frank grabbed a blanket, covered the naked woman, and called for one of his officers to fetch some bolt cutters and a blanket.

The officer ran to his squad car and retrieved a pair of bolt cutters and blanket, then ran back to the cellar. The officer handed Frank the bolt cutters then went and wrapped the blanket he had retrieved around the near naked woman. Frank, after a few attempts with the bolt cutters was able to set the women free. They then assisted the women up the cellar stairs and led them out to the front of the house where the ambulances were parked. Ambulance medics quickly attended to the women and placed them in a nearby ambulance where they received initial medical treatment before being taken to the nearest hospital.

The scene was now swarming with dozens of police officers. The police read the cult members their Miranda rights before arresting them and placing them into police custody vehicles. The deceased were placed in body bags to await the arrival of the coroner.

Castiel, Sophia, and Elijah stood and watched it all. Castiel said, "Well, guys, that wraps this up. Not much more we can do here."

"It's a good result, Castiel," Sophia said.

"Indeed," Elijah said, nodding.

Chapter 54 - Final Approval

When they arrived back in Elysium, Sophia, Castiel, and Elijah received instructions from Araton to go directly to the Capernaum Hall. Castiel led the way.

Outside the doorway to the hall Castiel said, "You have to go in first, Elijah. Sophia and I will follow on either side."

"Why?" asked Elijah.

"You'll see."

Elijah moved toward the door, which caused it to open automatically. The hall was incredibly large and constructed in the style of a stately old cathedral. A wide centre aisle led up the middle to a podium on the far side of the hall. On either side of the aisle were rows of seats filled with other angels, all of whom rose to their feet as Elijah entered.

Castiel gave Elijah a nudge. "Keep walking."

Araton was standing behind the podium and Elijah could see his angel friends—Dina, Uriel, Nemamiah, Suriel, Raphael, and Isis—standing on the podium behind him.

Araton spoke. "Please welcome, Elijah Hael, who is joined by Castiel, his support angel, and Sophia, who has served faithfully as Elijah's guardian angel."

The angels in the hall broke into spirited applause as they watched Elijah move forward towards the podium where Araton was standing. As he walked down the centre aisle, Elijah looked around in amazement at the sheer size of the hall and audience.

"Elijah, please come stand beside me," Araton said.

Elijah walked slowly, savouring the joy of the attention, applause, and grand welcome.

The trio ventured onto the slightly raised area at the end of the hallway and stood beside Araton.

Araton turned to face Elijah and said, "Elijah Hael, we have monitored your performance closely during your training to become an angel." Araton paused for a moment, letting Elijah's suspense build. "I wish to congratulate you on passing the requirements in Elysium." Elijah smiled and was about to say something just as Araton raised a hand to interrupt and said, "However, before we can pronounce you an angel officially, there is One who needs to give final approval. Please stand at the front of the podium and face the audience."

The audience took their seats and watched Elijah as he stood in front of the podium. Elijah was not sure what he was waiting for. Time passed and nothing was happening. Elijah squirmed a little and glanced back at Castiel out of the corner of his eye. Castiel in turn looked at Sophia and shrugged. Then a small gold glowing sphere, about the size of a marble, appeared slightly above the back of Elijah's head. The audience members' eyes lit up and they started to smile. Elijah was not sure what they could see. The gold sphere then spun around in a circle and vanished leaving a gold glowing halo hovering just above Elijah's head. Araton shouted, "All welcome Elijah Hael, our newest Angel!"

The audience all stood up as one, applauding, some whistling, others cheering, "Elijah, Elijah, Elijah." The noise was deafening. Elijah felt such a sense of honour bestowed upon him that words would never describe. Shivers scurried over every part of his body as endorphins flooded his system.

Castiel, Sophia, and Elijah's angel friends on the podium applauded along with the audience, expressing their own deep sense of joy that Elijah was now officially one of them.

When the applause at last began to settle down Araton continued: "We also wish to thank Castiel for leading Elijah through the transitional period."

Once again the applause, cheering, and whistling increased in volume.

Araton shouted louder. "And let's not forget to thank Sophia for her exemplary protection work throughout Elijah's life—as she ensured not only the safety of his body but, eternally more important, of his soul."

Sophia's name was now also included amongst the cheers for Elijah and Castiel, along with whistling and thunderous applause.

As the applause settled, the audience resumed their seats, Araton said, "Elijah, would you like to say something?"

Elijah moved behind the podium and addressed the audience, "I'm not very good at public speaking, but I'll do my best." Still overwhelmed, he hesitated to gather his thoughts. "Firstly, I would like to thank Araton for this great honour."

Looking at Castiel Elijah continued. "I would like to thank Castiel for his sustaining support after I passed from my earth life. Without his wise guidance, I'm not sure what choices I would have made."

Castiel nodded and whispered, "Thank you, and you're welcome."

Elijah looked towards Sophia. "And Sophia, I'm not sure where I can start…. Words cannot possibly express the loving gratitude I feel for you, for all you helped me through before and after my earth life."

Sophia smiled and blushed as Elijah continued. "You were, and still are, my angel."

Elijah looked back towards the audience. "I would also like to thank the angels who helped me along this journey and prepared me so well: Dina, Uriel, Nemamiah, Suriel, Raphael, and Isis. I am very grateful for all your support. Thank you also to all my fellow angels. I'm honoured to be a part of who we are."

The audience broke into another round of applause and cheering.

Elijah moved away from the podium, but then shifted back quickly, "And there is one more to thank." He raised his voice and shouted, "Thank God!"

The audience stood up and applauded with roaring applause that caused the very hall to shake.

Chapter 55 - The Ferris Wheel

It had been a long, arduous journey for Elijah, and he was given some leave time to do what he liked before starting his new duties and assignments as an angel. Elijah decided to spend that time in the Earth Realm, spending most of it around Juliana, Reece, and Kaley.

He spent each day watching them and being around them, giving them inspiration here and there, and providing some very subtle signs for his children to let them know he was around. He did not need to do subtle things around Juliana, for she seemed to sense when he was around. Many a time she would stare directly at where he was standing. Elijah often wanted to bestow upon her the ability to see him …. but he did not.

Deep down Elijah felt that one day Juliana would meet another man and move on. Until then, however, he promised himself he would be with her as often as he could.

His children were coping quite well. Elijah knew they would be okay. Separate angels guarded his children. They had been with his children from the moment they were born. Elijah had come to know the guardian angels and was delighted that they were there for his children. It was common for a deceased relative who became an angel to assume a kind of proxy guardian role.

Some days were tougher than others were for Elijah. He missed his family deeply and occasionally wished he had never died. It was a new kind of struggle that he had to learn to deal with. He knew, however, that being an angel was his destiny and that he had many adventures to come.

But, today he was spending time with his family in a very familiar place.

A year had passed since Elijah's death and Juliana had decided to take her children to Luna Park to ride the Ferris wheel, the very place where, 18 years ago, she and Elijah had gotten stuck during the blackout.

She asked the Ferris wheel operator for a favour. She explained her situation and how Elijah had passed away. She wanted to spend 10 minutes stationary at the topmost position of the Ferris wheel. After hearing her story, and looking at her children, and considering that it was a quiet night in Luna Park, the Ferris wheel operator granted her wish.

At the top of the Ferris wheel with Reece and Kaley, Juliana gazed at the night sky. It was almost identical to the night she and Elijah had spent together.

Elijah sat next to Juliana, in the very spot in which he had sat 18 years ago, watching her and his children. He felt touched by her gesture.

Juliana looked at Reece, who looked so much like Elijah, and said, "Eighteen years ago, your father and I were stuck up here during a blackout." She turned back towards the sky and added, "That night we both saw a falling star. It was a beautiful night." She paused a moment, continuing to gaze at the sky. "We both made a wish."

"What did you wish for, Mummy?" asked Reece.

Juliana turned back to look at Reece. "I wished he would kiss me."

"Did the wish come true?"

"We were just about to and then the power came back on." Juliana smiled and her eyes lit up. "But it was in that moment that I fell in love with your father."

Reece looked up at the sky and pointed to a distant star. "Is that where Daddy is now? Up there in the sky?"

"I think he is. I think he is up there somewhere looking over us."

Staring into the night sky, sensing Elijah's presence, Juliana added, "Actually I *know* he is. Elijah is an angel now ... our angel."

The End

Keep up to date with Elijah Hael at

Facebook

www.facebook.com/ElijahHaelTheLastJudgement

Official Web Site

www.ElijahHael.com

Authors Facebook Page

www.facebook.com/Steve.Goodwin

Authors Twitter Channel

www.twitter.com/fikeus

Printed in Great Britain
by Amazon.co.uk, Ltd.,
Marston Gate.